Hunger

Rob Preece

BooksForABuck.com

2008

Hunger

Rob Preece

Published by **BooksForABuck.com**

ISBN: 978-1-60215-078-2

Hunger

Chapter 1

Hunger hit like an icy spear through his gut.

Ewan shuffled forward behind the bent gray men. To him, they reeked of sweated alcohol and death.

He gripped his cheap plastic plate as they held theirs--his need was no less than theirs but his patience was trained by more bitter years than they could imagine.

Five still ahead of him. Now four.

He fought the compulsion to stare at the woman. He couldn't afford to frighten her, but need nearly shattered him.

Finally, he stood at the front of the line.

"Welcome to the Sisters of Faith Kitchen." Her soft Midwestern twang would have made her stand out on the east coast even if she'd lacked the glow of energy. "I haven't seen you here before, have I?"

Ewan shook his head, but his eyes never left her.

This woman could fill a hunger as vast as the empty space between galaxies.

Her brown hair glinted with golden highlights. Her deep brown eyes glistened with sympathy for his plight and that of the other homeless around him. Although her abundant curves, visible despite the baggy long skirt and apron she wore, might not be completely stylish, they suited her, pleased Ewan. A scattering of freckles across her nose showed she hadn't completely left the country behind her when she'd moved to New York City. The pulse in her neck beat strongly with life and strength.

Ewan's knuckles, already pale like the rest of him, whitened on his tightly gripped plate and he forced himself to relax—he couldn't let her run now. But his hunger raged.

The woman's lips quivered just slightly as she smiled.

He inhaled deeply, gathering the woman's scent of flowers and female over the rancid stenches of unwashed males and fatty, congealing gray mounds of food she and the other women served with salt and compassion as spice.

Her scent wasn't enough.

The woman's faith splashed abundantly, like water spurting from a geyser. Its power teased at him, but filled him as little as would the small gray mound, nominally food, she heaped on his plate.

She was looking at him and he realized she was still waiting for him to answer her question.

"I haven't always been homeless." Even to himself, his voice sounded rusty, unused.

"There's no shame in it." The woman handed her apron to another worker, plucked at Ewan's sleeve, and tugged him toward one of the tables.

"Guys, I want you to welcome a new brother."

She didn't ask for Ewan for his name--the homeless and destitute often have reasons to clutch their names tightly to themselves. Giving a true name yields power to others. Anonymity can sometimes protect those with no other defenses.

He gave it to her anyway. "Ewan."

Faded men, a mix of races and nationalities glared at him as he approached the table.

Fear collided with hunger. Did they recognize him as different? Alcohol, drugs, and insanity might separate them from the rest of the population, but those same things altered their perspectives, let them see what no normal person could imagine. But no, they begrudged him the food and the woman's attention. The world offered so little to the truly poor and hungry that they hoarded what they could.

Finally, two of the men shifted, opening up a space large enough for Ewan to squeeze into.

One of the men, a tall man whose tanned complexion and substantial muscles with more than a bit of fat made him stand out from the others held out a scarred hand. "They call me Big Red."

Intelligent gray eyes stared out from beneath Big Red's bushy white eyebrows. His head gleamed bald where it wasn't covered by a grimy, Russian-looking hat. If Big Red had ever been a redhead, he'd left those days behind decades earlier.

Ewan wasn't used to human touch. He consciously relaxed himself, ungrit his teeth, and managed the briefest possible handshake.

"You're cold as ice, brother. I'll scare you up some coffee." Big Red turned toward the woman, already heading back to the serving line. "Hey, Tia, be a pal. My man here is near-freezing to death. How about getting him a cup of coffee?"

"No problem." Her smile lit the room. "Cream and sugar, right?"

Ewan shrugged, then nodded. Coffee and calories could do nothing for the cold and hunger in him. Still, a mug would do as a prop, and would bring the woman, Tia, back again.

"You don't talk much, do you?" Big Red demanded as Tia hurried away. "You've got to get over the pride thing. Being on the street doesn't mean you're a loser. You just don't have a regular home. One mistake, getting sick at the wrong time, and lots of other people would be here instead. It's not us who've screwed up, it's society."

Ewan adjusted the plate in front of himself and arranged his arms protectively around it. The soup kitchen didn't give seconds, and anyone who lost his meal would go hungry. More than a few faces at the table looked disappointed. They'd hoped to take advantage of the new guy. Two looked more than disappointed—they looked angry.

He ignored them and turned to the man who wanted to befriend him.

"I guess they call you Big Red because of your politics, not size or color."

The big man laughed easily. "For sure it's not my hair." He removed his furry hat and ran a hand across his smooth dome. "Was a student activist after doing a hitch in 'Nam. After that, I never looked back. Most of the guys I hung

4

out with back then sold out. Sold out or are dead. So far I'm admitting to neither."

Tia appeared at Ewan's shoulder, a Styrofoam cup of steaming liquid in her hand.

"Cut the new guy a break, Red." She patted Ewan lightly on the back. "He needs something to eat and drink, not political slogans."

Tia's simple touch warmed Ewan far more than the coffee would. He barely resisted the urge to seize her now. But it was too soon.

"The great socialist leader Jesus said it best," Big Red opined. "'Man does not live by bread alone.' If I don't help the new guy, who will?"

"Jesus was not a socialist," Tia insisted.

"Read the Bible lately? Listen to what Jesus says, not to what others say about him."

"I have—"

"I don't need any help," Ewan said.

"That's something no man can truly say."

Big Red didn't know it, but Ewan was no human. And he didn't need help, exactly, but he definitely had needs.

"Our new friend needs sustenance, not polemic," Tia said. "Let him eat."

Big Red and Ewan both watched Tia as she walked back to the counter. Every man at the table wanted her. Ewan craved her more than he had words to describe.

"Wish I was thirty years--hell, ten years younger," Big Red told him. "A woman like that—oh, my."

Ewan nodded. Human lives flickered by so quickly, like single frames in a video. By the standards of the street, Big Red was ancient, but to Ewan the man seemed little more than a newborn.

"She's not for the likes of me," Big Red continued. "Not for Sam or Hank, either." He nodded down the long table at two of the men who'd refused to move when Ewan had approached the table.

"If either asks, maybe she'd go out with him." Ewan didn't need magic to see the loneliness that rode Tia like a jockey.

"Those two? They're the taking kind."

Which described Ewan as well. He'd take what he needed if he had no other choice. He wondered, though, if the sense of danger that had roused him from his long sleep had been only those two homeless men conspiring against Tia.

Ewan watched Tia for the next half hour as Big Red tried to raise his political consciousness.

That little distraction barely helped him ignore the hunger that clawed at his insides like a weasel trying to escape. The food and coffee helped not at all. He needed the woman, needed to consume her essence—and he wouldn't let anything stop him.

* * * *

It isn't really dark.

Tia Burns knew true darkness from long winter nights on the Nebraska prairie. Even on a moonless night, New York faded more than really sinking into blackness. Day and night were just different shades of gray.

Gray or black, the Atlantic's wet cold penetrated more completely than even the blizzard winds of home. Tia pulled her coat more tightly about her and tried to pick up her pace. She could have caught a cab, but she was running a bit short this month, and besides, she needed the exercise.

She recognized her mistake when two shadows she hadn't wanted to believe were following her transformed into men.

Walking faster was a mistake. Her leather boot bottoms slipped on ice and got away from her. Her butt hit the ground hard, knocking the wind out of her and her bag slid away.

The figures transmuted into Hank and Sam from the homeless shelter.

She tried to regain her feet, but Sam grabbed her shoulders and dragged her into a nearby ally, then pressed her down as her shoes skitted for traction and found none.

"What a nice surprise running into you here," he said.

Her ex-fiancé had warned her that New York was too dangerous. Maybe he'd been right. "My money is in my purse." She gestured toward the fallen bag. "Take it and leave me alone."

"Not happening," Sam said.

Her body dumped adrenaline into her bloodstream, but Sam held her tightly and her legs just thrashed against the ground.

"We rape her first," Hank said. "Then kill her. No witnesses, no mess."

This wasn't just a robbery. Oddly that knowledge calmed her. She forced herself to relax, as if giving up and then, when Sam's grip loosened just slightly, she twisted, bringing up her feet to kick at his head.

They never made it.

Hank smacked a filthy hand, open-faced, into her cheek, smacking her head back into the pavement.

His blow only knocked the fight out of he for a second, but that was all Sam needed to yank open her coat.

"Always did like those tits," Sam said.

"Well hold on to her, then. 'less you got a problem and want me to hold first.

"I've got a problem with this whole thing." The voice was quiet, nothing like the brash pseudo-confidence of her assailants, but it cut through the night like one of her roommate Lori's samurai katana blades.

The snick of Sam's lockback blade opening was loud enough to wake the dead. "Your problem is butting in where you aren't needed."

"If you ran now, you might still survive," the voice insisted.

The voice sounded familiar. Her spirits sank when she placed it--not a cop, just the new guy, Ewan, from the soup kitchen. The pale guy so gaunt he looked skeletal.

"Get away from here. Call the police," she screamed.

Hank slapped her again.

He must have been holding back the first time he'd hit her. Her head bounced off the concrete, then hit again and pain washed over her like an incapacitating wave.

"That was a mistake." Ewan's voice would chill an arctic wilderness.

Hank grinned, showing a mix of brown enamel and a gap where his upper front teeth should be. "Your mistake. Prob'ly your last."

"The guy behind me has a knife." Tia was past help, but Ewan had a chance if he took off running.

Instead, the idiot stepped forward. Like he was some maiden-rescuing knight.

"Run, moron!"

Sam dropped his grip on Tia's shoulders and stood. He cupped his switchblade against his wrist, hiding it as he faked what looked like a clumsy attack toward the new guy.

Ewan took an unhurried step out of the way, let the knife miss him by a tiny fraction of an inch, then struck twice—his hand moving so quickly it blurred.

As quickly as he's struck, he stepped back, his gaze flickering between Sam and Hank.

Sam stood perfectly still for a good second, then dropped the knife on the ground and collapsed like a lightning-struck tree.

Before Sam fell, though, Ewan had already gripped Hank by his collar and belt, lifted him away from Tia, and held him over his head like a professional wrestler about to launch a smack-down.

It shouldn't have been possible. Ewan had hardly looked strong enough to pick up a good-sized paperback.

"They've earned death." His voice sounded almost bored. "Shall I kill them for you?"

Bile fought its way up her throat. Why was everyone so violent? "Killing them would make you no different than they are."

"Nothing would make me like them." Still, he lowered Hank until he held the murder wanna-be comfortably at waist level. Then he shifted his hips and slid Hank across the ice like a hockey puck, smashing him into his still-grounded friend.

He turned from the two muggers as if they'd ceased existing. "I'll walk you home."

There was no way she'd let anyone connected with the shelter follow her home.

"I need to call the cops." She fumbled for her cell.

"You don't have to do it here."

She stared at him. His face was so gaunt, his high cheekbones threatened to burst through the skin of his face. His dark eyes seemed to absorb rather than reflect light. She'd have said they were black, but she couldn't even say whether that meant dark brown or dark blue. His too hair was black and he didn't wear a hat despite the night's bitter cold.

"Listen, Ewan. Of course I have to call the cops. And I appreciate your help, but I can get home by myself."

"I'll make sure of it."

Her blood felt as cold as the city sidewalk. He'd sat at the same table as Hank and Sam. Was this just a fight over dividing the spoils?

She watched him as she took out her phone and entered the 9-1-1.

The operator promised someone would check out the scene, but couldn't guarantee a time.

Ewan said nothing.

"Look, I'll be all right. I don't need your help." She stepped toward a nearby subway station.

She wobbled when she took her first step. Her knees shook so badly from the adrenaline reaction to her assault that they repeatedly buckled beneath her.

"You *will* be fine. I intend to make sure of that." He grasped her hand, helping her balance.

Her mittens covered her hands, but one of his long, slender fingers extended to that narrow gap between the mitten and her coat and touched the bare skin of her wrist.

His touch burned.

Big Red had claimed Ewan was cold. She'd assumed the loud but friendly religious socialist had meant chilly. But Ewan's touch was closer to the harsh cold of the worst Nebraska freeze, when the arctic air poured down from the north and froze every cloud from the sky.

She shuddered, then her feet skidded on an ice patch, and she slammed headfirst into his chest.

Ewan stood on the same slick patch of ice, but he seemed as set as hardened concrete.

"Sorry." Was all of his body so cold? The question was scary, and just a little sexy.

"No problem." He caught her shoulders, helping her balance.

He smelled wonderful, but it wasn't a cologne she recognized. His scent put her in mind of mountain forests—something piney, musky, but also secret and dark.

"You probably saved my life. Thank you."

"Yes, I did. You're quite welcome."

Not a modest response. But Ewan didn't seem the modest type.

"But I want you to leave me alone now."

His smile started at the corners of his lips but didn't even reach the middle, let alone his impossibly dark eyes. "You are frightened of me. We will need to change that."

His eyes looked like they were peeling away her skull to get inside her brain —no way was she not going to be scared. "I guess I'll see you next time I'm working the kitchen."

"Day after tomorrow? Yes. I shall be there." He paused, staring into her eyes. "I could hardly stay away."

* * * *

"I wish I'd been there. I would have kicked their butts for sure." Tia's roommate, Lori, pranced off her bar stool and threw two high kicks and three punches. She was nothing if not confident with her new orange sash in Kung Fu.

After Tia had taken a long shower, her roommate had called up a friend and the two had dragged her to the neighborhood bar and forced her to down a Tequila shot. It burned but it helped.

"No offense, babe," Lori's friend Marti said, "but I think Tia would rather get rescued by a sexy guy." Like Lori, Marti was an aspiring actor-slash-waitress. Both were beautiful, with size zero figures. Lori was an ebony-black African-American from the Maryland suburbs of Washington D.C. while Lori was a blond from Mississippi, but their shared love of the theater and the dramatic drew them together.

"Not a sexy guy, a homeless guy. Tia can do better than that." Lori said. "Besides, he might be a stone killer"

As usual when the three of them got together, the two actresses were, well, acting. Tia would generally create the topic of conversation and her roommates would take it in ridiculous directions--like the idea that she'd be interested in any guy from the soup kitchen.

Tia shivered as she remembered Ewan's eyes and touch. "He might be a stone killer. He would have killed Hank with as much thought as killing a cockroach."

"It's different when you're rescuing someone," Lori said.

"But why was he there at all? Ewan was following you," Marti insisted, her voice breathless.

"You're paranoid," Lori said. "The guy saved Tia. It isn't as if there are so many sexy men in New York that we can assume the worst about any of them. Especially not straight men."

"That's enough," Tia said. "I don't even know his last name. Unlike some women I could name, I don't just sleep with anything with a Y chromosome."

"Don't look at me," Marti protested. "I invite a guy home, he better not plan on sleeping." She waved at the bartender and ordered drinks. "My round. I'm acing my audition tomorrow so I'll have money."

Tia sighed. She'd gotten the two off the topic of Ewan. If only it were that easy to get him off her mind.

"Let's toast to new boyfriends," Marti suggested when the drinks arrived,

"I don't have a boyfriend."

"If you hung out with anyone other than homeless people, you'd have a boyfriend," Marti argued.

"He's not a—"

"You're right," Lori interrupted. "Let's review the evidence, sweetie. You found a mysterious man with a definite presence. He speaks flawless English, but uses the language as if he isn't used to it. He's homeless, but he

9

wears clean clothes and he doesn't stink. He's only seen at night. He manages not to go into the church sanctuary even though that's a requirement for getting the free meal and the other way out of the soup kitchen is locked. And, oh by the way, he can beat up knifemen without even breaking into a sweat and doesn't care whether they live or die. Know what that sounds like to me?"

"A ninja?" Marti suggested.

"No not a ninja. Tia, your new boyfriend is a vampire."

Chapter 2

His hunger grew stronger. He'd expended too much energy in collapsing probability states to keep Tia safe but so far he had nothing in return.

Ewan let the hungry and homeless press past him, grab their small heap of food, and elbow their way to one of the long tables laid out for them.

A dietitian might claim that the soup kitchen offered a complete and filling meal. Nothing solid could assuage the hunger that tore at him.

"Word on the street is, you had a little trouble." Big Red joined him at the back of the line.

The man was trying to be his friend—Ewan had never been a friend and wasn't ready to start. "I don't remember any trouble."

"That's not what I heard."

"I can't help what you heard."

Big Red ignored his brush-off. "I heard that you beat up Sam and Hank when they assaulted Tia. Considering they both outweigh you, that was good work."

"They weren't assaulting her," Ewan said. "They were going to murder her." But the warning signs hadn't gone away. Tia was still in danger.

Big Red nodded. "Had to be something like that. They're not the brightest bulbs, but even they'd know they couldn't come back if they left her alive to talk. Speaking of Tia, where is she?"

That was the question, all right.

Lacking her, the church was cold stone, its taste made even bitterer by the colder presence of an unwelcoming force.

He could alter probabilities but he couldn't completely protect her and he was too weak to follow her unseen. That's why he'd insisted she call him if she ever fell into danger. If she had, he would come to her no matter where she was, what troubles she faced.

But she was alive. He could taste that in the air.

"Wanted to mention something to you, by the way," Big Red said, interrupting his thoughts. "You snuck out after dinner, didn't stick around for the prayers."

The man must have been watching carefully. "I don't pray."

"Unlike you, I'm no atheist, but my faith runs a lot more on the side of keeping your prayers in the dark. Forced prayer seems like a poke in the eye to everyone, including the big guy upstairs. So, I'm hoping you'll share your escape route."

Ewan's reason for avoiding the church sanctuary was more practical than the boredom of ignorant ministers showering praise they didn't mean on gods who didn't need the worship. One thing Ewan definitely wasn't was an atheist.

"You can't travel my path."

Big Red's expression morphed from mystification to anger to resignation in less than a second. "Guess you're right, my friend. Too many sneak out, they'd notice. Then we might all suffer. Government money pays for the slop they feed us, but they still insist we listen to their prayers."

"Want a bit of advice?" Ewan hesitated a second before using a word that had never had much meaning to him. Finally he went ahead. "Friend."

"I'm not too proud to listen."

"You'd convince more people if you toned down the rhetoric. People can't even hear your meaning because of the way you say it."

Big Red laughed and slapped Ewan on the shoulder. "I know <u>that</u>. But I like being able to use my own words."

"Even if it means that your message doesn't always get through?"

"You know the line about standing at the door, knocking."

Pain rippled through him and Ewan shuddered. "I know <u>all</u> the lines."

Big Red looked at him more closely. "You just might at that. Anyway, I figure, I'm the guy at the door knocking. I tell people the truth. It's up to them what they do with it. They're ready, they hear. They aren't ready, maybe there's someone there who can dress up the truth for them so much its own mother wouldn't recognize it."

By then, though, Ewan wasn't listening. He felt Tia's glow though she was still outside.

She was rushing, knowing she was late, and her hurry added an extra glow to her presence.

Big Red followed Ewan's gaze, so both were staring the door for a good half-minute before Tia burst through it and rushed for the kitchen.

"You've got good ears," the aging radical said.

"I hear things many others miss."

"Maybe you can hear this, then. Tia Burns may look like a big strong girl, but she's fragile inside. Anyone tries to hurt her, they'll answer to me."

Ewan's hearing wasn't his only superior sense. He knew that Tia was breakable, knew that she was a candle, burning hot but easily and quickly snuffed out. Worse, he knew he might be the one who broke her.

But Tia was just a mortal and Ewan was dying of hunger and Tia was his sustenance. He didn't want to shatter her pure and precious faith, but some hungers can't be denied.

"You hear me, Ewan?"

"I hear you, Big Red."

Big Red had to know Ewan hadn't promised anything, but he had made his threat and Ewan had listened.

They joined the line of homeless and inched their way forward, plates held in front of them like shields.

* * * *

Ewan was here.

Tia had left work early enough, but her afternoon would have been slapstick if it hadn't been so dangerous. She'd barely survived one threat before walking into the next near-disaster. First, a car had come over the curb, barely missing her and running into a department store plate-glass window. Then a scary-looking man in a dark suit had followed her for a couple of blocks, only to get grabbed by a couple of even scarier looking guys. Okay, that was par for New York. What had happened afterwards had been really weird.

Tia didn't believe in magic. But what happened strained coincidence.

She'd noticed her shoelaces had come untied and bent to retie them just as an exploding car spewed gasoline exactly where she would have been if she'd kept walking. Even in New York, cars don't just explode for no reason.

Thanks to the car explosion, she'd been late for her train, and missed a derailment that closed the subway.

When she'd summoned a taxi, another guy had shoved her out of the way and jumped in, only to be confronted by a gun-wielding driver.

She finally arrived at the soup kitchen a good half-hour late and completely frazzled. Seeing Ewan frazzled her even more.

The strange man, the possible vampire if she were to believe her roommate, joined the back of the line while she slipped on her apron and hairnet. He acted exactly as if he'd been waiting for her to arrive.

She pushed her way into among the servers and smiled as she dished a scoop of the corned beef hash for Big Red.

Then Ewan stood before her.

She studied her rescuer carefully.

Until that moment, she'd treated Lori's vampire theory as a joke. Seeing his contrast with Big Red, his muscles practically flailed, his pale skin, and his tight skin clinging to the bones of his skull made her lose her concentration and dump his hash back in the serving pan.

But the idea was ridiculous. Human vampires were mythical. Goth-types might call themselves vampires, but actual undead had to be a scientific impossibility, not to mention questionable religious dogma. She shook her heads. That she'd only seen Ewan at night couldn't mean anything. She only saw any of the soup kitchen clients at night.

"Nice to—" her voice squeaked, so she cleared her throat and started over. "Nice to see you again, Ewan."

"You had some troubles, didn't you? Remember to call my name if you're ever in danger."

Yeah, right. She'd just call his name into the wind and a he'd appear like a genie, anxious to do her bidding. She might be from a farm in Nebraska, but she hadn't fallen off the cabbage truck.

Oddly, she *had* been thinking about him as she'd headed from her office to the kitchen, as the string of accidents had happened around her. But she wouldn't believe he'd had anything to do with her miraculous survival—or the random disasters.

"I appreciate the offer but I hardly think it's realistic."

He smiled, showing white even teeth. "Not everything is realistic. Some is just real."

Yeah, right. He must think he was Yoda or something. She dug out another spoonful and plopped the scoop of the corned beef hash on his plate. "Enjoy your dinner."

"Thank you. I'll walk you home afterwards."

"Not necessary. I'm—" She was talking to his back and let her voice trail off.

He wasn't a vampire—that was ridiculous. Still, she couldn't help watching him as he stepped toward an empty seat.

His dark overcoat had to be cashmere. His pants were so black that they caught her gaze and threatened to suck it in.

"Wonder how *he* became homeless," one of the other volunteers said. "Maybe I should take him home."

"I hope you're kidding."

The other volunteer laughed. "Guess my husband would have problems with that."

"You don't think he could be a vam—" Tia cut herself off, not able to even say the word. "I'll serve some coffee."

"Good idea, hon. Looks like Big Red's table could use some." Big Red's table being where Ewan sat.

Tia didn't like feeling pathetic, but Ewan fascinated her even as he frightened her. She just had to learn more about him, she decided. Maybe she just needed to be laugh at Lori for suggesting he was a vampire.

Most of the guys had finished dinner and were mopping their plates with slices of white bread to soak up any remaining crumbs or grease, polishing their plastic plates to a high sheen. Ewan had moved the hash around on his plate. She couldn't tell that he'd actually eaten any.

"Coffee, gentlemen?"

She started with Big Red, moving around the table clockwise and getting to Ewan last.

He put down the fork he'd pretended to eat with and held up his coffee mug, but Tia's eyes were glued to his fork where he'd set it on the table.

Impossibly, frost formed where his fingers had touched the metal. Now that was completely weird.

Nobody could be that cold. Nobody alive, at any rate.

"Enjoy your coffee." She filled his cup then hurried back to the serving line although everyone had been served and there was nothing but cleanup left.

While the homeless trickled upstairs to the church sanctuary, she straightened, dumped the remains of the hash into freezer bags, scrubbed the large pans so they could be used again the next day, and sorted recyclables from trash. Anything to avoid thinking about the frosty fingerprints on Ewan's fork.

She was still scrubbing pans when Ewan and Big Red finally headed upstairs. They were discussing Nietzsche's argument about God's death.

Big Red generally had strong opinions on everything, so the *topic* didn't surprise her. What did surprise her was that Big Red spent at least as much time listening to Ewan as he did talking. Since the outdated radical spent his day reading old philosophers, he didn't usually have much time for other people's uninformed opinions. He'd made time for Ewan.

Relief warred with a peculiar disappointment in Tia's emotions when she realized that Ewan hadn't followed up on his promise to walk her home.

Clearly Lori had been kidding about Ewan being a vampire. People enjoyed reading about the undead, but they didn't really believe in them. Still, Tia wished Lori had skipped that particular joke. Because now it was all she could think of —well, all except the magnetism the man, or whatever he was, exuded.

A few minutes later, she heard recorded hymns and relaxed. Everyone knew vampires couldn't enter consecrated ground. She might not believe in vampires, but she certainly did believe in the power of faith. Surely her beliefs would keep her safe from anything unnatural. Not, she reminded herself, that there was anything she needed to be kept safe from.

"I'm trying too hard to convince myself."

"What, hun?" The other volunteer looked up from the ten-quart coffeemaker she was cleaning.

"Nothing." She was really far-gone when she resorted to talking to herself.

Tia hung up the big pots that had held food, wiped down the counters and tables, and waited until a shuffle of footsteps told her that the homeless had finished paying for their dinner by listening to Rev. Thruston's prayers. They weren't required to pray themselves, but hearing the prayers wouldn't hurt them any.

Moments later, Rev. Thruston poked his head downstairs.

"Still here, Tia?"

"Just finishing up."

"You usually come up to pray. We missed you."

"I got busy." She paused, gathered her courage. "Can I ask you a question?"

"You can ask. I can only promise my best with the answer."

She took a deep breath. "Can vampires exist?"

He grinned. "I assume you're not talking about South American bats."

"I was thinking blood-sucking undead humans."

"Since you're asking a minister, you must want a religious answer. Here it is. The mythological vampire, like Dracula, is not inconsistent with the teachings of the church, although it raises interesting questions about the nature of the soul. From a scientific perspective, though, it's pretty unlikely. Where would vampirism have come from? Think about it. Human DNA is quite similar to the DNA of great apes and other primates. But I've never heard of a monkey vampire. Have you?"

She admitted she hadn't.

"Bottom line. Unless you've seen something to contradict it, I'd have to say that the vampires are nothing but myth."

"So you don't think Ewan could possibly be one?"

"Whom?"

"Ewan. A new guy at the kitchen. Good looking, tall, broad shoulders but really thin looking. Pale."

"Doesn't sound like anyone I saw."

Ewan stood out. Rev. Thruston should have seen him. It didn't mean he was a vampire, of course, but how else could he have avoided the mandatory prayer meeting? "Okay. Thanks, Reverend."

"Call me Paul."

"Right. I'll see you on Friday, then."

Rev. Thruston--she *couldn't* think of him as Paul—looked around. "Are you going to be all right going home, Tia? I heard something happened on Monday."

"I was in the wrong place at the wrong time." There seemed to be a lot of that going around.

He considered, then reached into his cassock. "Why don't you take this, then. It might help."

He held his closed fist to her.

She expected a cross, or maybe a St. Christopher medal—if Presbyterians believed in St. Christopher. Instead, he handed her a small can of pepper spray. "You need this more than I do. And my body doesn't inspire much desire."

He probably wanted her to argue that, but he was right. "Thanks, Reverend Thrus—uh, Paul."

He showed her out and locked the door behind her.

* * * *

Tia hurried home, Rev. Thruston's pepper spray heavy in the hand Tia kept in her coat pocket. Whenever another pedestrian stepped toward her, she had to fight the urge to pull it out and start spraying.

Only when she hit a deserted stretch of road did she finally relax.

Mistake.

"I'd almost think you were avoiding me." Ewan hadn't been there. Now he stood in front of her as solid as a statue. Desperately, she looked for a shadow but it was too dark.

She rocked back on her heels. "How... what... where—"

"I told you I'd walk you home." Ewan spoke as if she'd offered him some friendly greeting rather than a panicked sputter. "I've been thinking about what Sam and Hank were up to."

She nodded. She still had the pepper spray and Ewan hadn't done anything to her yet. Maybe she was just being paranoid. "Okay, we'll walk. I live this way." She pointed to her next turn.

"I know."

How could he know where she lived? The apartment wasn't in her name and she didn't plaster her address in men's restrooms. The answer--he couldn't know. He was lying.

"Can I ask you some questions?" she finally said.

"Of course."

"Why did you help me?"

"Any gentleman would have helped if he'd seen you being attacked."

He'd avoided giving her a real answer but she let that slide. For the time being, anyway.

"And you're walking with me now because you're concerned that Hank and Sam will pull something else?"

"What Sam and Hank did makes no sense. Why would they attack the one woman who could identify them?"

It had been odd. They hadn't really been interested in her money. They'd meant to rape her, but that had felt like an afterthought. Their main goal had been her death—which wouldn't benefit anyone.

"I'll bite, why?" She slapped a hand over her mouth at her poor choice of words. Mentioning biting to a suspected vampire had to be unwise.

"Perhaps they were carried away by lust." His eyes, which now seemed to hold just a hint of gray, appraised her, showing neither doubt nor approval. "Perhaps they were seeking something only you had to offer. Then again, perhaps they didn't choose you themselves. Can we consider the possibility that you were set up?"

Despite what Sam and Hank had said, Tia didn't like that possibility at all. "I'm a paralegal, not a supermodel. And I don't even work criminal law. The Internal Revenue Service might want our law firm shut down, but they're not going to hire Sam and Hank to take me out."

It was a feeble attempt at a joke, and Ewan didn't smile.

His gaze swallowed her, brushing against her form but also seeming to penetrate beneath her clothing, beneath her skin, into the essence that was Tia, whatever that essence might be. "You are more than a paralegal, Tia."

"I guess everyone is more than just their job." Even to herself, her voice sounded forced, breathy. "And speaking of jobs, why are you pretending to be homeless?"

His lips, barely less pale than his face turned up. His smile looked bitter. "But I am homeless."

"I'm *so* sure. You've changed your clothes since the last time I saw you. Maybe you don't know this, but homeless people don't keep spare sets of clothing around—because others steal them. You're clean but you don't smell like the disinfectants shelters use. And you're not hungry enough to eat the food we serve at the kitchen. Why don't you stop giving me your line and try the truth for once?"

"I'm more hungry than you can imagine." Ewan's smile faded. The expression that replaced it combined a world-weariness that went beyond anything she'd imagined with an ache that made a part of her want to clasp him to her breast.

"But—"

"I haven't lied to you, Tia. If I appear clean, that is largely an illusion. If I do not eat, it is because ordinary food does not begin to satisfy my hunger." He shrugged. "As for the rest, I can see why you would be confused, but I have not lied. I lost my ancient home and have no other."

Now *that* sounded scary. Hunger that food couldn't meet? Ancient home? Maybe Lori's joke wasn't so funny after all.

"What hunger?" She held up a hand. "Don't answer yet because I don't need any more lies. I saw the frost on your fork from where your fingers touched it. I know that you're not what you seem to be. I want the truth."

He nodded. "I do not lie. Never"

"Right. Give it to me straight." She looked at him, standing there in the near dark, his feet dry despite the icy slush on the ground, his coat immaculate, his face hungry and pale. "Are you a vampire?"

Chapter 3

For the first time in a thousand year, Ewan felt an urge to laugh. He'd sensed Tia's suspicion and confusion, her battle between desire and terror. He hadn't guessed her imagination had taken that turn.

"By vampire I assume you mean a formerly human person who has died and been transformed into a blood-sucking creature who can only be killed by a stake through his heart? I am not one of those."

She didn't look satisfied by his answer, which was unfortunate. He wanted to get her under his influence before he gave her the full truth.

"Are you some other kind of vampire?"

It was another question he could evade, answering truthfully but incompletely. "I don't suck blood."

"But you don't eat food, either."

"Not as you understand it."

Comprehension replaced confusion. "Got it. You're an alien, right? You're cold because you came from some planet that's further from its sun than Earth is from ours. Are you an explorer, or are you trying to decide whether we're ready for some great technological gift? Or are you maybe scooping Earth out for some destructive purpose—is that the sense that you're a vampire?"

"I am amazingly un-alien."

She stopped in the middle of the sidewalk. "I'm not letting you any closer to my apartment until you tell me what you are. Spill or get lost."

Her faith and honesty shined like a beacon. Just being this close to her fed him as he hadn't been fed in centuries. In all the years of his memory, he could think of only a few people who had that glow. Abraham, perhaps, that day when he'd come down from the mountain with his son still alive. Siddhartha, of course. Joan of Arc, too. But not many more. Then again, Ewan hadn't been aware of much for the past few centuries, until Tia had awakened him.

"I'm a god, Tia."

"Oh, Jesus." She rolled her eyes. "Why do I attract all the nutcases?"

The outpouring of her faith turned bitter to his taste and he reeled away. "Not *that* God. I was ancient when Moses talked to his burning bush and rallied the Hebrews in Egypt. But I was *not* his god."

"You're being blasphemous. There is only one God."

"You may be right." He shrugged. "But there are many, too."

"**Don't confuse me with made-up paradoxes. Is there one god, or many?**"

"There are tens of thousands. That doesn't mean there isn't only one."

"Spare me the bullshit."

He was surprised she could curse without affecting the glow of faith that surrounded her. But she managed.

"Have you ever studied the Hindu faith?"

She narrowed her eyes, staring at him as she decided whether to talk or run.

"I took comparative religion in college. Why?"

The temptation to reach into her brain, close a few synapses, make her decision for her nearly overwhelmed him.

The trickle of energy he absorbed from Tia was like an occasional drop of water teasing rather than satisfying a man dying of thirst.

But mental compulsion was dangerous. If he altered her mind and soul, he might destroy the wellsprings of her power—and himself. He had to stay be patient, survive on the random scraps from her bounty, and gradually persuade her to worship only him. He had time, after all. Tia was young. Once she stood behind him, he could reclaim his place among the powerful. With *all* of her faith, he could dominate the world and recreate what the ancient Romans had stolen from him.

Patience, he told himself.

"You are aware of the basics of the Hindu faith?" he asked.

"Three gods, right? Creator, Preserver, Destroyer. Brahma, Vishnu, Shiva. Lots of arms. Animal vehicles. Dancing."

He shook his head. "That misses the point. Hindus believe in a single god-spirit. This ultimate unitary god takes multiple aspects. The three you name, along with their female sides, are only the primary forms the single spirit takes. Three male and three female aspects make six. Each of these six primary gods self-creates avatars as needed—lesser gods. Hindus believe in a whole pantheon of these sub-gods, each more or less similar to the gods worshiped by the Greeks and Romans. Each of these gods, you understand, is an aspect of one of the three primary god pairs which, in turn, are reflections of the one."

"So you're saying that you are some aspect—"

He shrugged. "I've speculated on where I and the other gods might have come from, just as you humans speculate on why *you* are here. Like you, I don't *know*. I certainly don't remember a time when I was one with Yahweh, or Zeus, or Brahma—even if such a time existed."

She sighed. "This is the most absurd thing I've ever heard, Ewan. I don't even know why I'm having this conversation."

He waved a hand. "I can manage a burning bush if you really need confirmation."

* * * *

"Give me a break." Tia glared at the tiny burning shrub, then looked around for the video cameras.

She'd walked into it when she'd asked if he was a vampire but this had to be a gag. Considering she lived in New York, maybe someone was creating a TV pilot for *America's Most Gullible*.

She didn't see anyone who looked like a cameraman, but that didn't mean much. She'd spent enough time with Lori's actor-friends to know that tiny video cameras could be hidden anywhere.

"There's no one here but us."

If he hadn't lied, she could have handled this a lot better. Instead, she got mad. "What we're doing at the soup kitchen is important and you're mocking it. I don't want to see you there again. I don't want to see you anywhere. Get out of my life, Ewan. And stay out."

She pulled out the pepper spray Rev. Thruston had given her to make sure Ewan got the message, but she didn't need it. The wanna-be-god looked like he'd been caught in one of the gales that blew down on Nebraska from the north and half-backed, half-faded into the foggy night.

The rest of her trip home, she constantly checked behind her, making sure Ewan wasn't following, and thought about how he'd vanished—and his burning bush trick.

For a couple of blocks, she thought she heard footsteps, but she ducked into a magazine shop and checked. Despite the overcoat and black slacks, the man she'd been suspicious of wasn't Ewan. He was tall, muscular, and good looking, but he definitely wasn't Ewan. He was just another guy on the sidewalks of New York.

Still, the stranger grinned at her as if he knew she was afraid. But he did nothing.

She told herself not to be disappointed. She'd wanted Ewan gone, told him to get lost. Still, a part of her couldn't help feeling let down. Lori was right about one thing—really sexy guys didn't come along every day.

Naturally Lori was disappointed, too. In Tia, not in Ewan.

"Maybe he is a god."

Tia poured herself a second glass of the cheap red wine they kept around the apartment. She'd gulped down the first one before she'd even told her roommate what had happened. She wasn't a big drinker, but this was starting to be a pattern—see Ewan and get a drink.

"I know you're New Age, but even you don't believe that Gods hang out in homeless shelters, do you?"

Lori shrugged. "Your soup kitchen is in a church. Ever think about that?"

"That's different. And a little tiny burning bush floating about four feet above the ground? Come on—that's ridiculous."

"You *told* him you wanted a sign."

"He isn't a god. There is no such thing as gods wandering around."

"I used to sing in the choir you know," Lori reminded her. "I know about ordinary religion. I also know the *Bible* is a bit unclear on whether God is the only God, or if he's just the best God."

"It's not unclear at all. And even if it was, why would I bother with some god whose idea of a miracle is to burn a six inch bush?"

"Because he's sexy?"

"Not good enough."

"Because he saved your life."

"He might have set that up."

"If he'd set it up, would he just let you walk away?"

Tia poured two more glasses of wine. "He's just a weird guy. I'm not going to waste my life worrying about weird guys."

"One thing for sure," Lori said. "He's not doing a TV pilot. He'd need to get a model release form before he could do anything with the footage."

"Maybe he's trying to sell the concept?"

"He couldn't even do that. Besides, the idea is ridiculous. Who would advertise on a show about a guy who pretends to be a minor god? If somebody <u>was</u> dumb enough to want to make a series like that, they'd hire real actresses rather than pick someone off the street and come up with more convincing stunts than frost on a fork or a tiny burning shrub. I mean, how about that guy who made the Statue of Liberty disappear. That was a miracle."

"That was a trick," Tia reminded Lori. "There was nothing magic about that."

Lori sipped her wine. "And this isn't? There are just two possibilities. First, he's insane and he's behind all that bad stuff that happened to you, including setting you up for that attack a couple of nights ago. Or second, he's telling the truth."

"They're both impossible."

"Something odd is going on. It's interesting that he told you to call him if you got in trouble."

"He said to call but he didn't give me a number."

"He's a god. He can hear without a phone."

"That's crazy." Tia shouldn't have told Lori anything about Ewan. Her roommate was a mega-romantic and wanted everything to be just like in the movies. But they put those endings in the movies so people would pay twelve dollars to see what doesn't happen in real life.

"Know what Marti would say?"

Lori's friend Marti was devout. "She'd agree with me."

"She'd say he's the Antichrist."

"That's absurd."

"That's why I didn't say it."

Tia looked at the nearly full glass of wine and decided she'd had enough. "I'm going to bed. When I wake up, things will make more sense."

Lori sighed. "It doesn't matter whether he's a god or a vampire or whatever. If he's a good-looking guy, he won't have any problems finding more women than he can shake a stick at. If he's interested in you in particular, he has a reason."

"You always make me feel so desirable."

"You're not exactly low-hanging fruit. New York is full of women who'll do anything to snag a guy. Why work at it if he doesn't have to?"

"I don't know."

Lori seemed to think she'd made a point. "Well, I don't blame you for being scared, but I think you're going to have to figure out what he really wants."

"I'm not scared." But Tia was lying.

* * * *

She couldn't breathe.

I didn't even finish my second glass of wine was her first thought. What felt like the hangover to end hangovers threatened to split her head in two.

22

Somewhere in the distance, an annoying buzzer sounded—as her befuddled brain struggled to make sense of it.

Smoke detector. A mental picture of her father replacing the batteries in the detector when her family had visited New York over the Thanksgiving holidays flashed into her head. It had made a noise like that when he'd tested it. But this was no test. She inhaled. Something was burning.

Across the bedroom, Lori made a snarfing sound.

"Wake up. Something's burning."

"Huh?"

"That's the smoke detector. And I smell fire."

"But—"

"Get down, near the floor," Tia cautioned as Lori stumbled to her feet. She tried to remember long-ago fire safety lectures. "Put on shoes and jeans and let's see if we can get out of here." She dialed 9-1-1 and reported a fire.

The operator suggested they get out if they could.

After hurriedly dressing, Tia and Lori made their way to the door leading to the exterior hallway.

Lori reached for the knob, but Tia pushed her roommate's hand away. "Careful." She coughed a few times because she'd gotten a mouthful of smoke. Then she brought her finger close to the door.

Hot! And a dull red color glowed from the bottom of the door, where it didn't quite meet the jam.

"That's—" She coughed again, "Fire out there."

"What'll we do?" Lori demanded.

"Fire escape is down the hall. We can try the window, but I'd say it's time to pray."

Their room was on the tenth floor. Tia was almost certain fire department ladders wouldn't reach high enough. Jumping meant dying more quickly than burning.

"Maybe the fire department can put it out in time."

They could only hope. That and try to stay alive until the firefighters reached them.

Tia coughed again, harder. "Lori, wet some towels and let's stuff them in the doorjamb. I'll see if any firemen are in the street. Maybe they've set up some nets."

Jumping into a net from a hundred feet didn't sound much safer than jumping onto concrete, but looking offered an illusion of progress. Growing up on a farm had taught Tia that some things have to be accepted, but that you still gave them a good fight, just to make sure.

Seeing nothing below, she dialed 9-1-1 again. The operator told her that the fire department had been dispatched. When Tia said they were on the tenth floor, the operator hemmed for a moment, then fell silent. Tia knew what that meant. The firemen weren't going to be able to get them out.

"I wish I'd gotten to at least make the casting call for the *Guys and Dolls* revival tomorrow," Lori said. "The world needs a black Sarah Brown."

Despite the towels under the door, the smoke was growing thicker. Heat radiated through walls and the crackle of fire sounded loud over the more distant clamor of sirens and emergency radios.

"We're not dead yet." Tia's affirmation would have been stronger if she hadn't broken into another coughing fit at the end of it.

The two women sat on their living room rug and joined hands. Already the wood floors were hot to the touch.

"We should pray," Tia said.

"Know what I think?" Lori asked after a few moments of silence.

"That our parents were right and we should have stayed home and gotten married or something?"

Lori wrinkled her forehead. "I'm thinking this is another of your disasters and it's related to that god-guy at your kitchen. He said you should call if you need help. Well, do it. We sure need help."

Tia didn't want to believe Ewan had caused all of the problems she faced, but could it be coincidence? She pulled out her cell and stared at it. "I told you he didn't give me a number."

Lori sighed dramatically, with a cough at the end. "Hey, I'm almost ready for a Camille revival."

"I don't see how—"

"How many gods named Ewan are waiting for your call? Let's both say his name together. Like this." Lori took a deep breath and put her hands together in a prayer position. "Ewan. Ewan. Ewan. Come, we need you." She paused a moment. "I did say, *together*, didn't I? As in, both of us."

"Asking for help from some false god is wrong."

"Apologize to your minister *after* Ewan rescues us. Come on, Tia, he's waiting for *your* call. He knew we'd need help--that's why he told you to call him. So, do it. Come on Tia, on three. Ewan, Ewan, Ewan. Come on, god-man. Any time would be fine. The sooner the better."

Tia joined in the chant, but half-heartedly. Ewan couldn't be a god, and he wouldn't hear the call. Even if he heard, what could he do?

"Come on," Lori urged. "I'm too young to die."

Tia concentrated. "Ewan, if you're going to help, now would be a good time." She let her thoughts reach out to the universe. Not that she was praying to Ewan. Still, it couldn't be wrong to *hope* he'd find some way to rescue her.

Lori continued chanting Ewan's name, her voice weakening as smoke and poisonous fumes crept under the seal in the door and through the cracks and conduits that connected their apartment to the rest of the building.

The floor grew hotter and flames flickered outside their window, now. If they weren't rescued soon, it would be too late.

From open window, the sound of sirens and the chatter of helicopter blades rattled the night. But the fire's angry roar dominated everything.

Tia didn't even hear the chainsaw at first, couldn't believe its snarl was anything but more fire.

When tool's the sharp steel teeth cut through the floor near her feet, she couldn't deny it.

"What the devil?" Lori pulled herself back from the saw and the women watched as it traversed a circle through their floor, slicing off a substantial chunk of the Turkish carpet they hadn't really been able to afford but had bought anyway when Tia had gotten her job at the law firm.

A section of floor collapsed into the apartment beneath them and a helmeted head stuck through. A fireman, of course. Relief, coupled with just a hint of disappointment that it wasn't Ewan flooded through Tia even as an updraft of hot air smashed through the new opening so strongly it felt like an ocean wave crashing over her.

A rescue so soon after they'd sent their mental message to Ewan was nothing but coincidence.

The fireman passed up insulated blanket and shouted that they should wrap them around themselves. Then he gestured for the women to follow him downward through the hole he'd created in their floor.

They lowered themselves onto a dining room table in the fully engulfed apartment below their own. Tia looked around, but the fireman appeared to be alone. What was that about?

Red flames surged where they burned wood, blue where heat had exploded liquor bottles, and white where electrical appliances sparked and shorted. Despite the insulating blanket, hairs on Tia's arms shriveled in the intense heat and her head, already woozy from fumes, threatened to explode.

"Hold your breath," the fireman said. Follow me."

Another hole led further downward to the level below and, abruptly, they were out of the heat, fumes and noise.

Tia gasped for fresh air as the fireman led them out of the eighth floor apartment and down the hall to the stairwell.

"Someone started the fire on the ninth floor, directly beneath your apartment."

Without the background roar of fire, she recognized the voice.

"Ewan?"

"You called me, didn't you?"

Chapter 4

His hunger had distracted him, almost fatally.

Ewan wasn't omniscient. The people who had worshiped back when the world had moved from the Stone Age to the Bronze Age had believed in gods who could be fooled, who could be bargained with, who could be as petty and as narrow minded as themselves. Those weaknesses had nearly killed Tia and her friend, had nearly destroyed him.

He should have been more alert. Tia stood directly in a bull's eye, and Ewan had no idea who targeted her. Which made him responsible for this near-disaster.

Despite his anger, his lips curled up into something vaguely like a smile. For just a few seconds as she'd called him, she'd flooded him with power. It wasn't all that she had to offer, of course, but she had believed in him a bit. It gave him a hint of what he'd enjoy once he persuaded her to yield to him, to worship him, to give him everything she had.

First, though, he had to keep her alive. He hurried the women down the fire escape, then stripped off his fireman uniform and was back in his dark topcoat and pants.

It took almost no effort to encourage the police holding back the curious to ignore them as he and the women walked past the police line and into a cab that had pulled alongside to gawk.

"Take us to a hotel. A nice one. Close."

"Solita all right?"

A clear picture of the hotel came from the driver's mind. "Fine."

The driver took off, not bothering with his meter. Ewan hadn't been aware for long, but he knew about meters and money. Better to take what he needed.

The cabby pulled up in front of the hotel, wished them a happy stay, loaded up a new passenger and took off.

"He didn't ask us to pay him?" Tia sounded like she'd just witnessed a bigger miracle than Ewan responding to her psychic call or chilling his fork to frosty temperatures.

"He caught a very good fare at the hotel to make up for carrying us for free."

"What? Forgotten gods don't carry cash?"

With power, getting money would be easy. A small electrical glitch in a bank computer and he'd have an account with whatever amount he wanted. With money, he could use Tia's power as a base to establish himself as a dominant god in the weird world he found himself in. But he needed Tia before he could do anything. And he needed her alive for that to happen.

Tia and her roommate, Lori, inspected the hotel lobby with some trepidation.

"It was nice of you to rescue us, but we can't afford to stay here," Lori said.

Oddly, this black woman believed in him. He couldn't remember ever having a black believer but the taste of her manna was identical to any believer. Unfortunately, Lori's manna was an infinitesimal fraction of the pure power that Tia commanded.

"Have faith in me. Money won't be a problem," he said. Or rather, faith would solve any problems.

The hotel manager met them at the door, presented them each with a key to a minisuite, and thanked them for staying at her hotel. After inquiring whether they needed bell help with their baggage, she vanished back into her office.

"You're magicking these people, aren't you, Ewan?" Tia sounded disapproving. Her disapproval cut back in the spillage he picked up from her.

Ewan was more familiar with *establishing* moral rules than *following* someone else's. Still, he thought he understood where Tia was coming from.

He waited to answer until the elevator had deposited them outside the top-floor room and put his key in the door. Nice they way these electronic things worked. Almost magic.

"This suite wasn't being used. It will cost the manager nothing to allow you to stay there while you recover from the attack."

"But I'm not sure it's right." Tia fumbled out a credit card. "Maybe I could pay for a couple of nights. Uh, how much is it?"

He shook his head. People of great faith could be so difficult. "You've been assaulted, nearly destroyed by obviously created accidents, and now someone set fire to your apartment. Your credit card record would appear in a computer, which would be as good as an invitation to attack you again."

"Well, you say you're a god. Maybe you can tell me who is supposed to be doing all these things, and why. Tia crossed her arms across her chest. "One thing I know for sure, Sam and Hank couldn't have derailed a subway, exploded a car, or set that fire. And who else would care?"

Ewan lifted a hand to Tia's face, skimming just beyond its surface, healing the minor burns that she probably hadn't even noticed in the adrenaline rush of escape, but that could fester if left unaided. He had enough strength to heal her and her friend. It was little enough for him to do, considering that he stole his strength from her.

"You're right. Sam and Hank are just tools. Another is behind the fire, behind Sam and Hank's attack, too."

The three of them stood in front of the half-opened suite door. Lori poked him with a finger to his chest.

"'Another?' As in you have no clue? You're supposed to be a god. Wave your hand, shoot a lightning bolt. Make all those badguys disappear."

Tia looked shocked. "Come on, Lori. You can't just go around killing people."

Ewan had been certain Tia would take that view. She hadn't even allowed him to kill Hank after the man had tried to rape and murder her. Killing others, even those responsible for arson, was outside Tia's nature. Balancing Tia's moral beliefs with reality was going to be tough. Keeping her in the dark just might be the easier--as long as she didn't ask inconvenient questions.

"You said yourself that *accidents*—" Lori made two-finger quote marks in the air, "—keep happening near you. But now we know they weren't really accidents at all. Someone tried to kill you by driving a car up onto the sidewalk. Someone sabotaged the subway you were supposed to be riding. Did you hear that twenty-three people were hospitalized as a result of that *accident*? And now the fire. Another <u>accident</u> that could have hurt a lot of people. Someone is playing hardball. We can't let them get away with it."

Tia shook her head stubbornly. "Killing doesn't solve problems."

"As it happens," Ewan said, "I can't just zap them. *They* know about Tia, and therefore me. But *I'm* clueless about who they are. The motive is easy enough to guess, but there are many who might share that motivation."

"What motive?"

He sighed. "They're using you to get to me."

"Boy, that makes me feel real important."

Ewan had nothing to say to that. Whether she knew it or not, Tia was incredibly important. Old worn-out gods were a dime a dozen. Humans who generated faith like Tia, what the gods called 'manna pumps,' came along once every few hundred years.

Tia pushed the suite door the rest of the way open and looked around. "Wow. This is really nice."

The women flopped into couches set around an expansive living area. Ewan prowled. Waiting should be easy for him considering he'd spent the previous two thousand years in a sort of stasis. It wasn't. He needed to be on the hunt.

As long as Tia remained in danger, he was vulnerable. He needed to use Tia's manna to create new power for himself. He didn't need to get distracted by the details of her life. He certainly didn't need the weird desire he felt for her. He hadn't been a fertility god in five thousand years—if he had to have sex with her, it would be about manipulation, not desire.

"As long as you stay inside, call for room service, don't let anyone else know you're here, you should be safe. You'll need to move in a week but I'll help you find another place then. One with stronger protections."

"You want us to stay here like lumps?" Tia sounded shocked. "I've got a job and my volunteer work."

"Can't do it," Lori added. "I've got three auditions this week. Do you have any idea how unusual that is? I'm not going to sit in a hotel room and let other people take my slots."

"You've got to stay safe," he argued. "Once I discover your enemies, you can get back to your normal lives." Normal lives that lasted a few short years. A god could normally be patient, but Ewan couldn't—not when something could happen to Tia at any time.

"What enemies?" Tia stood and blocked the door like the angel defending the Garden of Eden. *Did he really remember that angel?*

"And why me?" she continued. "You say they're using me to get to you, but why should you care? Until three days ago, you didn't even know I existed."

"I knew." He'd been vaguely aware of her since her birth. But her work with the homeless had transformed her, like a cup of gasoline transforms smoldering ashes into a blazing flame. The faint trickle of power that had made him aware of the world increased until he could move again, could pull himself free of the faded bonds that had held him. He'd come as quickly as he could, but clearly he hadn't been the only being to sense Tia's power.

Tia's anger cut him like a blade, denying him even those wasted splashes of faith that could sustain him. "Why me?"

"Someone is using you to pull my strings like a puppet-master, intending me to dance their tune."

"I'm like anyone else."

He shook his head. "You generate more power than a ten thousand ordinary people. Without you, I'd either wither or have to kowtow to whomever is behind the threat."

She shook her head. "I don't believe in you."

He gestured to himself. "Which is why I'm only a shadow. Do you know why my hands feel cold? Because the vacuum of space fills my emptiness."

"That's weird, Ewan," Lori said. "What about me? I believe in you."

He smiled at the young actor. "That helps. But Tia is a faith-freak-- something that happens only rarely in human history.

"So they want to grab me and use me?"

"More likely, they see you as a dangerous independent power source."

"So, according to you, they'd kill me just to free you up? Even if I believed in you, I don't think I'd believe that."

Anger surged through the emptiness that was he. Weak and hungry, he might be, but he was a god. The powers of a god were not meant for humans to exploit.

"Imagine being able to control a god. You Americans have an expression about something being 'an act of God.' Go with that idea. Using me, they could determine who gets struck by lightning, what man in a crowd clutches his chest, hit with a heart attack. For lack of a better term, gods are, well, godlike."

"Why am I having a hard time believing this?"

"You were prepared to believe I was a vampire or an alien and you don't even believe in them. You do believe in gods, but you have a hard time with that."

"That's different."

"A god *needs* faith like a mythological vampire needs blood. Without it, we shrivel, we die. Gods and humans are symbiotic. You shape us, give us our power through your faith, your prayers. And we, in return, do what you created us to do."

"Well, *I* didn't shape or create you. I don't even believe in you. I have my own faith, my own God. The real God."

Yeah, Ewan knew that.

He could kill her as easily as a human could breathe. He could reach inside her mind and make her forget this conversation. His powers over the human mind were vast, but they were largely destructive. To tamper with Tia's beliefs in any fundamental way would be like trying to re-do the electrical circuitry at a nuclear generating plant—while it was operating. Despite the potential power she offered him, he didn't dare reach in and re-direct her worship. And that didn't even consider what the competition might do if Ewan messed with His creature.

"I'm…" he paused looking for the right word, "I'm an addict."

"Wow. That's flattering."

"Let's make a deal. Worship me and I'll give you whatever you want."

"End world hunger. A cure for cancer."

He considered. "Those would take time." Time and more manna even than Tia could generate. Still, given time—

"That's what I thought. You're not a god, you're a pervert."

He sighed. "I don't lie. For whatever reason, your faith, the power of your manna, dragged me here. It could have reached to any of the millions of gods stuck in limbo, caught between power and extinction. It turned out to be me. Imagine suffering from withdrawal pains from the most addictive drug in the world, then multiply that a thousand times and you'll have an idea of what I'll face should anything happen to you. Whoever's after you has been waiting, who knows for how long, for this to happen. If we don't act together, they'll kill you and control me."

She stared at him, her anger fading, but fear and uncertainty taking its place.

"We are so screwed."

Chapter 5

Ewan's words, the sincere look on his face, had the ring of truth.

Tia didn't want to believe he might really be a god. She knew from her comparative religion classes that there had been a time in Biblical history when the Hebrew tribes who'd created the Old Testament of the *Bible* had believed in multiple Gods, holding Yahweh as best but not alone. But those were ancient Hebrews, before the revelation had been complete. Her own belief structure didn't include multiple gods, nor gods who depended on mere humans for energy and power.

The frosted fork could have been a trick. A little dry ice and zap, instant miracle.

The bush was the kind of trick thousands of stage magicians pull.

He might have heard about the fire on a police scanner. Hell, maybe he'd set the fire himself just to be a hero.

Making a New York taxi driver forget his fare and a hotel manager give them a free suite would take a real miracle, but he could have set that up too.

"I've got to investigate, try to find out who's behind the fire now," Ewan announced.

"What about me?"

"The only sensible thing for you to do is to hide and stay safe. Call down for room service. Watch television. Enjoy a vacation."

She shook her head grimly. God or not, he didn't have much of a clue about the way New York worked.

"Not going to happen, Ewan. Lori has auditions to go to. And I'm not going to let them down at the homeless kitchen. You may be able to take care of yourself, but the people at the kitchen need me."

"I need you."

She shivered. Once she got past the god stuff, Ewan was a sexy guy. Even though she'd never seen him without his overcoat, she could tell he had a terrific body, even if he could do with a bit more meat on him. From what she'd overheard in his discussions with Big Red, as well as in their own conversations, he was intelligent too. Plus, he'd saved her life at least twice. And he said he *needed* her. In a lot of ways, he was the perfect answer to a mythical personal ad. 'Wanted: Godlike male to sweep lonely ex-Corn-Husker off her feet in New York.' Unfortunately, if he was telling the truth, he didn't need her for her wit, her looks, or her sense of humor. He needed her the way a mosquito needs blood. And anyone with her manna, or whatever he called it, would do the job.

"You may need me, Ewan, but I'm not going to hide up here."

"Know what we should do?" Lori asked. "We should find out who's trying to hurt you. You're a paralegal, you should be able to do it."

Tia specialized in taxes, not murder-for-hire heretics. Still, she had to do something.

"Good idea."

"You'd be a fool to put yourself in danger," Ewan said.

He might not have cut so deeply if her parents and college boyfriend hadn't used almost the exact words when she'd announced she was moving to New York three years earlier. She'd be a fool to move, a fool to abandon the safety of Nebraska, a fool to try anything that didn't follow exactly in the path someone else had laid out for her.

Maybe they were right. But she wasn't going to live her life sitting around being anyone's doormat, not even someone who said he was a god. "I appreciate the rescue, Ewan. But I've got to be at work early tomorrow and I need some sleep. So, I'll see you around, huh?"

"But—"

"Go."

He reached out, touched his fingertips to her face, then backed away so suddenly it was as if he was being sucked into a vacuum cleaner like so much filth.

She didn't even hear the door close, but he was gone.

"Well, if you don't want him, you think maybe you could send him my way?" Lori asked. "He can bounce my bedsprings any time he wants."

"He paid for the cab and the hotel in advance and is faking us out with the miracle stuff."

"Yeah? So?"

Tia's skin still tingled from the brief sensation of his hand on her cheek. He hadn't radiated the extreme cold she'd felt from him before, but it hadn't been normal, either. This was something else—something she had no words to describe.

"Ridiculous."

"Who's being ridiculous, Tia? He could have done those things, but why bother? A guy who looks like that doesn't need to go to this much trouble to get laid."

"He's crazy."

"You're in serious denial," Lori said. "I'm going back to bed. And I'm going to dream about my own god coming on to me. If you won't share Ewan, maybe he's got a friend."

Tia shook her head. "He isn't coming on to me. He just wants my manna." She stepped into the bathroom before her roommate could tell her she'd just lost that argument.

One look in the mirror was more than enough to persuade her that Ewan wasn't stalking her for her sexy looks.

She was a mess. She wasn't wearing makeup, had dust bunnies clinging to her jeans and sweatshirt. Her face and hands were so covered with soot, she looked like a depression-era photo of coal miners. And she looked exactly like a woman who hadn't gotten enough sleep.

Ewan might not be a god or a vampire, although the jury was still out on both of those. For sure he wasn't a normal guy, because no normal guy would give her a second look. As she looked in the mirror, she realized something else. Nobody could walk through the fires without getting smudged, but Ewan had remained as clean as anyone she'd ever seen. Even his fire jacket had remained spotless.

That didn't make him a god, but it meant something. She just wasn't sure what.

Tia washed off as much of the soot as she could, then went out to face Lori.

"The way he touched you was so sweet." Lori put her hands together near her heart and sighed, not letting Tia get a word in edgewise. Oh, yeah. She was an actress.

"How would you like it if you found out that this super-sexy guy wanted you because of your money."

Lori giggled. "I don't have any money."

"Drop the ditz act. You know what I mean."

Lori wrinkled her forehead, but only for an instant. She worried about how every gesture would impact her skin's elasticity. "If a guy only wanted me for my hypothetical money, it would really suck. Because even if he really fell in love with me later, I'd never know."

"Well, that's my problem with Ewan. Even if he is telling the truth--" And she had to admit to herself that he seemed to be telling at least part of the truth. "—the reason he's interested in me is because I'm a manna-spewing freak of nature. It's not because of my charming wit, my Rubenesque body, or any sort of hormonal urges on his part. I could be anyone, just as long as I had the manna. Before you go on gushing about this being my one great love, put that in your pipe."

"You don't have a Rubenesque body—it's just lush. Since you're not an actor, you don't have to worry about the camera making you look twenty pounds heavier, so it's okay for you."

"Don't be deliberately obtuse."

"Me?" Lori protested. "What about you? Sure Ewan noticed you first because of your manna action. But that's just where it started. Think about this. How is your relationship so much different from the usual thing of a guy being attracted to you because you've got nice tits or a pretty face? Guys are always superficial at first. But it can grow from there."

"Even if you're right, how would I ever know whether it's grown or it's the same thing? If he's telling the truth, I'm is the only chick with magical manna action."

Lori shrugged. "Well, if you can *never* know, who cares? If it's got a body like Ewan's, does it really matter whether it's true love as long as it looks and acts exactly like true love? It isn't as if he's going to spend all your manna and go on to the next chick. Even when you get old, he won't go out looking for younger women. You're like a fire hydrant, he said, right? He's like a dog who can't stay away."

That wasn't an image Tia wanted to hold in her mind. Still, Lori's argument made sense, to a point. If it looked and acted like love, why care? Unfortunately, Tia cared.

* * * *

Ewan brooded.

He'd gone back to Tia's apartment, passing through the police line like a wraith, drifting up an out-of-service elevator shaft, and finally floating over the charred remains of what had once been a typical New York apartment.

The arson investigator walked from room to room on Tia's floor and the floor below it, speaking into his dictation device while remaining completely unconcerned about Ewan's obvious eavesdropping. Thanks to a tiny suggestion Ewan had planted, he saw Ewan as part of the team.

Ewan allowed himself a small smile. That kind of manipulation, the simple alteration of human perception, was easy. People wanted to believe that everything was normal. He simply nudged them in the direction they wished to go.

Considering that he'd already dissipated much of the energy surge Tia had sent him with her prayer, and her recent blast of anger still kept him from getting more, it was just as well he wasn't being called on to work any serious miracles.

"Extensive evidence of accelerants throughout the ninth and tenth floors," the arson investigator mumbled into his digital recording device. "The highly organized burn patterns and the chemical residuals indicate a gelatinized petroleum product. From preliminary indications, I would say it is weaponized material. We appear to have a well-equipped arsonist here. Note to self, call contacts in the FBI and find out if this is a government operation." He paused briefly, then stepped carefully across the charred floorboards until he got to the impromptu exit hole Ewan had cut. "The perforations in the floor on levels nine and ten are clearly post-conflagration and appear consistent with an informal rescue. This may explain the apparent lack of casualties."

Ewan hadn't doubted that it was arson, an attack on the spillover of faith that kept him from Limbo. But gelatinized petroleum meant planning, organization, money, and even government involvement. The chance their enemy was a greedy student of the occult vanished. Whoever was after him was more dangerous than even he had guessed.

They'd subverted Hank and Sam within minutes of when he'd first made physical contact with his source. Tia had also barely avoided being killed on her way to the soup kitchen. And they'd struck again two days later. Managing three or more separate hit attempts meant organization and experience in the criminal side of life.

He looked out the fire-broken windows of Tia's apartment. The sun, rising over the Atlantic, shed a dusty red light over Manhattan. *Red sky at morning.* That had been a cautionary proverb way back in those long-lost days when he'd been at his prime, when he'd realistically envisioned a day when the entire world worshipped him, showered him with their faith. Those dreams had been lost, but he dared to dream again. The danger of a storm remained.

34

Hunger

Once he turned Tia, persuaded her that he was the proper recipient of her praise and worship, he could bat aside whoever was stalking him as if they were pesky mosquitoes. He could even reclaim his iron-age dreams. He *could* deliver miracles, *would* reward his followers. Why shouldn't he become the god he'd almost been before Roman armies and Roman gods had smashed the faith of his followers?

But he needed Tia first. A man would have accepted his offer: worship in exchange for wealth, power, anything her heart could desire.

Women, though, were more complicated than men. Tia didn't care about being the high priestess in a new religion. He'd need to take the slower path. He could play the love game, win Tia over. To his surprise, playing at love sounded like a lot of fun. Maybe the days when he was a fertility god were not completely lost after all.

What he couldn't do was wait until he won Tia over. His enemies, whomever they might be, had struck quickly and powerfully. They'd continue to do so until he eliminated their abilities to strike at all.

He nodded firmly. Once he finished this investigation, he'd go back to the hotel where he'd left Tia and woo her, seduce her, charm her, use every ounce understanding and insight he'd accumulated over thousands of years of interacting with humans to win her over.

First, though, he had to find the attackers. He closed his eyes to the physical reality of the room and opened his true sight into the inner realities of what had happened.

People left a bit of themselves behind, like a snail trail that lingers through dimensions humans can't sense but that Ewan had once called home.

In the vast open spaces his clans had once controlled, those residuals were easy to follow even months after someone had passed.

New York overwhelmed him. The city was a teaming population in Brownian motion. Dozens, maybe hundreds of residents came and went every day. Firemen, cops, investigators had tromped through Tia's apartment building, overlaying and overwriting the signs left by the arsonists. Air already breathed by thousands of New Yorkers touched and dissipated what remained.

But Ewan wasn't a human psychic investigator limited by poorly understood tools and human blindness. He might be a depleted shadow of himself, but he remained a god, with a god's vision and with the patience he'd learned from more than two thousand years of powerless suspension in Limbo.

He relaxed his hold on his physical form and sank his essence into the multidimensional space that was the real essence of the charred and dripping hole that had once been the apartment beneath Tia's.

The arson investigator glanced his way, momentarily recognizing that something had changed.

But everyone who should be there remained and the investigator shook his head and went on with his work. Perhaps he really needed to take that vacation his wife had been hinting at over the past couple of months.

Ewan's essence drifted through the memories left behind in the apartments.

The primary traces were from a couple who had lived in the apartment for several years, had loved, fought, made up, and fought again throughout that period.

Their emotional rages contaminated everything, over-washing even later visitors.

He patiently catalogued every characteristic of the battling couple. Once he'd fully comprehended the two individuals, he stripped those emotional excesses away, exposing traces that had been overwhelmed by the noise.

The next step was to unravel the newest strands—the rescued women, the cops, firefighters, rescue workers, and arson investigators who'd tromped through the apartment in their successful efforts to combat the blaze and to ensure that no one had been harmed by the fire.

One of the cops had a crush on a paramedic. A firefighter was afraid his wife was having an affair. Another suffered from losing of two members of his unit earlier that year.

Ewan used human emotion, manipulated them, but he didn't trust or like them. They got in his way. Like iron walls, they kept him from insinuating his subtle hints into the human mind, forced him to use brute force, waste his energies.

He gritted his psychic teeth and continued.

One by one, he comprehended, encompassed, and stripped away the emotional signatures left by post-fire visitors.

What remained were the incidentals. Brief visits, people passing through.

Somewhere buried amongst hundreds of casual contacts, was the arsonist.

Ewan went through the memories. Each absorbed a fractional second of time he couldn't afford and energy he couldn't replace.

The apartment manager had visited to make sure the apartment was ready to rent to new tenants. A deliveryman had brought a package.

Could that package have been an incendiary device? No. Whoever had set the fire had done so with a degree of precision, of science. A randomly left package wouldn't do.

But realizing that gave him what he needed to grasp the threads left behind by the actual arsonist.

He'd been looking for emotion—for the near-orgasmic thrill that was the universal 'tell' of a firebug. But that was misdirection. The man who'd created this blaze was merely doing a job. He hadn't cared about what he was doing, hadn't gotten any thrill from the fire that would result. His only emotional tie was a sense of professional pride and accomplishment. He'd laid out his kerosene-polystyrene accelerants in a way that provided minimum risk of collateral casualties with maximum certainty that the tenants of Tia's apartment would die in the blaze. He'd timed the operation to allow himself to escape undetected, even using a motion sensor to ensure that the women in Tia's apartment were sleeping.

Ewan *heard* the arsonist's final thought as he'd connected wires to a small battery operated alarm travel clock constructed completely out of flammable plastic. *It would take an act of god to save those women.*

And that was all. The arsonist didn't consider of his identity, didn't even identify himself as a male or female, although some trace of frustration when he considered the women he intended to kill led Ewan to assume he was male. He certainly didn't do anything helpful like consider his street address or phone number while he was setting the incendiaries.

The police would need a great deal of luck to track down the arsonist. Ewan didn't think the organization behind this operation would let the police get that lucky.

But Ewan *could* track down the arsonist, persuade him to talk. It would take time Ewan could scarcely afford, but he finally had a strand to pull on. Like a cat with a half-knit sweater, he'd keep pulling until the entire plot unraveled. Until both he and Tia were free from threat.

He gathered himself, slowly reassembling his human form in three-dimensional space, making sure that none of his ectoplasm escaped into the N-dimensional hyperplane that was the abode of the gods.

It shocked him to see how ephemeral he had become. Better than two thousand years of starvation had drained him in ways that the trickle of manna he received from Tia, and that infinitesimal drip from Lori as well, did little to fill. His hunger for more nearly overwhelmed him.

His weakness gave his enemies their chance. Science had progressed in the millennia during which he'd been dying, cut off from sensation and knowledge. Science apparently gave them some means of detecting the manna flow. Science would also let them limit his ability to escape their grasp, to collapse the quantum state. He was too weak to change observed reality.

In literature, it might be noble and tragic to set humans against gods. In reality, as Ewan saw it, anyway, setting humans against gods was worse than dangerous. Just as children should be kept from nuclear weapons, so humans must be denied the power of the divine.

Anger at their plan and at his lack of power gave him a sense of purpose. For a god, he was pitifully weak. But those who meddle with gods had better make sure their first shot hits home. They'd missed on their first chance. He didn't intend to give them a second.

* * * *

"I'm with Umbright, Chancey and Forester," Tia explained for the fifth time since she'd returned to her apartment building, flirting, charming and bullying her way through multiple lines of police. "We're looking into possible actionable violations on the part of the apartment management." She flashed her law firm ID at the latest roadblock, a worried looking arson investigator with a small twitch in his left eye. She pretended to believe that a law firm ID gave her some right to be there and hoped he would be too tired to argue.

"I guess we're just about done," the investigator admitted. "But I can't tell you anything. You'll have to wait for my report."

"My clients need to know whether this fire was the result of faulty wiring." She laid her best smile on him wishing she'd grabbed something a little more flattering than a U of N sweatshirt before her apartment went up in flames.

The investigator blushed. "If faulty wiring can lay a napalm bomb, then maybe."

"I see." She scribbled the word *napalm* in her Palm.

Jeez. Napalm. Whoever was after her wasn't just playing around.

She hadn't realized how deep-seated she was in her denial. She hadn't wanted to believe Ewan's explanations, hadn't been willing to buy into the hocus-pocus and conspiracy-theory stuff that underlay everything he'd told her. So far, though, his story checked. It wasn't as if she and Lori had enemies. Sure her ex-boyfriend back in Nebraska was still mad she'd left town and come to New York, but he wasn't the type to get violent, let alone leave Nebraska to visit what he saw as the core of sin and evil in America. Even if he were, she didn't think he had access to napalm.

She still wasn't prepared to believe that Ewan was a god. She was equally not prepared to believe he would napalm-bomb her apartment. Thinking of him as an alien helped—a little.

She stared at the remains of what had once been a relatively nice, if outrageously expensive by Nebraska standards, apartment.

Her living room was incinerated. The small bureau that had held her clothes now held nothing but a dripping mass of cotton and silk ashes and melted polyester.

The apartment's single bedroom wasn't much better. She rescued her mother's gold locket, but Lori's prized antique pearl necklace was shattered, with only a few of the pearls surviving the intense heat.

Tia was so intent on what little remained of the earthly possessions of three women that she didn't hear Ewan approach. That was the line she gave herself, anyway. He couldn't just materialize in the middle of what had once been her living room.

"Hi Ewan. Fancy meeting you here."

Anger darkened his face. "This isn't safe."

"Wake up, Ewan. Women might have been passive little things when you were a godling, but it's the twenty-first century. We don't just huddle in our caves and wait for the cavemen to bring us dinosaur meat to cook."

"You have an astoundingly bad concept of history and geological time. And I'm not a godling."

"Oh, really? You have exactly zero worshipers and nobody alive over the past thousand years has even heard of you. I'd say that makes you pretty minor."

His expression said he didn't like her analysis, but he didn't argue. "I need to get you someplace safe."

"As my nine-year-old nephew would say, 'you aren't the boss of me.'"

He looked ready to dispute that, but said nothing.

Instead, he closed the distance between them, brought his hand to her arm and tugged her close.

Sexual desire surged in her, but oddly, it didn't stop her from noticing that his footsteps left no marks in the ashes that covered what had once been her floor.

Watching him walk across a floor covered with ash lighter than confectionary sugar leaving not a trace of his presence behind him shattered what remained of her denial. Everything else could have been faked. But how do you fake something like that? Even an alien would leave traces in the dust.

Abruptly, he was there, inside her personal space, so close he filled her vision.

"What do you think—"

His lips descended on hers, cutting short her question.

She expected pain, a return of the bitter cold that his hand had caused in his touch that could leave frost on plastic utensils.

She gritted her teeth against the punishment she knew was coming and decided to duck away—but her body wanted to find out what was coming and didn't listen to her brain's command.

She shivered as he pressed his lips to hers, as his strong arms drew her against his body. That shiver began in expectation of the freezing sensation of his touch, but it transformed itself into something else as his lips claimed hers, as her lips involuntarily softened, parted against his. Oh, no. That shiver did not come from cold.

Molten rivers of pure sensation streamed through her body. It was insane, impossible. Tia had graduated from University of Nebraska, a hotbed of hormones and desire. She'd kissed and been kissed plenty of times. But nothing in her experience compared with the pressure of Ewan's hard body against the yielding curves of her own, of his lips that first brushed against hers like the wings of butterflies, then settling in, taking, conquering, claiming, plundering.

Her legs went rubbery, her knees abruptly unable to support her weight. Reflexively, she leaned against Ewan's strong body for support.

When his lips finally left hers, he didn't back away. Instead, he kissed a trail of fire down her cheek, nibbled on her ear.

She caught herself making embarrassing moan-y noises but couldn't stop, couldn't move, couldn't do anything but savor the moment, the sensation of Ewan's lips against her skin, the power of his strong arms around her, the gentle touch of his fingers in her hair.

"You *will* stay safe," Ewan said, his voice confident and seductive. "You *will* go back to the hotel. You *will* hide there until I've discovered our enemies and eliminated them."

Chapter 6

Ewan refused to smile but his plan was working. Women had been suckers for that emotional stuff at least since he'd taught them to farm. Tia would do what he—

"That's complete crap." Tia spit the words like poison. "Are you trying to mind-control me, Ewan? Well, guess what? I don't go for dominant-male bullshit. And get your paws off of me. I don't let manipulating jerks touch me."

It took him a moment to realize Tia was pounding her fists against his chest. He'd intended that his kiss manipulate *her* senses, but somehow he'd gotten caught up in it himself, in the pure lush physicality of Tia's body against his own, in the way her lips had parted, opened, welcomed his tongue into her.

She was supposed to be helpless putty in his hands, ready to follow his instructions like the basically good human she was. Instead, her sharp brown eyes blazed with anger, not lust.

He backed away, barely maintaining contact. "Try to be logical."

"I told you I'm not going to sit still. They're trying to kill *me*, remember? I have a right to be involved in figuring out who they are and deciding how to handle it."

"*I've* already decided how to handle them." Mortals who dare manipulate a god could not expect mercy.

She yanked the rest of the way out of his grasp. In all of the anger and emotion, he hadn't quite gotten around to removing his fingers from her long, silky-soft hair.

For a moment he tried to remember if he'd ever really noticed a woman's hair before. Was other women's hair so cool to the touch? Had it ever before felt so vivid as it slid through his fingers, had it forced him to think about how it could slide against every inch of his body?

Tia's angry voice yanked him back to the three-dimensional human plane. "*You've* decided? Let me get this straight. You're only here because I'm powering you, right? You're like an appliance, and I'm the battery."

She stopped briefly, blushing bright red as she caught some allusion he didn't exactly follow. "Never mind that analogy and please forget the appliance thing. The point is, it takes both of us, right? As in a partnership— we decide things together. Not as in, you decide and I meekly follow along."

No. Meek was not the word to describe Tia.

He'd had priestesses once. In the very early days of his godhood, women controlled religious functions in his tribes. Although they'd been female, they'd been biddable. They understood the need for distance between human and god, between worshiper and object of worship. Sure, some of those priestesses had been stubborn, took a while to understand what he wanted them to do. But when he finally got the message through, they'd bent over backwards to deliver.

He had no problems getting his message through to Tia. She just didn't bend an inch.

"I am a god," he reminded her. "Of course we do what I say. I know about these kinds of people. Do you really believe this is the first time someone has attempted to force the power of gods? Why do you think there is a Biblical prohibition against taking the name of the Lord in vain? It's because primitive people attempted to use the true names of gods for magic, forcing their God to do their will rather than his own. Humans always do that, and gods always fight back."

Tia blocked his way, her hands balled into fists, shaking her head at him as if he'd been spouting nonsense rather than simple truths confirmed in her own Bible.

"Tell you what. Get a note from *my* God, the *real* God, and I'll think about following your orders. In the meantime, we either work together or I go against these murderers on my own."

He considered. If she wouldn't stay safe, he could best protect her by staying near. There was something more, too. His reaction to the kiss hadn't been hunger alone. Women were unpredictable. Who knew? Staying close might allow opportunities to experiment with that strange mix of physical and psychic bonding that he'd felt during those brief seconds of their kiss. Of course, it would also give him time to persuade her to shift her worship his way. Defeating their enemies and not winning her worship would be an empty victory since Tia was human, had a limited lifespan.

"If you refuse to be sensible," he said, "I guess you must come with me. I'll do my best to keep you safe."

"Partners." She stuck out a hand in an ancient gesture of a bargain.

Did she realize what a bargain with a god meant? Humans could walk away from their bargains. Once a deity accepted a bargain, he was stuck with it.

"How about we just say that we'll work together for the time being."

She snatched her hand away. "So you can dump me when you think it's expedient? Not happening. Partners or nothing."

"I don't think you understand—"

She stuck her hand back out. Her arm trembled with anger, but she was still offering. "It's *you* who doesn't understand. I don't think it's because you're stupid. So it's got to be that you're a sexist pig."

"It has nothing to do with your sex."

"Then, partners. Shake on it."

No god partnered with a human. Not even Abraham had insisted on so much. Then again, no god had ever been so weak. He sensed her preparing to withdraw, cut him off even more. He didn't know for certain, but he suspected she wouldn't walk out of this building without meeting a fatal *accident* unless protected by him.

"How about we agree to a temporary and limited partnership. Strictly for purposes of—"

"Hello. Somebody isn't listening. I thought gods could look into human hearts. Well, look into mine. I'm not budging. But I will walk away if you don't stick your hand out and shake mine within the next five seconds. Walk away and continue the investigation on my own. And you'd better believe I won't be calling for *your* help if I get into trouble."

Tia didn't know what she was asking, but Ewan did look into her heart and saw she was unwilling to compromise. He had to choose. He could accept her deal, make himself her partner, or let her walk into dangers that she could not comprehend and that she almost definitely would not survive.

"Partners." He grasped her hand in his own.

She flinched when their palms touched.

The physical body he wore in the fraction of the true universe tangible to humans was a translation into three spatial dimensions of a horribly attenuated divine form that stretched across a multitude of spatial, temporal, and spiritual dimensions. The extreme cold that Tia had noticed before was simply a symptom of his hunger, of the vast rents in the fabric of his being. Thousands of years of starvation had left him so empty that he manifested at a temperature close to absolute zero. Only a trick of manna surrounded him with an electrical charge that kept away a dripping mass of nitrogen and oxygen congealing from the atmosphere.

That electrical charge, together with the expenditure of just a little desperately needed manna, let him protect Tia from the bitter cold of his touch. She wouldn't die when she touched his hand, just as she hadn't died when he'd kissed her. Whether he could maintain that control if their physical contact went beyond a momentary kiss, was beyond his experience. Then again, extended physical contact with him seemed low on Tia's priority list. He needed to change that—both to win her worship and to satisfy an urge within him that he didn't understand.

She shivered as her small hand fit into his larger one. She returned his grip, not in the kind of macho contest human males engaged in, but in a grip of friendship, of equality. When she finally pulled away, she did so slowly, as if she to were unwilling to end that physical contact. "You're doing that on purpose, aren't you?"

"What?"

"Sending erotic thoughts into my head every time we touch. It's exploitative and cruel."

He let Tia release her grasp but left his fingertips in contact with her own. A slow, unplanned smile crossed his face and he didn't even bother to damp it down.

Given his very limited power and the disastrous results of getting it wrong, he wasn't about to directly manipulate Tia's feelings. Whatever erotic sensations Tia felt, she generated them all by herself.

If a god couldn't use genuine erotic feelings to control the situation, he should turn in his halo and get a day job.

He considered explaining, letting her know she had come up with those daydreams of doing the nasty all by herself, but she wouldn't believe him.

"Perhaps we should get on with our investigation." He paused a beat. "Partner."

* * * *

Ohmigod. Had she really said that? Tia couldn't believe she'd just come right out and accused Ewan of getting her all hot and bothered. It wasn't as if his oversized ego needed any stroking. The worst part was, she wasn't absolutely certain those sexy visions weren't straight from her own libido.

Besides, telling him that was as good as admitting she believed his god story. She couldn't, wouldn't do that. Whatever he was, and she was ready to admit he wasn't a normal person, he couldn't be a god.

She took a deep breath and went professional on him. She'd insisted that they be partners. It was her chance to let him know he'd made the right choice.

"I spoke to the arson investigator on my way here. He said the fire was started with napalm," she reported.

"A modern, militarized version of napalm," Ewan added, letting her know he was on the job, too. "Old-fashioned gasoline-based napalm would have been easier—you can get recipes for that on the Internet. Whoever we're after has access to military, and therefore other government resources. Which I would have told you if you'd given me a chance to explain. Are you still sure you want to come along?"

She'd decided on a legal career when she'd seen the movie *Erin Brokovitch* back when she'd been a teenager. She was all over *the idea* of taking on the government and mysterious evil corporations. The *reality* was a lot scarier. Until Ewan had explained the napalm thing, the danger had seemed amorphous. Sure the fire had been a horror, and the Sam and Hank incident had been disgusting, but this was scary in a different way.

Still, they'd tried to kill her and would have killed Lori just because she was there. While Tia wanted to believe Ewan was delusional, she suspected their unidentified enemy would keep trying to kill her until they either succeeded or were stopped.

"I've taken unpaid leave from work, but I can still go into the office and search the databases. There might be something about missing military supplies."

"You'd put your co-workers at risk unless I went with you, which your bosses might not like. Besides, I've got a trace on the arsonist."

"Really? How'd you manage that if the cops couldn't?"

"A miracle. Come on."

"Where? And what are we going to do to him?"

"I don't know where but I know the direction. My plan is to find him and make him squeal."

Tia's nephew was a fan of the Greek myths and had roped her into reading him both the kidified editions and some of the more adult version of those stories when she'd been back in Nebraska for Christmas. If one clear message came through from just about every one of those legends, humans, especially women, who spent time with gods, always got hurt.

The longer she spent with Ewan, the more she suspected that whoever had created those myths knew what they were talking about.

That's when she realized she was starting to believe he really was a god. Of course, watching him fade in and out of the charred walls of her apartment was a lot more convincing than a six-inch burning bush.

"All right," she said. "Let's start with the arsonist."

Tia input Ewan's direction and distance into her Palm, then used her Palm's GPS to bring up the neighborhood.

Turned out, it was in Brooklyn. "We can take the subway."

Ewan was reluctant. He muttered something about being an aboveground sort of god, not an underworld sort of god, but Tia wasn't going for it. She felt guilty enough about ripping off the hotel and the taxi driver a few hours earlier. No way was she going to let Ewan's cheat more cabbies of their fares. And she sure didn't want to pay a bunch of fares herself when the subway was right there. She'd exaggerated when she told Ewan she was taking leave without pay. If their adventure took longer than a week, she'd be unemployed.

She pitched a bit of a fit but finally convinced Ewan to give the subway a try. She grabbed a coffee and bagel from one of the street merchants for a bit of energy, smiled when Ewan turned down her offer to buy him one, and headed down just in time to catch a train.

She had her Metrocard ready. Ewan walked through the solid turnstile without seeming to touch it.

They'd missed rush hour and the subway wasn't too full. A few harried-looking businessmen, a couple of attractive young women who looked vaguely familiar and were probably in the acting, modeling and waitressing circuit with Lori, a Catholic priest, a Hasidic Jew, and a pair of tattooed punks reminded Tia that they were in New York, the original melting pot.

Ewan looked intently around, assessing everyone in the car before joining Tia on the seat.

"You picked something up from your apartment, right?" he said. "Can you show me?"

She hadn't thought he'd noticed, hadn't even thought he was in the apartment when she'd grabbed them. "Just a couple of keepsakes. A locket of mine and a ruined necklace that Lori loved because it belonged to her grandmother back in the fifties."

"Ruined how?"

"The fire cracked some of the pearls and just burned others to ashes. It's pretty much worthless, now, but I thought she would like to have it anyway, because it was a family hand-me-down. I guess you don't get the idea of family, right?"

He smiled gently but shook his head. "Some gods belong to families, like Jupiter and Venus. But thinking about the gods who've gone before reminds us that we might be next."

"Sometimes people are like that. But a lot of times, we want to remember." She needed to keep reminding herself of the differences. Differences like the way Ewan had just walked through the subway turnstile. Differences like, she feared she was falling for him and he thought of her as an energy pump.

He reached for the ruined necklace. "May I see it?"

Flashing jewelry around on a subway was a quick road to trouble, but she didn't think anyone would be interested in the mess that Lori's necklace had become. She pulled the clear plastic sandwich bag she'd put it in from her purse and handed it over.

"In my day," Ewan mused, "at least in my part of the world, pearls were rare. Only a few mollusks produced them."

She'd noticed his strong hands, his long slender fingers before. They appeared hypnotic as he unfastened the sealed top of the sandwich bag and reached in.

"That was before the Japanese invented cultured pearls. They put in a starter and the oysters produce."

"Larger pearls are still more valuable?" Ewan's fingers tightened around one of the ruined pearls.

"Well, yeah."

He pulled the necklace from the bag. "Here, then."

She let out an embarrassing peep before shutting herself down. She'd been super-careful when she'd put the remains of the necklace in the bag, since many of the pearls were coming apart. Now, though, all were lustrous, and completely whole. And big. Each pearl was about half again as big as it had been, straining on the chain that held the necklace together rather than flopping between the knots. Each pearl now gleamed far more brightly than ever.

"You just—"

"They're the same pearls they were. I just allowed them to fulfill their potential."

"But—"

"I saw how you looked at me when you offered to buy me coffee." A touch of anger colored his voice. "A god is not a useless expense to be pitied and lugged around like a white elephant, Tia." His smile only partially mitigated the anger in his voice. "Weak as I am, I have a certain control over what your scientists call 'collapsing the probabilities in a quantum state'."

She stared at the restored pearl necklace. Yes, Lori would be happy to see it. And yes, she could see that Ewan wasn't just high-quality eye-candy. She hadn't studied quantum states in college, Lori thought quantum mechanics was woo-woo and had tried to explain them to Tia. Unless Tia'd misunderstood everything Lori had told her, someone capable of 'controlling the collapse of quantum probability states' on a large scale could do just about anything. Someone like that was close to being a god.

"Could you make diamonds out of coal, like *Superman*?"

He considered, staring at her until she abruptly realized she was pulling the knowledge of *Superman* and his diamond trick from her brain.

"No."

"No?" Scratch one fantasy.

"No. This *Superman* mythical individual used pure strength to create enough pressure and heat to turn a lump of coal into a faceted, cut diamond. It's a brute force method. Give me a million worshipers and I could do that. As I am, it's beyond me."

"So much for my idea of going into the diamond business once we've resolved this mess, huh?"

"I didn't say I couldn't make diamonds. I can't make them like your *Superman* does. Watch."

He picked an abandoned copy of the *Times* from the floor, peeled out the business page, and folded it neatly.

Then he turned it and folded again. And again. And again. Continuing to turn and fold so many times that she lost count.

"I believe this type of creation is called origami," Ewan said as he handed over what appeared to be a perfectly clear brilliant-cut diamond—a jewel measuring approximately three-eighths of an inch across. To think that Bobby, her ex-boyfriend, had tried to tempt her with a diamond chip weighing something like a twentieth of a carat.

"Jeez, Ewan. You can't go doing things like that on a subway." She stuck the diamond in her purse and looked around worriedly. Someone *had* to have seen what Ewan was doing with the diamond and the pearls.

Sure enough, a pair of dirty-looking teenage punk-types whispered among themselves, nudging and elbowing one another in an obvious attempt to build up their nerve.

"I see them." His lips didn't move, but she heard him clearly.

"Don't start anything."

He shrugged. "Me?"

Well, he could afford to joke. They weren't going to try to hurt Ewan.

Clearly ignoring her warning, he approached the two teens and held out his hand. "Want to see another magic trick?"

"You mean that diamond thing was fake?"

He laughed. "You're kidding, right? You really think a person could change newspaper into a diamond?"

She watched intently, her brain racing as it analyzed what Ewan was doing. He didn't lie to them, exactly, but he let them believe a lie. Did he lie to her like that? Would he let her believe lies? She'd have to watch him more carefully. Not that watching Ewan was any hardship.

"Well, it sure looked like you managed it," the younger punk said.

"I do street magic. You ever see David Blaine on T.V.?"

"Yeah? He does good tricks." The younger punk scratched his head and Tia shuddered, trying not to think about the zillions of head-lice he was probably spreading around the train.

"Here's the real trick, though," the older punk said. "It doesn't matter whether the diamond came from the newspaper or your pocket. I think it's worth something. So, make your bitch hand it over."

Ewan got very still. "My partner doesn't like it when people call her that."

"Yeah?" The punk puffed out his chest. "Well, I don't like it when people don't do what I say. That clear enough for you?"

"Tell you what. I'll show you a trick. If you can figure out how I do it, maybe I'll give you the rock."

"What trick?" The teens were understandably suspicious. Tia was suspicious as well. Ewan had already shown that he didn't care whether people lived or died. If his trick was stopping their hearts, they were all going to be in trouble—and Tia was going to have to rethink her crazy idea of being partners with him. What had she been thinking, anyway?

Ewan made a hand gesture and came up with a switchblade about six inches long—before opening. From her angle, Tia could tell it had simply materialized in his hand.

"This is your knife, right?"

"How'd you get that?"

"That would be telling. You have to figure it out." He flicked the blade open, then closed it with a snap of his wrist. "Nice knife. Stainless steel blade, right? Made in China, but what isn't these days. Here's the real trick though. I need you guys to watch closely."

He flicked the knife opened, again. As the two youths watched, intent despite their effort to appear tough, Ewan passed his free hand over the deadly blade several times.

She thought it was her imagination at first, but a brown stain appeared on the knife. With seconds, the entire knife crumbled to rusty powder on Ewan's hand.

He blew on the ashes and nothing remained but a small puff of dust and a rusty stain on the subway floor.

"Nice, huh? If either of you can tell me how I did that, I'll give you the woman's rock."

"Hey, that was my knife."

"You're right." Without any apparent movement, Ewan had the punk's collar in his hand. He lifted him off the ground without a hint of effort. A hint of a smile crossed his lips as the punk's face turned purple.

"Guess what, kid. Turning a stainless steel knife to rust is a lot harder than turning you into meat. So, take a word to the wise. Don't call women bitches, and don't mess with strangers. The next one might not have a moralistic friend urging them to hold back."

Friend. Tia sort of liked the sound of that word.

* * * *

Fear isn't as good as faith, but Ewan took what he could get. Those two punks had jumped off at the next subway stop. If he read their souls right, they were going to do some heavy thinking about their futures. They wouldn't send any manna his way but that was fine. Gods who were worshipped by the hateful and intolerant became as twisted as their followers.

He turned back to Tia and noticed her expression.

"What?"

"You didn't have to threaten them about calling me a bi—" she paused. "You know, that 'B' word. You know the saying about sticks and stones, right?"

He shook his head. "No."

She laughed. "I thought you knew everything. You knew about Superman. It's something we say in kindergarten. Sticks and stones will…"

"I know the *saying*. I meant, no, it's a lie. Words matter. And when someone calls you a name, it hurts you inside. Until you open to me, worship me the way I need your worship, I don't dare reach in to heal the damage their kind can do. So I'm doing my best to cut it off as quickly as I can."

"I'm not going to worship you and I don't need you defending me."

"I don't need your permission for that."

She shook her head. "You're pretty weird, Ewan."

"And you base this on how many gods you've personally known?"

She looked out the window as the subway squealed to a stop. "This is where we're going. Come on."

The psychic traces of the arsonist were stronger as they emerged from the subway.

The one- and two-story homes of Dyker Heights were as alien to Ewan as were the high-rises of Manhattan.

"It's funny but I've never come out this far," Tia admitted. "It's almost like another world from the East Village, although I'd guess the people living here mostly commute into The City for work. Back in Nebraska, we never think anything of driving fifty miles to do something. Here, anything outside of Manhattan seems like forever away."

A brick church climbed toward the steel-gray sky. From within it, organ music sent up hymns of praise. It could only be a small weekday service, but still, manna pulsed from it like blood from a beating heart. Like blood of the wrong type, it was poison to Ewan.

Further down the street, a group of men met in a small synagogue. Uniting in their prayers, they too sent streams of power up to their deity.

Like a vampire outside a locked bloodbank, Ewan watched in envy. In this entire city of so many million, no one remembered his name, recited the carefully constructed liturgy that had been his worship. No one could name the miracles he'd created for his people, the ways he'd protected them from their enemies or how he'd so often brought them safely home when they'd been lost in the snow.

With Tia's worship, though, he could begin to change that. He could become the god worshipped by millions. His miracles would, once again, be on people's lips and in their hearts.

"If you're just going to stand there, let me know and I'll get something to eat."

It didn't take any great skill to pick up annoyance in Tia's voice. Or in the way she put her hands on her hips and glared at him.

"I beg your pardon."

"You've been standing there for close to an hour. I'm freezing and I'm getting hungry again."

He considered reminding her that he'd been hungry for thousands of years. Could she really blame him for being like a child pushing his nose against the window to a chocolate shop? But he didn't want her pity. Even a hungry god has his pride.

"I was considering the ways your modern worship varies from the traditions I was accustomed to." The truth, if less than the entire truth.

"I hoped you were tracking down the guys who were trying to kill us. That is what we're trying to accomplish, right? Or did you drag me out to nowhere-land to keep me away from the action?"

"I learned that, too."

"Well, what are we waiting for?"

He shot another quick look at the church. Abruptly, the church bells joined the organ in peeling out praise for the God so many worshiped.

"I'm done waiting. Let's get him."

Chapter 7

He'd scared her.

Tia had over-reacted, but he'd stood there on the street for so long, perfectly still, staring at nothing at all—she knew this because she'd moved her hand in front of his eyes and they hadn't tracked—and he'd seemed to grow thinner, even a bit transparent.

She'd been afraid he was going back to wherever he'd been before her weird powers had pulled him into the modern world. Sure she would go on without him, but she wasn't ready to be left alone.

Which was strange. If he left, presumably she would be safe again, could resume her normal life without being worried about government-connected evil corporations, or anything that made her question her faith. She didn't need him: he needed her.

I was just weirded out, she told herself. She wasn't convinced.

Ewan led her down Thirteenth Street, turned onto 78th, and stopped in front of a two-story home that could have graced a postcard. Colorful lights outlined all the trees and the home's eves. A glowing Santa Claus clung to a brick chimney and a reindeer-pulled sleigh perched at the top of the roof.

This had to be home for some perfect family. She waited for Ewan to move on.

Instead he turned up the walkway.

"No way some arsonist lives here."

"I know what I'm doing."

He hesitated before putting his hand to the door, then opened it without knocking.

He didn't blur, he simply stood in the doorway one second, then he was gone.

Nice Nebraska girls don't walk into strangers' homes without being invited. And nice Nebraska girls don't confront evil arsonists by themselves. But Nebraska girls, nice or not, don't abandon their partners. She didn't believe that Ewan had abandoned her so she had no choice but to follow this investigation and see where it went.

The home's interior was every bit as precious as the Christmas decorations outside. Hummel figurines, an eggcup collection, and what looked like antique Victorian furniture gave a homey feel—like visiting your grandmother. Like a stage set, she suddenly realized. Nobody is that perfect.

There was no sign of Ewan on the first floor and she reluctantly climbed the stairs to the second.

And wished she hadn't.

In the bedroom, blood splashed across the bed, spattered all the way to the ceiling, and dripping from the nightstand.

Ewan knelt over his victim, holding the man's head in his hands like some sort of horrific lover.

A scream bubbled up in Tia's throat, but she turned it into a sob.

"He won't be starting any more fires," Ewan observed.

That was true, and Tia shouldn't waste much sympathy on the man who had attempted to kill her and her roommates. This was a horrible reminder. She couldn't be attracted to Ewan, couldn't fall for someone who could kill so quickly and casually.

Ewan's victim didn't look like a fearsome arsonist. He'd been in his late fifties, probably. Wispy gray hair had been losing a battle with baldness. Scattered but dying plugs showed that a transplant hadn't taken. Acne scars showed he'd lost similar battles with his complexion as a teenager.

Although it was the middle of the afternoon, the man must have been sleeping when they'd arrived. He'd worn only a t-shirt and a pair of briefs. Blood, still flowing sluggishly from his nearly severed neck was so thick that Tia could barely make out the NYU logo on the formerly white t-shirt.

Well, he'd never sleep again—unless they let you sleep in Hell. Tia believed in a forgiving God, but she had a hard time wishing forgiveness on this guy.

The stench of blood mixed with that of feces. The arsonist had shat himself as he'd been dying.

"Did you forget, Ewan, that our objective was to find out who had sent him? Why kill him?"

Ewan raised a bloody hand from the dead man's forehead and the man's head lolled back, connected to the neck by a few strands of skin and gristle.

"He hasn't been dead long enough for his brain to be wiped clean, but I still can't get anything."

"You might have thought about that before you killed him."

He stared at her for a second. "You think this is *my* work? I'm no death-god. I draw energy from the living. Your arsonist was dead when I arrived."

The blood was still wet, still dripping. She'd seen the welling of blood that meant the heart was still trying to beat blood through increasingly empty veins. "But that means—"

"Yes, indeed." A strange voice, not Ewan's, answered the question she'd only started to phrase.

"You're quite right." A stranger stepped from the closet where he'd been hiding. Several other men came out of the bathroom and one climbed down from the attic. All except the speaker carried electronic equipment that they kept pointed at Ewan. "It means that the killers are still here," the man continued. "You took a bit longer than we'd anticipated, which meant poor Harten here had to put up with our company for longer than he really wanted. Frankly, we were getting a little worried about your long stay at the subway exit. But you're finally here. Thank you, Ms. Burns, for delivering Mr. uh, Ewan, into our hands."

* * * *

The speaker looked like nothing more than a thirty-something businessman. Tia recognized the type—her college boyfriend was turning into one himself. The guy would have been good looking if he hadn't been so smug. His blond hair and Nordic carved face made him look like a model for an expensive

German carmaker.

Ewan froze in an impossible stance, half-standing from where he'd been examining the dead arsonist, half-twisting to face the businessman.

"Got him, boss." The four guys who'd popped out with the businessman looked like technicians or scientists. Three of them pointed what looked like satellite dishes at Ewan. A fourth clicked at a tablet PC's screen with a stylus, adjusting something that could only be a part of whatever they were using to trap Ewan.

"How long will it hold him, Farner?"

The man with the PC shrugged. "He's our first god, you know. We're still learning. He's soaking up some serious energy."

The businessman, apparently named Travers, laughed. "Well hold onto him. Catching a god isn't so hard after all. A little chum in the water, a bit of bloody bait, and bam, you have one."

Tia suspected *she* was the chum Travers was talking about. Which meant, now that they'd caught Ewan, they wouldn't need her. No wonder the attacks had failed. They hadn't really intended to kill her, yet. They'd just been making sure Ewan was fully involved with protecting her.

With Ewan in their control, it was up to her to rescue both herself and the god. She wasn't sure what one woman could do against five guys who'd already killed once, but she intended to find out.

She relied on what she'd learned dating Bobby, her Nebraska ex-boyfriend. Guys like him, and she suspected like Travers, always want a chance to tell how clever they are. Maybe she could delay things, give Ewan the time he needed to get free.

"This is amazing," she gushed. "How could you possibly have known that we'd track down the arsonist? He didn't leave any evidence at all."

Travers leered at her. "No evidence? Not for a cop, maybe. We knew Ewan could follow the psychic path. A professional torch was perfect. If Harten got you in the fire, Ewan would fall into our hands like a ripe peach. If he rescued you, he'd follow the traces—leading to us. Too bad for you he brought you along."

"So you knew Ewan was a god all along?"

Travers' face darkened. "You're trying to distract me, aren't you? Kasper, kill her."

"Me?" one of the technicians--the one covered in blood--protested. "I killed Harten. How come it's not Farner's turn?"

Tia didn't wait to see how that argument worked itself out. Instead, she ducked under the dish to get at one of the scientists, hoping he'd be distracted by the argument.

No such luck. He brought the dish down hard on her back.

She fought for her balance, reaching for him as she fell.

He grinned and smashed the dish again, hitting her lower spine.

Her legs wobbled under her, then gave way.

Sorry, Ewan. She wanted to get up and keep fighting, but her legs didn't answer when she called on them.

Apparently Kasper had gotten the message that Travers didn't appreciate his complaining because he pulled a bloody knife from his pocket and walked toward her. He might have *preferred* not to kill her, but his face showed about as much emotion as your average head of lettuce.

Ewan moved.

Apparently her back had put a bit of a dent in the satellite dish they'd been pointing at Ewan because the guy with the tablet PC poked harder and faster, but Ewan kept moving.

"Stand still or we kill the girl," Travers said.

Ewan's laugh seemed filled with the pain of millennia of loss. "With this?"

He waved his hand and abruptly Kasper's knife was in his own hand.

"No. With this." Travers pulled a large gauge pistol-like device from a holster under his tailored suit jacket and pointed it at Tia. "Bring him back under control, Farner. You said he wouldn't be able to move once you hit him with your god-zapper."

"Working on it." Sweat rolled down the technician's face as he stabbed at his slate.

Whatever he was doing was having an effect. Ewan seemed caught in slow motion, each step an agony of pushing back unbelievable forces.

Tia's legs didn't work, but she reached up and grabbed the satellite dish that had bashed her, yanking it down so it didn't aim at Ewan any more.

This time the technician didn't even bother hitting her with the dish. Instead, he kicked her in the head.

Stars danced across her eyes. Damn, pretty.

She forced herself to concentrate. *Come on, Ewan. You can do it.*

She didn't say the words out loud, but she believed he could hear them.

Ewan's face was a brutal grimace of pain and effort but he took another step toward Travers.

"I don't want to hurt you, but I will if I have to."

"An insignificant ant like you hurt a god?" Each word, each syllable ground out like extruded steel.

"Ten seconds. Hold him off for ten seconds and I'll have him," Farner reported.

But Travers didn't have ten seconds. As slowly as Ewan was moving, he would close the distance in half of that.

She saw the moment when panic gained control of the businessman.

Travers took two steps back, then jumped to the side to avoid Ewan's knife.

Ewan adjusted his aim.

Travers fired.

Tia had assumed that bullets would bounce off of Ewan like they did off of *Superman* in the movies.

Maybe regular bullets would have. This weapon had been designed with a god in mind. Projectiles ripped through his manifested flesh like termites boring through balsawood, then hammered a ten-foot circular hole though the house's exterior wall.

Ewan staggered.

Amber blood, glowing like molten metal, gushed from a hole in his chest where his heart should be.

The liquid blood seemed to dry the instant it hit the air, then fell with a sound like a strand of pearls breaking, each bead striking the ground a moment behind the last.

Ewan put a hand over the hole in his chest, a hand she clearly saw through the exit wound in his back. Inevitably, like an imploding building, the god fell.

In his earthly form, Ewan wasn't much taller than six feet, but his fall seemed to be that of a giant rather than a man.

Travers shouted in triumph, then fired again.

The bullet's impact twisted Ewan so he faced away from Travers. He gave Tia a satisfied nod, as if he'd intended this to happen.

Behind Ewan, Farner gave a short cry and crumpled, his tablet PC smashing to the ground. The bullet left another hole through Ewan. It simply eliminated the lower half of Farner's body. He looked down at his torso, at where his legs and groin had once been, then died without making another sound.

Ewan reached for Tia, grasped her arm, and turned away, taking her with him.

She couldn't give a better description than 'turned away.' He turned away from her, from the arsonist's house, definitely from Travers and the other killers. But he didn't turn *toward* anything she knew.

The two plunged into a world of impossible colors—yellow skies, green clouds, orange trees. Except yellow wasn't yellow. Blue wasn't blue. And Tia suspected that mixing the two colors together would yield nothing remotely similar to green.

Ewan looked different, too, although the differences had nothing to do with color.

He moved through an atmosphere that was far too solid for anything as mundane as human breath, crossing miles, maybe light years with each step.

The two holes Travers' bullets had drilled through his body seemed as big as craters on the moon. His amber blood combusted when it hit the ground, leaving a trail of fire behind them as he strode through uncounted miles.

She couldn't breathe. She opened her mouth to tell him, but she couldn't speak.

This was no place for a human. Ewan had rescued her from the killers, but his rescue looked to be every bit as fatal. At least for her.

All of her doubts vanished. Ewan really was a god.

* * * *

Travers and his scientists had cooked up something that could hurt, even kill a god. And Ewan knew killing gods wasn't easy. In many ways, though, the electro-manna grid they'd used to trap him had been worse than the projectile.

Hunger

At least there was precedent for deicide. Nobody had actually trapped a god since Hephaestus had trapped Aphrodite in a divine net or Zeus tied Prometheus to a rock. That mere mortals could develop such a tool was worse than blasphemous—it was dangerous to both the gods and the humans.

Still, the projectiles had hurt plenty. Acting like mini-black holes, they'd sucking his multidimensional form into a singularity, growing more ravenous as they moved. They left huge gaps in him, gaps that he lacked the power to close.

Ichor flowed from him, draining him of still more energy he could not spare. In his arms, Tia too was dying. He'd translated himself into n-dimension God-space to allow his escape, but she couldn't stay here.

If Tia died, he would die too. He would lose every trace of the manna that gave him his small grip on reality. Even without his injuries, he would be pushed through Limbo and into Tartarus, the oblivion of lost gods. Her death would implode him like a dying star leaving nothing but darkness behind.

He twisted again.

Female screaming surrounded him. Fists pounded on his battered body. The loss of ichor, and the horrible damage those impossible bullets of something both science and theology insisted could not exist, left his brain moving slowly.

If his body hadn't been slowed as much as his mind, he would have reacted, would have killed before he'd realized it was only Lori, Tia's roommate, responding to his sudden appearance with Tia's apparently lifeless body in his arms.

Instead of killing her, he ignored Lori.

He brushed the remains of what had obviously been a thorough shopping trip from the sofa and set Tia down on it.

Her face was purple and her fingers clawed at her throat, but her brain had forgotten how to breathe.

"What did you do to her? And what's happened to you?" Lori had stopped beating on his back but the tiny trickle of faith she'd been sending his way since the fire vanished.

"Wait." He covered Tia's mouth with his own and exhaled.

Her lungs filled, but stayed filled when he broke the seal.

Gently, so as not to damage her, he pressed down on her chest, forcing her to exhale. Then he breathed into her once more.

Incongruously, his senses responded to the warmth of her lips against his own, the soft roundness of the breasts he could not avoid touching as he reminded her body to breathe.

"Jeez. You're both messed up, aren't you? Is she going to be all right? I hope the other guy looks even worse."

When he had called upon his powers to stop their hearts, all five men should have collapsed instantly. Instead, their machines had drained his manna from like water being sucked in an undertow.

They'd prepared for a divine attack, knew exactly who they were dealing with. Clearly they'd been studying, had been preparing for years.

For an instant, Ewan wondered if Tia might be involved. Travers had known about Tia, about her power, about the psychic connection her manna created with Ewan.

The idea was ridiculous and he dismissed it as quickly as he'd brought it to mind. With Tia on their side, Travers and his men would have manipulated Ewan even more competently.

As it was, Travers's panic had allowed Ewan and Tia to escape. If the man had kept his cool, simply kept backing away from Ewan as he'd advanced, Ewan wouldn't have reached him before Farner's computerized trap had compensated for Tia's distraction and tightened on him once more. But Ewan had read Travers's soul, had counted on the man's panic, had positioned himself so that bullets passing through him would hit Farner and his device. Bullets that could injure a god had obliterated both the man and the machine.

Unfortunately, Ewan suspected whatever organization Travers worked with would be back with more.

A god can endure a lot of damage. Still, Ewan's escape had required a superhuman effort from Tia, precise calculation of every angle, and a good deal of luck. Even with all of that going for him, he had barely gotten away. The next time, he couldn't rely on luck.

And there would be a next time, unless he failed to save Tia. In which case, he'd cheat them by vanishing into nothingness.

He wasn't sure what a nearly powerless shadow could do against men who could murder a god. But he intended to find out. First, he had to save Tia.

He filled her lungs again, pushed out the air, then breathed into her one more time.

"Live, dammit," he said.

He didn't dare use his power on her, not that he had much left. Even near death, Tia's faith in another god kept him from reaching into her and fixing what needed repair. Killing was easy. Keeping someone alive was much tougher.

It could only be coincidence that Tia responded to his words. She coughed, choked, then, when he was certain she was dying despite everything he could do, she took a breath on her own.

He backed away but she reached her arms around him and pulled him back.

His kiss had nothing to do with breathing and everything to do with lust.

She opened her expressive brown eyes and he fell in.

Fell, at any rate.

Abruptly, his knees buckled and he collapsed to the floor.

He tried to make the twist back to multidimensional space, but found he was too weak even for that.

Although he manifested here, ichor poured from his body not in the simple three dimensions of the human world, but in every one of the near-infinity of dimensions through which his true form extended. He'd saved Tia, but he wasn't sure she could save him.

He feared that Travers might come after Tia even with him vanished, but there wasn't anything he could do about that. He was fading and didn't have a clue how to stop the damage.

* * * *

Indigo had whispered soft nothings into Tia's ears. Ethereal symphonies painted tastes better than chocolate in her mouth. Sweetness pressed against her skin. Heat and sensation created visible images in her eyes.

For the first time, Tia understood the sacrifice of the enlightened one, the Buddha or Christ. It must have been horribly difficult for them to achieve oneness with God. To give up the bliss of unity with the divine simply to bring their message to the unwilling Earth would have been an act of supreme self-sacrifice.

At least the enlightened had a message to share. Since a god had dragged Tia through the realm of the divine, she had nothing in particular to share with the ordinary world. She'd wanted to stay.

She'd tried to ignore the voices calling her back. What were mere human concerns, human joys, compared to the richness of infinite dimensions?

But one of those voices was too insistent, too demanding to ignore.

The strength of that voice had dragged her from bliss, yanked her into the ordinary world.

Her senses collapsed. Lights she had never known existed darkened, winked out. Tastes she'd only dreamed of faded.

But a touch of it remained.

Her lips tingled with a sensation she knew, yet couldn't really comprehend. Until memory returned.

Oh, yes. Ewan's lips pressed against her own. That sensation brought her close to the bliss she left behind.

If she was going to be denied enlightenment, she wasn't going to be denied his touch.

She'd wrapped her arms around him and pulled him to her, brought his lips back to her own, kissed him with all of her heart.

At first, Ewan had responded greedily, needing her as much as she needed him.

A part of Tia knew she was cheating. She was falling for him, pretending that Ewan might feel the same for her. But it wasn't like that for him. He was an addict dependent on her as his needle. And the first thing she'd been taught when she agreed to volunteer to work with the homeless is that addicts cannot truly love.

Tia refused to let herself care. Maybe later. For the time, Ewan's kiss was enough.

But something was wrong.

Even as he kissed her, he seemed to be collapsing.

Memory streamed back. He'd been shot. The holes blown through him would have killed anyone. Hell, one glancing shot that had already penetrated through Ewan disintegrated Farner's entire lower body and killed him instantly. Ewan had endured two point-blank shots.

She opened her eyes—and wished she hadn't.

57

They were back in the hotel suite Ewan had stolen for her, but Ewan was dying.

Being in that strange other world had changed Tia, it had done nothing good for Ewan. Amber blood still flooded from his wounds, still solidified and dropped to the ground. That solid blood lay on the floor in piles so deep she wondered it would fill the entire room.

"Don't just stand there," she told Lori. "Let's get him patched up."

"I didn't know gods could bleed." Lori hesitated, then grabbed a sheet from the bed and pressed it against Ewan's chest.

Tia grabbed a couple of towels from the bathroom, pulled Ewan onto the couch where she'd been laying, and tried to close his wounds with them.

"Don't you dare go away, Ewan. We need you."

"Believe in him," Lori said. "You're the Niagara Falls of manna, remember? You can give him strength if you just believe in him."

"I can't worship him," she said. But she could have feelings for him. Could that be enough? *Don't you dare leave us*, she projected. It was as close to worship as she could manage.

"Trying." His voice was barely a whisper.

"Try harder."

Lori wrapped a couple more sheets around him, like a full body tourniquet, using the sheets to keep the towels pressed against his wounds.

Tia pressed her body against his. She told herself she was keeping him warm, trying to prevent shock. She did it as much for herself as for Ewan, though.

"Let's get some liquids into him. There should be some tea in the minibar. And Lori, I'm doing the best I can on the manna side but I can't do enough."

Lori brought her a glass of chai tea, then ordered chili from room service.

Tia shifted to put Ewan's head on her lap and coaxed him into drinking the over-sweet tea.

His throat moved as he swallowed and he clenched her hand in his own.

She had less luck getting the chili into him, though. He managed one swallow, then stopped.

"Come on, babe. You've got to take it."

His head lolled to one side and he stopped breathing.

"I think he's dead," Lori said.

Chapter 8

He led his people on a wave of conquest, spreading their culture, technology and their certainty in his power from the steppes of Turkmenistan into Anatolia, down to Mesopotamia and eastward into what later became Persia.

His outnumbered mounted tribesmen faced the iron legions of Rome, while he confronted the ranked lines of the Roman gods. Together, he and his people smashed legions that had conquered the known world, killed their generals, laughed at the gods who thought they could steal the faith of his people.

But the Romans and their gods didn't give up. A generation later, he stood again against Rome. This time, superior numbers and organization, and the power of so many millions praying for their gods, overcame his warriors, swamped his people while their gods held him immobilized. He, along with those most faithful to him, were dragged before the mocking citizens of Rome. Along with thousands of other gods, brought by the Romans from their many conquests, he was held captive until his power diminished, until his name was forgotten, until he became nothing but a wraith of godhood.

With Christianity, the captors became victims themselves. A few of his erstwhile enemies among the Roman gods transformed themselves, becoming Christian Saints or voodoo gods. Most, though, joined him in limbo, their powers eclipsed by new gods, new faiths.

Thanks to Virgil and Bullfinch, *they* were still remembered. They still had a few worshipers, a little power. They were conscious, aware, capable of doing a little here and there.

Ewan had drifted, but he hadn't been truly dead.

Now, though, he was fading toward the final death, the death from which no god returns.

As he whirled through the *true world*, falling fast toward Tartarus, and from there, into the destruction of complete oblivion, he ripped past many of those old gods. Fellow captives, former captors, all barely surviving on the dregs of what had once been divine omnipotence.

He nodded, recognizing them, trying to pause in his rush toward oblivion.

"If they can use you, they can use all of us." Fierce Mars battered a bronze spear on the ground and lectured him on the obvious.

Ewan forced his battered body to shrug. "They've killed me, putting me beyond their power. You may be next."

Those who worshiped Mars were mostly punks or fools who knew nothing of the horrors of war, but he didn't tell the war-god that. He didn't owe the Roman gods anything, but he didn't want them captured and twisted by Travers, either.

"You've got to return and fix the problems you created." Dressed in blue, with her owl perched on her shoulder whispering secrets in her ear, Minerva/Athena was tougher to argue with than was Mars.

"How?" It wasn't as if he *wanted* Travers to win. But painful millennia had taught him that wanting doesn't equate to *doing*—even for a god. Without power, all the wanting in the universe was wasted.

"Get the female to worship you and you can heal yourself, defeat our enemies."

"Too late. I'm dying."

Athena turned to Pluto. "Well?"

A black helmet covered the death-god's face and a black cloak his body. Skeletal hands grasped a scepter of bone, twisted it as he considered. "We can *lend* you power. For a little time."

Mars reached out his spear, catching Ewan with its shaft and holding him in place.

Ewan didn't trust Pluto, but he recognized that deity's might. Death-gods were different. The world constantly created new deaths, churned out new manna for a death-god, even a death-god of a lost faith.

"I'm hardly in a position to repay."

"Get it from the woman or give it to us from your death-manna. The woman wants to love you—use her love and transform it to worship. We can sustain you for..." Pluto paused and looked at the faded ranks of the other Roman gods, gods who had been Ewan's enemies for centuries before becoming his fellow captives in limbo. "For two weeks, Earth-time. Maybe."

Ewan didn't trust the Romans, and trusted Pluto least of all. But any chance was better than annihilation. "I'll try."

Pluto gestured and pain etched itself across the faces of each of those Roman gods. Ichor dripped from gaping wounds in *their* previously flawless skin. Hunger tightened their skins against their bones.

With every drop of their ichor, Ewan's body healed. With each gasp of pain from the Romans, his own agony receded.

"Two weeks," Pluto repeated. Then the god turned and plunged himself into a memory of a Hades filled with newly dead worshipers.

Tartarus no longer pulled at him. He wouldn't vanish into oblivion. Not yet, anyway.

Ewan twisted himself dimensionally, folding down to the three special dimensions of the middle earth. Agony ripped through him as he tried but failed to translate.

Those gods believed themselves to be stronger than they were. The accumulated manna from more than a dozen Roman gods could sustain him in limbo. Until he healed, it was too little to let him return to Tia, to confront their shared enemies. And with his remaining wounds, he couldn't heal.

* * * *

"He disappeared. That's impossible." Lori gaped at the space Ewan's body had just left.

"You don't think a god's body would just lay around for people to gawk at, do you?" Tia bent down and picked up a perfect amber sphere. Those solidified remains of his blood were all that remained of the vanished god.

Hunger

She wanted to crawl under the covers of the comfortable hotel bed and stay there forever, but she owed it to the memory of Ewan to keep going, to make sure that Travers and his scientist-killers didn't hunt down any more gods.

"We'd better start thinking about what we do next."

"Why not stay here?" Lori demanded. "It's what Ewan wanted."

"Now that he's not around to confuse the hotel management, how long do you think it's going to be before they realize we're not paying for their suite?"

Lori wrinkled her nose. "Too bad. I could get used to living like this"

"I'll find someplace safe for you, then I'll go after the creeps who killed Ewan," Tia said. "With Ewan dead, they won't be expecting any danger."

Lori shook her head. "Oh, no. Ewan might be your boyfriend, but I liked him too. And I'm not going to let you go into danger without being there to help."

As if Ewan was her boyfriend. "What do you think you can do?"

"I don't suppose Kung Fu is much use against someone who can kill a god, but two of us are better than just one."

If she were really a good person, Tia would refuse Lori's help and insist that she find someplace safe to wait out whatever Travers and his sidekicks did next. But Ewan's death left her alone, damaged. She needed support and assistance. If Lori volunteered, Tia couldn't turn it down.

"All right. It's the two of us against the big bad wolf."

"Does that make us piggies?" Lori pinched a bit of skin around her tiny waist and considered it.

Tia looked at her impossibly thin roommate. "Definitely no more than one pig here. We're the billy goats, gruff."

"That's us," Lori agreed. "Although you're mixing fairy tales now. Anyway, we'll boot that troll right off his bridge. But first, we're going to find out who he is, and where he hides. Lucky I've got my super-paralegal researcher here."

"Ewan thought it would be dangerous to go to my office."

"They haven't kicked us out of this suite yet, and we've got a Web-TV connection." Lori gestured to the large flatscreen TV hanging on the wall like a picture frame. "So, let's get to work."

'Us getting to work' consisted mostly of Tia working while Lori looked over her shoulder and cooed at the way she accessed private databases.

Ten minutes later, Tia realized this wasn't going anywhere. There were 62,000 Google entries for 'Travers+businessman.' The man they were looking for didn't show up in the first hundred, and it would take weeks to wade through all of the entries with no reason to be certain they'd find him even if they had weeks.

"Time to call on the network," Lori said. "I don't know much about computers, but I sure know phones. I need to get some we can use without being traced."

Tia knew what that meant. Lori was going to hook up with a guy she knew with connections. "No drugs. This isn't the time for that."

Lori wasn't a big user, but she was known to use the amphetamine crutch when she thought she needed to lose a pound or two.

"No drugs," Lori agreed. "Just phones."

While Tia cleaned up the worst of the mess in the hotel room, Lori vanished into New York's underworld.

An hour later, she were back with an armload of untraceable cellphones, her girlfriend Marti, and the news that a blond man named Travers was known in the underworld as a party guy and a dependable over-payer for cocaine and rohypnol. Unfortunately, Marti's contact hadn't known more than that, couldn't give a last name, a business connection, or an address.

"Sounds like a complete jerk." Lori examined the phones. Most were cheap models—the kind you can buy on street corners and throw away once you'd used the hundred minutes. Some, though, were fancy Palms and Blackberries. Tia didn't want to ask where they came from.

Equipped with the most indispensable tools of the New York entertainer, Lori and Marti started dialing, connecting with the hundreds of women they knew from waiting in lines at casting calls, sitting in modeling agencies' waiting rooms, and from working as booth bimbos in trade shows around New York. New York was full of beautiful women aching for the chance to be discovered, to become the next big thing, and most of them lived with their phones, waiting for their breakout call. And it seemed that Lori and Marti knew all of them. And one of them would know Travers. In New York, six degrees of separation was more like two.

Or so Tia had thought. None of their friends had any luck identifying the scientist types. But good-looking businessmen-types were a tradable commodity in the girlfriend-net world. It turned out a man named Travers had asked several of the women out and was generally known as a creep. Although none of the women confirmed that Travers had drugged them, word was he liked things rough.

Their description matched the Travers Tia had met to a 'T.' Sadistic tendencies. Nordic good looks but an inclination to dominate. A swelled head.

When they learned that Lori and Tia planned to go after the creep, their friends became even more forthcoming. Not only did they get multiple volunteers to hold Travers down while they got a sharp knife and removed certain items from his anatomy, they also got a first name, Edmond to go with Travers.

Considering Tia had been looking for Travers as a first name, that narrowed things down. Google brought results.

An Edmond Travers was Vice President for Corporate Events Management for The Iconic Security Corporation of Holmdel, New Jersey.

"Never heard of it," Lori said.

Tia hadn't either, but between Web-TV and the financial databases her paralegal job gave her access to, she ran a profile of the company.

"Supposedly they make security products for government and corporate accounts. But they've pumped about fifty million dollars into development and only have a couple of minor products to show for it. Total sales of less than a hundred thousand last year."

She clicked another link. "Uh-oh."

"What?" Lori got off her cell and leaned over the back of her chair to check out the screen.

"They bought the company that made the two products they're selling. Which means they have exactly nothing to show for fifty million dollars in R&D."

"Guess they're better at spending their money than getting things for it. Figures when they hire a jerk like Travers as a Vice President."

Lori wrinkled her forehead briefly, then caught herself and pressed her fingers over any possible wrinkles. "That's sort of funny. Except, where did an incompetent bunch come up with fifty million to burn?"

Losing money could mean money laundering, so Tia clicked another couple of links but came up blank. "Unnamed angel investors are the supposed source of their funding," she reported. "Unfortunately, private corporations don't file financial details the way publicly traded companies do. These guys sure haven't filed anything they didn't absolutely have to."

Lori paced between the television on which Tia displayed her results, and the balcony. "How about checking out their corporate operations on *GoogleEarth*? At least we can take a look at their plant."

It was a good thought. What *GoogleEarth* showed, though, was nothing like a corporate research campus that could go through millions of dollars a year. Instead, the address was an ordinary looking office building on an ordinary street in Holmdel.

"Boring," she reported.

"So do a search on the address," Lori suggested.

The search results mystified Tia although, from the way she'd made the suggestion, Lori had guessed what would happen. Dozens of companies were listed at the same address as Iconic Security. The building wasn't *that* big.

"This location is a mail drop," Lori said.

Tia didn't think of her roommate as an airhead, exactly. But she was surprised Lori was so knowledgeable. Lori was supposed to be beautiful. Tia was supposed to be the smart one, the professional researcher.

Time to show a little of that savvy. "Their research and development group must be in the god-catching business. They've got to have a real location, a lab, a manufacturing facility."

Lori reached into her purse for rarely seen glasses and perched them on her nose. Her prop in place, she studied the *GoogleEarth* satellite photograph of the Holmdel location.

"For sure they aren't making anything in <u>that</u> location. This isn't the city, remember? A company out in the 'burbs needs parking for their employees. And there isn't any. Did you find anything about other locations on Google?"

"Just the corporate headquarters."

"Then let's get back to work on this Travers creep. He's got to have a home."

That made sense. It also coincided with what Tia's worst instincts wanted her to do—find out more about the man who'd threatened her and killed her—what? She couldn't even put a name on what Ewan was to her. He might be a god, but he wasn't *her* God. He might be a heavenly kisser, but he wasn't her lover. Still, he might have become one—if Travers hadn't killed him first.

* * * *

Edmond Travers, Vice President, wasn't as stealthy as his company.

It only took a couple of minutes to learn that Travers had grown up in Connecticut, attended college at Yale and gotten his MBA at Georgetown. He lived in Manhattan, had a Mercedes as a corporate car, and despite an attractive salary of three hundred thousand a year plus all sorts of corporate perks, his Visa Signature Card carried a balance of better than fifty thousand dollars.

Private databases available to paralegals let Tia see exactly what he'd spent that money on.

"Dang girl, you can learn just about anything about a person, can't you?" Lori said. "I just have one question."

"Hmm?" Tia was scrolling down the charges trying to see a pattern.

"How come you didn't tell me that Richard was two-timing me? If you'd looked at his credit cards, you could have seen he was going out with someone else."

"You were so starry-eyed about that jerk, you wouldn't have believed me and you wouldn't have forgiven me."

"Yeah, but—"

"Here's something interesting. Just about all of the charges are in the city. Except these Hawaii charges."

"Probably a vacation," Lori guessed.

"Maybe," Tia agreed. "I wouldn't guess there are many research labs on Maui. Unfortunately, we still don't have an office address."

Lori rubbed her hands together. "He lives in New York. We've got his address there. What do you say we give him a visit?"

The last time Tia had tracked down a suspect, things hadn't worked out very well. "We could call the police."

"And tell them what?" Lori asked. "That this Travers is engaged in deicide? Friends don't let friends do anything that stupid. Besides, where's the body? All we've got left is some amber jewels that we can claim are his blood and a hotel penthouse we aren't supposed to be in. We'll be the ones going to jail."

"It might not even be illegal to kill a god," Tia admitted. "Hiring someone to commit arson is against the law, though. And they didn't just kill Ewan. They also killed Harten, the arsonist."

Lori considered. "Use one of the no-name cells, tell the police where they can find Harten's body. After you make the call, we'll take that cell and mash it with a hammer so the cops can't track it back to us. Because you know what? Somebody reports a body, the easiest thing for the police to assume is that the people who found it are the people who did it. Especially if one of us is black and we're trying finger rich white guys with a CIA connection."

"Nobody said anything about a CIA connection," Tia protested.

"Where else are you going to get fifty million dollars to play with technology to trap a god?"

Tia could think of places—even worse places. Organized crime was high on the list. Corporations who wanted to take the easy way to making obscene profits might be there as well. The former KGB was another possibility now that it had gone private. But the American government was so vast, so complicated, so secret, it was always a safe bet. Besides, it didn't matter. No matter who was behind Ewan's death, they were bound to have more sway with the cops than she did.

"We'll do it your way," she decided. "I'll make the call and then you can smash the phone."

She dialed 9-1-1, reported Harten's location, and hung up as soon as the dispatch operator started asking questions about who she was, how she knew this, and where she was calling from.

The instant Tia hung up, Lori snatched the phone, threw it against the suite's hardwood floor so hard it left a dent in the polished wood, and whacked it with a newly purchased spike-heel shoe until the liquid crystal display flew off and the battery pack dangled.

Tia gathered up what was left and flushed it down the toilet.

"They'll be able to trace it to the nearest cell tower, but there's no way they can connect it with us," Lori reported. "I hope."

"Now we wait and learn what the cops discover and what they do next," Tia said. "With luck, they'll discover evidence that points at Travers and he'll be in jail before we have to do anything.

"One problem." Lori said. "It's not like they're going to tell us, even if they do find anything."

"There's a website that tunes into the police bands," Tia said. "We can listen to dispatch"

"I didn't know that. Don't they do most of their stuff by cell these days?" Lori asked.

"Nah. They all like to listen in on each other. That way they can all find out where the action is."

Less than an hour later, a cop reported back from Harten's place. They'd found a couple of big holes in the walls, but no evidence of a body.

"Holes may indicate something," the dispatcher remarked. "Make sure you check it out completely."

"Yeah, yeah."

Twenty minutes later, the same cop reported back.

"Complete waste of time," the duty cop reported. "We luminoled the place. Best we can figure, it's an abandoned home that got broken into. There's no ownership paperwork on the place. Not in the database, anyway."

"Roger," dispatch replied. "Is the location secure?"

"Better get someone to put plywood on the holes, cause they go all the way through. I'm surprised they don't have homeless people moving in."

"Roger that. Guess you can return to patrol."

Tia clicked off the browser window. "No way. I thought Luminol was supposed to pick up blood traces even after you'd tried to clean it up." Evenings watching CSI with the homeless were more helpful now than her job as a paralegal.

"Iconic Security," Lori said. "How hard is it to believe that kind would eliminate the mess? Or, if not, of persuading the cops that they, and their families, would be safer by keeping their eyes shut?"

Tia looked at her roommate. "It's up to us."

Chapter 9

"How do we get into his apartment?" Tia asked.

Lori had insisted that they dress in black jeans and black t-shirts, and she'd stopped by her dojo and picked up some martial arts weapons she claimed would have anybody helpless in no time.

They looked exactly like a pair of hardware-intense cat burglars as they stood outside of Travers' mid-town apartment.

In their apartment, security had consisted a doorbell buzzer. Anyone could get around their building's security by pushing a lot of doorbells—someone would buzz them in.

Travers' place took security more seriously. A guard sat as a desk surrounded by what looked like bulletproof glass. Closed-circuit television monitors showed every foot of the external access and alternating views of the different hallways within the building. The pistol at the guard's hip looked dangerous. The man himself looked like someone who couldn't get a job anywhere else. Food-crumbs marched up the front of his uniform tunic and he'd cut himself shaving in four different places. Lori's Kung Fu or not, it didn't take a genius to shoot a gun.

"I'll get us in," Lori promised.

She sashayed up to the guard, gave him a hip-twitch and let him look down her scoop-necked t-shirt. Not that she had much to show there, skinny as she was. Still, her modeling career had taught her to use what she had to full advantage and the bra she wore provided maximum magnification.

A couple of minutes later, she waved Tia in.

"I had to explain to Tommy here that Travers' birthday present is a *surprise*." She was acting, using a sultry voice that carried the molasses sweetness of the Deep South rather than the harsher accent of her mid-Atlantic suburban upbringing. "Poor Tommy can't get away from his desk to come up and see us do our little act, but he sure is interested."

"Couple weeks ago I turn thirty-five," Tommy said. "Some of my buds took me out for beer. That's it." The guard's eyes were big as he looked from one of the women to the next. He stared at Tia's breasts for a bit, but finally decided that Lori, with her five-foot ten frame and black hair down to her butt, was the one to concentrate on. "Any of you girls want to continue the party a little later, I get off at two."

"We'll keep you in mind."

Tommy's eyes just got bigger.

Finally he assayed a chuckle. "I don't think any one guy is going to tire both of you out. 'Specially not a business stiff like Travers."

"The sooner you let us up, boyfriend, the sooner we'll be back down. Back down to go down if you know what we mean."

"Heh-heh. Oh, yeah." Tommy's fingers shook so hard he missed the access key the first time he stabbed at it, but he finally managed to let them back into the secure area of the apartment building without calling ahead a warning.

They clomped into the elevator. "Twentieth floor. Got to be the penthouse. Nice." Tia pressed the number and the elevator slid up the shaft. "Think we can knock down his door when we get there? Go in like commandos and take control?"

"You've been watching the wrong TV shows. Not happening." Lori held the elevator door open when it dinged at the building's top floor and the women exited. "I've been in this kind of apartment before. First of all, our friend the guard is watching us on the closed circuit. Second, the doors are steel on the inside. We've got to persuade Travers to let us in."

"He'll recognize me."

"We sure could use a god about now." Lori stroked a fire extinguisher, studied Travers' door, then put the tube back on the wall.

"We don't have a god along to do our dirty work, although I will try a bit of prayer," Tia pulled down her top so more of her cleavage showed. "We get in here the same way you got through the guard. How much you want to bet that Travers won't admit to being the wrong address if he thinks he's getting laid? I'll just move so he can't see my face when he looks through his viewer."

Lori tied up her t-shirts at the waist to expose more tummy that Tia would ever let a stranger see, then Tia rang Travers' doorbell.

"Yeah?" His familiar voice sent chills down Tia's back.

"Strip-o-gram with all the extras for Steve. His co-workers at the hospital sent us."

"For Steve, you say?"

"That's right, sugar. Steve Johnson," Tia let her voice go all throaty. She hoped it sounded sexy, but at least it didn't sound anything like her normal voice. "They said the birthday boy needed the special two-woman treatment."

Tia could almost hear Travers's brain working. *All the extras* had to mean ol' Steve was going to get laid. And free sex under false pretenses was right up Travers's alley.

"If the guys at work wanted me to have this, I guess I can't turn it down."

Tia noticed he didn't quite claim to be the mythical Steve Johnson. He did open the door, though.

She trailed behind Lori, for once glad of her smaller height, and closed the door behind them.

Travers' place was the kind of apartment she'd dreamed of before moving to New York. A huge living room with pure white carpeting extended to a kitchen surrounded by bars and open space. The latest and most expensive appliances filled the kitchen and copper cooking pots hung from the ceiling. Two huge mahogany wine cabinets lined the dining room. A zillion-dollar entertainment system with what had to be a hundred-inch flat panel TV covered an entire wall of his living room. From the gyrating nude figures on the TV, she figured Travers had been watching porn when they'd gotten there. Sexy women at the door were the answer to any perpetual teenager's prayers.

Travers' greedy eyes checked out Lori, but his gaze froze when he got to

Tia. "You."

"Get him." Lori pulled a nunchaku from where she'd stuck them in her jeans and threw herself at Travers before she'd even finished talking, wrapping her arms around him and trying to tackle him to the ground.

Travers stripped the weapon from Lori's hand, tossed it across the room, then smacked a fist into her face.

Lori crumpled to the ground, blood flowing from her nose. "Jeez, I think he broke it." Her tone was that of a little girl.

Two against one had seemed like plenty when she and Lori had been grabbing weapons at the Lori's dojo. It didn't look so great any more as Travers stalked toward Tia.

"I told the guys you could have gotten out one of the holes in the wall but they didn't believe me." Travers punctuated his statement by grabbing for her.

She slapped at his hand and felt like she was slapping a concrete wall. The guy was strong.

He shoved through her attempt to push him away, snagged a bit of her t-shirt and yanked.

Tia saw pictures of herself joining Lori on the ground with a broken nose—or worse—and jerked away as hard as she could.

Fortunately the shirt material ripped, leaving her barely decent in a sports bra but out of range from Travers' big fists. For the moment, at least.

"Do you seriously think you can tap the power of a god?" she demanded. "He'll rip you into shreds like you did my top, and send your soul down to hell."

"Gods," he scoffed. "They call themselves 'gods' but they're nothing but energy entities. I'll bet Ewan didn't tell you he's only here because he's stealing power from you. Those so-called gods are like vampires. They suck power off the faith of people too dumb to know any better. People like you. We owe it to our country to get that power back and to use it for our own benefit."

Without a break in his words, he swung a punch at her.

Some sixth sense had warned Tia, though, and she leaned away just as he threw the punch. Instead of landing on her nose and knocking her down, it hit her shoulder and drove her backwards.

Travers cursed and rubbed his fist—apparently he wasn't big on hitting hard targets but Tia suspected he could take more of that damage than she could. She skittered out of the way, hoping he'd follow, and hoping even more that Lori would stop whining and start helping.

"The way we figure it," Travers continued, exactly as if he hadn't just attempted to knock her block off, "we at Iconic Security are like repo men. We collect the power energy entities steal from innocent people."

He kept moving, backing her toward his kitchen.

"It's not like they're hurting—"

He threw another punch. She avoided his fist by jumping to her right again, but Travers had seen a pattern and was waiting for her move. He grabbed her before she could get her balance and twisted Tia's arm behind her back until she felt something snap.

Pain, like a thousand root canals without anesthesia, shot through her body.

"Here's the deal. You go along peacefully and I'll take you to the plant. Ewan will have to follow and we'll catch him for sure. As far as your friend, I figure she can just deliver what she promised good ole' Steve."

He propelled Tia straight into the stone fireplace. Something went crunch.

* * * *

Tia gritted her teeth. Her arm didn't respond when she tried to get up. Fortunately, Lori chose that moment to pull out her second nunchaku. She managed to clip Travers in the ankle with it before he kicked it out of her hand.

"What do you say," Travers told Lori. "Pretty thing like you has probably learned some tricks in bed."

"I guess most of your dates don't do much. Rophenal means they're willing but not exactly active, huh?"

"Here I thought we might have magic moments." Lori had gotten to her knees so he punctuated his words with an open-handed slap that sent her rolling across the room.

To Tia's surprise, Lori turned her fall into a somersault, ending in one of the Kung Fu stances she practiced around their apartment. "That's it. I'm going to kick your butt."

"I didn't realize you were the Karate Kid. I should have recognized a ninja from the black push-up bra."

He threw another lazy punch toward Lori, then laughed when she kicked him in his gut. "Is that the best you can do, Wonder Woman?"

Travers wasn't paying any attention to her so Tia crawled over and grabbed the nunchaku Travers had knocked loose then struggled to her feet. Her right arm was still numb. She wouldn't give up, but she didn't have much hope, either.

Surprising him in his apartment, armed as they were with martial arts weapons, was supposed to give them the advantage. It hadn't happened.

Travers swung a ponderous slap at Lori's midsection.

Her roommate had plenty of time to block the slap, which she did. Sort of.

His arm went through her block, forcing her block back into her gut.

Lori oofed, looked sick, and backed up—straight into a corner, followed by the amused Travers.

"Catching the two of you is just what I need to get Winsor off my back. I never heard anyone so mad."

Lori dodged to the left but Travers headed her off. This time his punch was straighter, faster and harder.

Lori had learned something in her Kung Fu class. She ducked out of the way, slapping his fist as it went past her. Not to stop it because that didn't work, but just to redirect it enough that it would miss.

Travers hadn't expected that move. His fist smashed into the wall instead of Lori's face.

Tia saw a little shake go down Travers' spine. This was her chance.

70

She rushed at him, swinging the nunchaku like a tennis racket.

Travers had seemed completely involved with his own pain, but he must have spotted Tia with his peripheral vision. He grabbed Lori and swung her around between him and the weapon.

Oh, shit. Tia was swinging to hard to stop. All she could do was change her aim so the nunchaku hit Lori in the butt instead of the ribs where she had been aiming.

"Ouch."

"Sorry."

Travers shook Lori like a terrier shaking a rat. "Drop the ninja thing, Tia. Or your friend will get hurt."

Lori screamed in pain but didn't stop fighting. She used her forward momentum to try a knee to his groin.

Travers must have grown up in a schoolyard where groin shots were popular. He blocked Lori's move almost casually, lifting one leg to interpose a muscular thigh between her knee and his family jewels.

Travers's movement put all his weight on the other leg.

Tia sidestepped to get around her roommate, then tackled that leg.

He caved backwards, falling over her body.

Tia had hoped the surprise would break his grip on Lori.

No such luck. When he fell, he held onto Lori like a drowning man grabbing a life buoy.

Lori struggled for balance, then yielded to the inevitable. There her Kung Fu training paid off for the second time. She twisted to land on top of Travers rather than underneath, bunching up her elbows to hit him in the ribs as she landed.

Travers laughed. The woman was just too light, and Travers had too much muscle for Lori to do much damage. And now he had her in his control.

The businessman yanked Lori's hair until her face was near his, then put his fat hands around her neck and squeezed.

"Say good-bye if you can, Wonder Woman."

Tia was a mess but she wasn't going to let Lori die in a fight that wasn't her own. The pen she grabbed off Travers's desk felt awkward in her left hand, but she shoved it next to his eye. "Let her go. Now."

Lori took a tortured breath as Travers relaxed his grip, but he didn't let their roommate go.

"We seem to be at an impasse. If I let Wonder Woman go, you'd probably stick me anyway. If you hurt me before I let her go, I'll kill her. Any suggestions to get us out of this mess."

"I'll kill you before you can hurt her."

"I'm hard to kill." Travers paused. "But I don't want to lose an eye. Tell you what. If the two of you leave now, we can pretend this never happened. Just back away slowly. I'll let Wonder Woman go once you're near the door."

"Are you kidding? The second I back away, you're going to choke her and then come after me."

"Good point."

"Anyway," Lori said. "We didn't come here to walk away empty-handed. We want to know about the program. What weapon did you use against Ewan? What were you planning to do with all of that power?"

"And we want you to stop," Tia added.

"You're asking me for things I can't deliver." Travers kept his voice as reasonable as if he'd been having a discussion in a corporate boardroom rather than negotiating with a pen point a few millimeters from his eyeball. "You know I'd be lying if I promised to shut the program down. Couldn't even if I wanted to. I'm just a project guy, not someone who makes the policy decisions.

"Here's the deal, girls," he continued. "The best deal you're likely to get. If you make me fight you, I will and I'll take both of you. I might be a one-eyed guy when the fight is over, but if I am, neither of you will be around to laugh at me."

"You're sick," Tia said.

"At least I'm not panting after some long-forgotten manifestation of human ignorance the way you are. Ewan hasn't been worshiped since the Romans smashed his obscure culture from the Caucasus region. How minor is that? Anyway, that's my best and final offer. Get out or take your chances."

"If we kill him, we won't learn anything," Lori said.

The sound of Travers' phone broke into the impasse. It rang four times before his answering machine picked up. "Travers? It's Winsor from corporate security. We're picking up too much chatter out there about you. Someone is searching on you, searching hard. We'll, uh, talk about it when I get there. See you in a couple."

Travers hadn't looked afraid when Tia stuck her pen the width of a few eyelashes from his eyeball, but he paled when he heard the corporate security operative's icy voice.

Lori must have sensed his fear because she wrenched away from him. She left a wad of her hair in his grip but she was alive.

"We've got to get out of here." Tia still couldn't use one arm, and every breath strained against damaged ribs, but she headed for the door in a half-crouched limp. "Travers alone was all we could handle."

"As if two chicks could handle me." Travers couldn't resist the shot, but his heart wasn't in it.

"Maybe you should run too." Tia kept the pen point over his eyeball, tracking the small movements he made. "Sounds like you've become a corporate liability."

"Shut-up, bitch."

Lori called an elevator while Tia kept the pen tip pointed at Travers's eye. When the elevator dinged, signaling its arrival, she jumped away from the executive.

Travers grabbed at her the instant the pen moved. His big hand smacked into her thigh but he used the hand he'd rammed into the wall and his grip failed. Instead, his attack just pushed Tia away. He was still rolling onto his hands and knees when Tia slammed Travers' door and jumped into the elevator.

Another elevator dinged as it reached Travers' floor, but their own door closed and they headed down.

"What the heck is that?" Tia asked, pointing at the large mirror on the back wall of the elevator.

The letters *R-e-o* were already fading from the otherwise spotless silver of the mirror. The characters themselves were insubstantial haze, as if someone had breathed them onto the chill surface of the elevator wall.

"Someone likes ancient rock music?"

"It wasn't there when we got on." Lori glared around the elevator as if expecting to find a third person hidden in a corner. "I saw it appear."

Irrational hope flooded Tia's heart. Although the letters evaporated, they *had* been there. Ewan was communicating with her from beyond his death. One of the things Tia remembered from her college comparative religion class was that it was hard to kill a god, and that even murdered gods tend to show up again.

"Ewan's sending us a message," she said. "I just wish I knew what it meant."

Chapter 10

Security guard Tommy had been so shocked to see the damage the two women had taken that he didn't stop them or ask questions. Which was lucky for him because Tia wasn't feeling friendly.

She and Lori took stock of their situation once they'd gotten out of eyesight of the building.

"We can't take the subway looking like this," Lori said.

"We also can't just stand here so near Travers's high-rise." The January wind cut through Tia's thin jog bra like one of those late-night-television knives cutting through tomatoes.

"What do you suppose that writing meant? I mean, *Red,* what's that about?" Lori led them through an alley then down a block, putting as much distance as they could between themselves and any future search.

Tia felt like an idiot. "Red? I thought it said R. E. O."

"I wondered what you meant about rock groups. The tail on the D must have melted before you saw it."

"Red has to mean Big Red. He's a guy at the homeless kitchen. Ewan sort of made friends with him."

"So Ewan is talking to us from beyond the grave just to suggest we get in touch with a homeless person? Boy, he is some useless divinity."

Tia didn't know why she should feel defensive of Ewan, but she did. "Considering what happened, we're lucky he can communicate at all."

"Okay, so, where does Red stay?" Lori started giggling almost at once, then couldn't stop as the tension of their brush with doom dissipated.

"What?"

Lori's giggles threatened to turn hysterical. "Where does Red stay? What kind of idiotic question was that? I mean, the whole point of the kitchen is that he's homeless, right? He doesn't have a home. He's somewhere on the zillion miles of streets that make up New York."

"It's not impossible," Tia said. "There's a shelter affiliated with the kitchen. We'll start there. And I don't think your question is stupid at all. To get help from Big Red, we need to figure where he is right now."

Lori hiccupped a couple of times but her giggles finally subsided. "We need to go back to the hotel first. We're freezing our butts off, and we need to get patched up."

That made sense but it didn't feel right to Tia. "If it were safe for us to go back to the hotel, Ewan could have contacted us there."

"Uh, yeah. I'm not sure that manager would be as glad to see us without your god, either."

Tia froze. She'd gotten used to thinking of Ewan as a god, but she didn't really equate that with her beliefs. Maybe she should follow Travers's example and think of him as an energy being. "He's not my god."

Lori nodded. "So you keep saying."

"Hey, you know something. You don't have to come with me." Travers kept calling you Wonder Woman because he didn't know who you really were. Lori had gone way past the lines of being a good roommate, and in return Tia had almost gotten her killed.

"But—"

"One of your actor-buddies can probably take you in until you find a new place. I can look for Big Red by myself."

"Oh, no. That jerk hit me. Now it's my fight, too."

Fortunately, it was late, which meant there were actually vacant cabs. Tia flagged one down, ignoring the fact that any driver who would pick up two bloody women was probably blind.

At least he had a heater that worked.

* * * *

The city of New York felt like a restless animal as Tia gave the driver directions to the kitchen where she volunteered. Omaha, the biggest city in Nebraska, rolled up its sidewalks at six in the evenings. At one in the morning, New York traffic whizzed by, pedestrians walked the sidewalks clutching coats close about them in the cold, and hungry looking rats peered up from garbage bags stacked near hole-in-the-wall restaurants and assessed the taxi's passengers as possible upgrades from their slops.

It wasn't New York's activity that disturbed her, though. That liveliness had been a major part of the attraction for Tia in moving to the city in the first place.

Tonight had a different, more sinister, feel. A chill vaguely like that she'd felt when Ewan's icy fingers first touched her skin seemed to hang over the soot-darkened buildings. The distant sound of a lighthouse, blasting its horn to alert ships of foggy and dangerous reefs, seemed laden with messages that were meant for Tia—if only she could interpret the dismal signal.

"Times like this, I wonder why I moved here." Lori's words eerily echoed Tia's thoughts.

"You moved here same as everyone," their driver announced. 'Cause New York is the pump, sending energy into the whole country."

Considering that he'd picked them up even with them looking like wrecks, Tia wasn't sure whether she should take the driver's philosophy too seriously. It did, though, sound a lot like Ewan's description of what she was to him.

"What are you saying?"

"Just that the rest of the country don't appreciate what the City does for 'em. They like to complain about us, like we're not really Americans. You ask me, without us, there'd be a big hole in the whole country."

She had asked him, so Tia nodded. The driver had perfectly described the attitude her parents and ex-boyfriend had taken when she'd decided to move to New York.

She and Lori had to pool resources to pay their driver, but they managed a nice tip and suggested he stay clear of anyone with a Lincoln Town Car. They'd seen that car, still steaming, outside of Travers's apartment.

"You ladies all right? Looks like you got banged up a bit," the driver belatedly observed. "I can take you to the cops if you want. Off meter, even."

It was the second time in two days that a New York cabby had offered a free ride. Miracles were flowing a little too thickly for Tia to believe it was coincidence.

"No need for the police," Lori said. "But thanks. And you're right about New York. I mean, where else would we even have a shot at making a living doing what we love?"

"Oh, I get it. You girls do horror movies, right? Lots of shooting at night. Guess it gives atmosphere. Your makeup is completely convincing, by the way. Total Zombie look."

"Thanks."

The driver sped away, leaving them coated in the golden glow of a nearby streetlight.

The Presbyterian Church that housed the soup kitchen looked like something out of a gothic romance—all dark and shadowy bricks and stones. It didn't have gargoyles, but that night it felt as if monsters were staring down at them from its high spires.

"You come *here* to volunteer?" Lori sounded impressed.

"We all give back in the best way we know how." She sounded stuffy, but she meant it. The guys who ate at the homeless kitchen were mostly victims, not perpetrators. Blessed with a job, her health, and plenty of spare time due to her boyfriend-less state, Tia got a lot of satisfaction from her volunteer work. At least she had until Ewan had walked into the scene.

"Okay, we're here. Now what?" Lori asked.

"This late, the kitchen is closed, but the shelter is across the street."

Full, the shelter had locked its doors hours before. The attendant, Benny Bags, wiped sleep from his eyes and glared at them through the door bars, one side of his hair sticking straight up toward the ceiling.

"Closed."

"We've got to talk to Big Red. Is he there?"

"You're a volunteer, Tia. You should know the rules. After lockdown, nobody comes in, nobody goes out."

"This is an emergency."

"It's *always* an emergency. And the rules don't change unless there's a fire or a warrant."

"We don't have to come in. Maybe we could just talk to him."

Benny sighed. "First it's talk. After a bit, then maybe you just want to give him something. After that, it would be a little visit. You know why we have rules? So people can follow them. You want Big Red, come by in a few hours. We open the doors at six."

"I could flirt with this guy," Lori whispered.

"Looked in a mirror lately?"

"I forgot."

"There's an all night coffee place not too far from here," Tia said. "Let's wait there. Unless you have a better idea."

* * * *

"I don't normally have women looking in on me this time of the night."

They'd been in the coffee shop for an hour and had done the best they could to patch themselves back together. Lori had mostly stopped the flow of blood from her newly lopsided nose and Tia kept wet paper towels pressed to her bruises.

They'd been so intent on their own misery they hadn't even noticed the tall, slightly chubby man approach their table.

"Big Red. I thought you were locked in until six."

"When I got out of the service, there were still a lot of the old depression-era movement guys alive. Guys who rode the rails with heroes of the struggle—even met Woodie Guthrie a few times when he lived her in New York. Those guys taught me to get out of prisons a lot tougher than a homeless lockup."

He paused, lowering his voice. "We safe to talk here?"

After the past couple of days, Tia wasn't going to put down anyone for a bit of paranoia. She'd been attacked on the street, had her apartment burned down, gotten Ewan killed, and managed to get her roommates beat up. It was a pretty dismal string of failure. Still, a spy would be pretty hard-up to hang out in an all-night coffee shop just hoping someone would say something. Huddled by himself in the corner, a gray-haired man who looked to be a hundred, but was probably half that, nursed a coffee but looked longingly at the bar across the road. A pair of young lovers, probably dancers from an off-Broadway show, held hands and whispered to each other at the counter. All three of them had been there when Tia and Lori had walked in. Other than them and the café manager, who was reading *Crime and Punishment*, it was just the girls and Big Red. "I think we're okay."

"Really? Well, *I* don't think so. I think we're going to have to go underground. You two need to be safe, and Big Red is the man to do it."

Irrationally, relief washed over Tia. Sure she was an independent woman. That didn't mean she wanted to make all the decisions. Common sense reasserted itself a moment later. This was Big Red, a homeless person. When he said 'underground,' he probably meant literally. A hole in the ground with a cardboard roof didn't have much appeal.

Big Red checked the women out. "Corporate goons got to you, did they? They can't defeat the workers if we stick together. I figured you'd be safe with that Ewan guy. He's solid, plain folk."

Lori guffawed, which started the blood flowing from her nose again. If there was one thing Ewan was not, it was plain folks.

Going underground sounded like an even better idea when, in response to a call from Big Red, a tousled thirty-something guy pulled up in a beat-up Volvo.

"I wish you'd just move in with me, Dad," were the first words from the man's lips. "Rather than just call me when disaster strikes. You could still do your organizing, but you'd have someplace warm to come home to at night."

The man's voice trailed off when he got a look at Lori. "Uh, hi."

Lori looked like she'd been struck by lightening. She adjusted her hair, simultaneously pushed forward and pulled back, and generally acted like she'd just seen the man of her dreams. "Hi back at you."

Big Red either didn't see the attraction or didn't have time for it. "I'll stop organizing when I die, boy-o. And nighttime is primetime when it comes to talking with those weighed down by the system. These here are sisters in the cause, beat up by corporate goons when they dared to stand up and be counted. I need your help mending them up and getting them back on the picket line."

"Sure, Dad. I'll be happy to do anything I can."

Tia didn't think she misheard a special emphasis on the word *anything*.

"Take 'em with you," Big Red continued. "I'll go back to the shelter. We're going through Volume Two of *Das Kapital*. The old compare and contrast to the *Gospel of St. Luke* lesson. You know those are sometimes hard going."

Big Red's son laughed. "Rather operate on myself without anesthesia than sit through Volume Two, with or without St. Luke." He turned toward the women, but with a special smile for Lori. "Let me introduce myself. I'm Joe-Hill Linteman. I'm happy to help out. Looks like I need to get you to the hospital. You've got some serious injuries."

"No hospitals," Big Red insisted. "Corporations will be watching."

Joe-Hill didn't sigh, roll his eyes, or do any of the things her parents would have done if she'd said something like that. "Okay, I'll take them to my place. But then I'm going to need your help, Dad."

Big Red grumbled but he finally agreed to give the guys in the shelter a break from Karl Marx. Just to help out, he assured his son.

Tia didn't think an aging radical would be much help but she couldn't blame Joe-Hill for using her as an excuse to get his dad off the streets for a night or two.

Lori beat everyone into the front seat, next to Joe-Hill, while Tia squeezed in back with Big Red.

"Your dad is partly right about the corporate goons," Tia said as they headed onto the Cross-Bronx Expressway. "But this story is going to sound really weird and I'm going to have to ask you to hear me out before you start asking questions or trying to poke holes in it. That okay?"

"I've heard weird stories in my day," Big Red announced. "There was this time we were—"

"Dad!"

"Save it for later? Okay. Go ahead, Tia. I want to hear your story."

She took a deep breath and explained everything while they drove from Manhattan into the Bronx, then pulled off the expressway and into a little neighborhood that seemed in the midst of gentrification, deteriorating tenements with laundry hanging from fire escapes mixing with renovated lofts.

She still didn't want to think of Ewan as a god, but she had little choice, unless she wanted to call him an energy being, which pretty much meant the same thing.

Tia finished as Joe-Hill turned onto one of the small side streets. She waited for Volvo-driving Joe-Hill to pull into one of the renovated places. Instead, he stopped in front of one of the worst looking buildings on the street. A paper 'Closed' sign decorated the front door of a free clinic.

"Are you a doctor?" Lori asked.

"Probably the poorest doctor in New York," Joe-Hill admitted cheerfully. "I charge what people can afford. Around here, that isn't much."

"You could make more money at a big hospital."

Joe-Hill glanced at his father. "I grew up on the road and dreamed of finding a place where I could put down roots. I still agree with my father about people needing help."

"Oh." Lori looked back at Tia and mouthed, "he's for you."

Tia didn't think so. The way Joe-Hill looked at Lori, nobody else would even catch his attention.

"There are a thousand explanations for the word Red appearing on an elevator wall." Joe-Hill unlocked the clinic and led them inside. "And unfortunately we can't call the cops on this Travers guy. He was over the line, but you did sneak past his guard, go up to his place, and attack him. Let's get you fixed up," he concluded cheerfully. "Then we can discuss the god part of your story."

Tia stiffened. "You don't believe me, do you?"

"Come on, Tia. You've got ancient gods walking the streets of New York, with evil corporate types tracking them down with satellite dishes. You've got professional arsonists who disappear so completely that the police can't find any evidence of blood that was spattered everywhere. Sounds like a Dan Brown thriller, not reality."

"Listen, buster." Lori got in his face. "I was there when Ewan popped into existence from nowhere. I was there when he faded out from the sofa. Maybe he's not a god, but he's sure something and it's not human."

Joe-Hill backed down in a hurry. "Uh, right. Let's get you looked at, then we'll figure out what to do."

Despite her pain, Tia couldn't help being excited for her roommate. Lori was *never* interested in anybody. Although she dated occasionally, those dates seemed to be more about her career than any actual interest in a guy. Tia worried horribly that her own story and problems, might get in the way of the first real boy-girl attraction Lori formed in the eighteen months she'd known her roommate.

"Believe what you want," she said. "We just need to recuperate and plan what to do next."

"Wrong." Lori wasn't giving up. "Ewan said we needed Big Red's help and Big Red called on Joe-Hill for backup. Can't you see? Their help is meant to be."

* * * *

Meant to be or not, Joe-Hill clearly didn't believe anything they said.

He had probably learned skepticism while listening to his father predict a wonderful future coming with the revolution. *Waiting for Godot* might be good theater, but waiting for the revolution would have been boring. In self-defense, he would have given up on fairy tales.

Sexual zing with Lori or not, Joe-Hill was all doctor. He ran Tia and Lori through x-rays, set and bandaged Lori's nose, looked at Tia's arm and assured her it was strained, not broken, smeared antibiotic ointments where Tia had scraped herself and then made all them, including his dad, eat huge bowls of stew he pulled from his refrigerator.

"Some people don't have enough money for their bills. They pay me with food," he explained. "I always have more than I can eat so don't hold back."

* * * *

The sun was peeking its way over the horizon when Big Red plopped down on a chair and rubbed his eyes. "You tried to do it alone and failed. Seems to me you need your man back."

"Ewan isn't my man."

Joe-Hill looked from his dad to Tia. "If he's not yours, we aren't going to be able to do anything."

Lori pounced on that. "So, you believe us now?"

Joe-Hill frowned. "There isn't a doctor in the world who can honestly say he doesn't believe in miracles. This one seems unlikely, but you were there and I wasn't."

Tia wanted Ewan back more than she'd ever wanted anything in her life. She wanted the taste of his lips on hers, the sight of his broad chest and his impossibly black eyes, the scent of old-growth forest on his body. But Ewan had fled from her world, bleeding and dying. Calling him back into her normal world would bring him back into danger, allow Travers and the scientists from Iconic Security an opportunity to claim him, harness him to their engines, suck him as dry as if they were the vampires Lori had warned Tia of.

"Maybe we should leave him alone, let him heal in peace," she said.

Big Red shook his head. "Ewan is part of the struggle. Coming here to get fixed up doesn't mean you're running away from the fight. Same with Ewan. He came to New York for a reason, and that reason is connected with you. As long as you're here, he'll want to be here with you. Soon as he can, he'll return to the struggle. Ewan's a good guy. He won't shirk his duty on the picket line."

Big Red was at least partly right, Tia thought. Ewan probably would return if he could. Not because he wanted to participate in Big Red's struggle, though. He'd come back because he was drawn to Tia like a fly to horse dung because she was a manna pump, because he wanted to grab become the being he once had been.

Tia needed to keep reminding herself of that. Travers and the others at Iconic Security might be greedy jerks, but ultimately, what they wanted and what Ewan wanted were the same—to use the power of a god for selfish reasons.

Still, if he was hurting, she needed to help him. It wasn't in her personality to leave him suffering just because she didn't trust what he'd do if he were healthy.

Chapter 11

"If he wants our help, he'll contact us," Lori said. She'd taken a quick nap and was fully recharged. "The problem is, we'll need to watch for it. Remember how fast his message faded? If we hadn't been looking right at it, we would have missed it."

Joe-Hill's face twisted just slightly, barely avoiding a smirk. He still didn't believe them, but Tia couldn't really blame him. If she hadn't lived through it, she wouldn't believe, either. Still, he didn't have to be superior about it.

"You're suggesting a séance, right?" Joe-Hill said. "Some way for him to communicate with you from beyond the veil."

"Nothing like that," Tia snapped. "We just need something that doesn't require too much energy. You can't imagine how badly wounded he was, so we need something that won't wear him out. And something low-tech. Ewan has picked up some basic understanding of modern life, but he spent most of his life in an era where bronze was considered super-sophisticated."

"I'm open to suggestions."

"Look at your car," Lori said.

"I hardly think—"

"Stop arguing and look out your window, dummy."

Ewan, if it was Ewan, had used the same trick. The palest hint of haze, as if from a shallow breath, crossed Joe-Hill's windshield—and froze into frost on the ice-cold glass.

"Blee? What the heck does that mean," Lori asked.

"Wait." The movement was painfully slow, but Tia noticed just a bit more haze added to the end of the last 'e.' Which meant Ewan was still writing.

"He's here. Now you can't argue."

"One of you could have done something to my car when I wasn't looking. I mean—"

"Right. Like I'd get my nose broken just so we could fool you with an impossible story," Lori snapped. "This is real, Joe-Hill. So, it's time for you to expand your imagination."

As they watched, the letter 'd' appeared. Followed by 'i,' 'n,' and 'g.'

"Bleeding. Well, that makes sense, even if it doesn't give us any new information." Lori fished into a pocket and pulled out one of the perfectly round drops of hardened ichor that she had picked up from their hotel suite floor and held it out for them to see. "He was bleeding hard yesterday. Unlike us, he didn't have a doctor to patch him up."

"That's got to be it," Tia said. "He needs Joe-Hill. He's like Prometheus, don't you see? The continual bleeding won't let him heal."

"I wouldn't know how to start with a god," Joe-Hill took the marble-sized drop from Lori and rested it on his palm. "I don't even know what this is. One thing it isn't is blood."

"Call it what you want," Lori said. "It pumped out of the holes in his body

81

like blood spurting from a wound. Whatever does that is close enough to blood for me. I thought you doctors had to swear some kind of oath about helping those who need help. Is there a 'no gods allowed' exception in that promise?"

Tia thought that was a little low, considering that Joe-Hill worked in an area where most doctors would fear to drive, let alone set up a clinic.

"Ewan wouldn't ask if there wasn't something you could do," she said. "You have a problem with that?"

Joe-Hill looked like he had all kinds of problems with that. He'd gotten up in the middle of the night to rescue his firebrand father and a pair of flaky women. His clinic was due to open at any minute and he hadn't showered, had a cup of coffee, or anything to eat, let alone a chance to sleep. And now they were demanding that he do more.

"I'll pay you," Tia added when it became clear that Joe-Hill wasn't going to answer.

"This isn't about money."

"Well, it's about something." She wasn't being fair—Tia knew that. She also knew that if they didn't help Ewan soon, worse things were going to happen. Both to Ewan and to the entire world.

Lori glared at Joe-Hill, daring him to refuse.

"I'll gather up my kit."

"You're a good man, Joe-Hill," Lori said.

* * * *

Ewan had painstakingly and painfully written the message four times before Lori had finally noticed it. Now, he laid back to rest. He'd known Tia was smart, counted on her to understand what he needed.

What would happen if she failed tore at him as much as the bullet holes did.

Ewan had never really considered the fate of any particular worshiper before. People lived, then they died—that was what it meant to be human. At the peak of his power, he'd had tens of thousands of followers. He'd been aware of each of them. But they flickered into and back out of existence so quickly he couldn't keep track. He'd never thought to question whether one life might end too quickly. His godhood had been about *the people*, not about any single individual.

But Tia was different. If he brought her to him and she died, he would die. Once she worshiped him, things would be easy—he's protect her, make sure she was comfortable. In the meantime, he wove a bit of protection, something that would let them survive a bit longer, then gathered his strength and pulled.

* * * *

I should have warned Joe-Hill.

Tia was back in a universe where her skin saw colors, her eyes tasted salt and sweet. Although her lungs refused to inhale, her nose savored the roar of a million Niagara Falls.

Joe-Hill's presence was like that of a tiny doll-like figure beside the bleeding giant that was Ewan.

The change in perspective made her dizzy. It wasn't that she and Joe-Hill had shrunk. She was seeing the real Ewan, rather than how he manifested himself in their human reality.

Ewan looked like Gulliver in the land of the Lilliputians. For the first time, she truly believed Ewan's story. Travers had been wrong. Ewan wasn't just an energy vampire, he still wasn't *her* god, but he *had* been a god to others. Ewan had been alive before the dawn of recorded history. He had watched humans emerge from their caves and learn to chip weapons from flints, control the first fire, discover the mixtures of copper and tin that made bronze, plant primitive grains. That he needed her to help him filled her with the sort of awe she normally felt only during an especially moving hymn at church.

The tiny bit of a crush she'd felt for him, she was willing to admit to that much—surely it wasn't more than a crush—was clearly ridiculous. When she considered the scope of the repair job ahead of them, she realized getting busy would help take the sting out of the death of any fantasizes she might have had about him.

Ewan lacked only eagles sent by Zeus to complete the picture of Prometheus, torn and dying.

"Would you look at that? He's bigger than a football field. It would take New York's whole garment district to sew him up."

Joe-Hill's words spoke directly to her brain. Then again, he probably couldn't breathe, either.

"We'd better get to work then. It can't be long before we collapse from lack of oxygen." She projected her thoughts back to Joe-Hill, trying to work her mouth to say them out loud at the same time. She didn't think talking would work, and it didn't. But thinking about the mechanics of speaking helped her project. She wasn't used to telepathy, after all.

She sensed a nod, then accepted the bag Joe-Hill offered her, took out a swab, and handed him a needle and thread.

The tiny needle seemed hopeless for the huge job before them. Ewan was acres of damaged but still beautiful flesh and muscle. A flood of amber blood stretched for miles around him. Imagining that they could fix him was comparable to imagining that an ant-sized doctor could heal a human of fatal wounds.

"Swab here." Impossible task or not, Joe-Hill was a doctor. He'd do his part.

Tia wiped down the area Joe-Hill had indicated, watched the doctor get to work, then moved ahead of him preparing new flesh for the doctor's needle.

Joe-Hill must have had plenty of experience with bullet and knife wounds in his clinic. He dispensed with the needle and used a staple-like device that let him quickly close yards of ripped flesh.

Large parts of Ewan were completely missing and Joe-Hill had to make do with what he could, piecing together what little remained in the empty caverns of Ewan's wounds, folding flesh over itself and stapling and taping.

Oddly, there always seemed to be more tape, more staples, more disinfectants, no matter how much they used.

Tia stayed just ahead, trying not to think about how long she could hold her breath. She pushing together pieces of Ewan where Joe-Hill instructed, wiped open wounds with gunky yellow goop, and tried not to think about how long they'd been there, how soon their bodies would collapse from lack of oxygen.

Clearly her sense of time had gone badly wrong because it seemed they kept going, yard after yard, down huge expanses of Ewan. She stifled a giggle when she wondered if he was biologically proportionate, then had to ignore Joe-Hill's inquiring glance. There was no way she was going to get into that discussion with him—or with anyone except maybe a girlfriend.

Once doctoring became routine, Tia let herself look around. Ewan seemed to respond to her touch, gaining color where she touched him. She concentrated on becoming the best manna-pump she could. Just as injured humans need blood transfusions as well as repairs of injuries, Ewan needed more than the huge holes in his body sealed up. He needed the strength and power that came from millions or billions of worshipers sending their god prayers of thanks and entreaty.

Tia couldn't provide that, whatever her exceptional skills in manna generation might be. But she did what she could, sending lots of affection and affirmation Ewan's way. Ewan would never be her god, but she considered him her friend.

* * * *

For the first time since he'd been shot, manna trickled into him and didn't instantly drain through the holes Travers's missiles had ripped through his body.

The doctor's hands fumbled, but then he found his stapler and tacked another part of the bleeding hole shut.

The shields Ewan had surrounded his people with were failing. He needed to get the Joe-Hill and Tia to their own plane before they tried to breathe the multidimensional aether that served as air in this N-dimensional space.

He twisted at the fabric of N-dimensional space, creating a sort of moebius strip that opened a pathway between dimensions for an infinitely short amount of time that was, nevertheless, long enough to shove the doctor and the woman through, back to their own world, back to where they could breathe the air, eat the food, swallow the water.

Opening that momentary pathway was easier—a lot easier this time. Maybe they'd done enough.

He stretched out an arm.

Muscles tingled as ichor found its way to extremities has body had abandoned to death. Pain, which had overloaded his senses and negated itself, abruptly returned. Hunger, an ever-present concern, became a raging fire in his gut.

Far more slowly than he should have, he stood.

A god's perceptions dwarf those of humans. From his viewpoint, looking into the limited human plane was easy. His people were back, but all was not well. Desperately, Tia breathed into the exhausted doctor while Lori pounded on his chest.

A momentary concern flitted through his mind. He didn't like the way Tia's lips molded themselves over those of the doctor. It brought back memories of experiences he'd savored when *he'd* reminded Tia's body how to breathe and live again.

Jealousy wasn't new to him. Gods are jealous beings, just as Tia's Bible recounted. This feeling was different. Never before had he concerned himself with the mating habits of his worshipers—Tia was his people but not his worshiper.

He peered into the doctor's internal organs and structures.

Yes, there was the problem. He reached carefully, grasped the man's heart, and squeezed.

* * * *

"Something's happening."

Joe-Hill jerked, away from Tia as if he'd been hit by a million volts of electricity.

He coughed and finally inhaled a huge breath of air.

"You can stop hitting his chest," Tia told Lori. "He's safe."

"This is safe?" Joe-Hill's face was gray and his voice was a contorted croak. "It feels more likes someone reached inside of me, grabbed my heart, and squeezed the juice out of it."

"We were giving you CPR," Lori explained.

"I just had some of the strangest hallucinations I've ever experienced."

Hallucinations? Trust the skeptical doctor to dismiss what he'd experienced as one of his father's drug-dreams.

Wordlessly, Tia grabbed his medical bag from the floor, where she'd dropped it when they'd returned from Ewan, and handed it to Joe-Hill.

"What am I supposed to do with this?"

"Open it up. If what we just went through really was a hallucination, everything will be there the way it was when you left. If it was real, you'll see that things were disarrayed, used."

Joe-Hill opened the bag, peered inside, and set it down. His face had been pale from lack of a heartbeat but it grew even paler. "That was real?"

"Every bit of it."

"But I'm an atheist."

"Are you sure?" Big Red demanded.

Joe-Hill opened his mouth, then shut it without saying anything. He ran his hands over his body, pressing on his heart. "I'm not *sure* about anything," he finally admitted.

"Maybe it's time you opened yourself to the universe," Tia's new-age roommate instructed. "And by the way, I thought you were going to bring Ewan home with you. We need his help." She rubbed nose bandages that made her look like an understudy for *Cyrano de Bergerac*.

"He was too injured to talk." Tia admitted.

"Then how'd you get back?"

How *had* they gotten back? "He must have been getting better."

"Assuming he isn't coming, then, what can we do without him?"

"One thing we can do," Big Red said. "We can help Joe-Hill out with his clinic. He's not going to be a hundred percent and he's already got patients lining up outside. We'll take turns doing admitting them and finding out what they need. When you're off-duty catch some shut-eye. I don't think any of us got any sleep last night."

"We can't stop Travers if we're sleeping." Lori fought back a yawn even as she protested.

"One of the most important lessons I ever learned, I got from an old hobo who rode the rails during the depression. He'd go from place to place, wherever workers were striking, helping them organize. He'd pitch in and lend his skills and knowledge, then head back to the rails. He told me, 'you've got to sleep when you can, eat what's available, and stay warm if it's possible. Because you never know where your next meal is going to come from, or when you'll have a moment to rest'."

That sounded like good advice. Despite her sense of urgency, it wasn't as if Tia had something specific to do. She took the first sleep-shift while Lori helped out with Joe-Hill.

* * * *

The instant she closed her eyes, Tia was back in that eerie otherworld.

She knew she was dreaming, though, because Ewan was wearing his cashmere coat again, was apparently uninjured, and was down to human size.

"Are you okay?" She knew it was a stupid question the second she asked it. This was a dream, right? What would dream-Ewan know about real-Ewan?

He smiled, but shook his head. "Other gods lent me strength. It's kept me from fading, but when they demand repayment, it will empty me."

"Forever?"

He nodded. "Forever."

"I've tried to send you manna."

"But Manna comes from faith, and your faith is still to someone else."

"I guess I'm pretty set in my religion." Which was funny if she thought about it. Believing in Ewan should be easier than believing her own church. She'd touched Ewan, spoke to him, seen the miracles he could work. But believing that Ewan was *real*, was *a god*, didn't make him *her god*.

"I've got to wrap up the Iconic Security thing in two weeks because that's when they pull their powers back."

"The other gods must be in as much danger as you. Why such a short timetable?"

"They're afraid to wait longer." He sighed. "All of us are hungry, Tia— desperately hungry. You can't understand what it feels like to be filled with manna, to be strong enough to pull hurricanes from the oceans and smash them into your enemies. To have that, then to have all of that power shrivel up until you're an empty husk is horrible. So we hoard what little manna they have left, begrudge every drop we share. That they were willing to share at all is a sure sign that they take Iconic terribly seriously."

Hunger

Which meant this was as good as it was going to get. Tia tried to put the best face on it. "Okay, then. Two weeks is pretty long. We've only known each other for a couple of days and look what's happened already."

"So far we've both been killed. They've been ahead of us every step, manipulating us into doing what they wanted. It took divine power and luck to escape them."

"Maybe." She paused. "When are you coming back?" She dreaded his answer but had to ask. This dream was strangely lucid dream. A dream so real that even though Tia knew she was dreaming, she believed she was talking to the real Ewan rather than some imaginary figment.

She didn't know what she'd do if he said no. If she never saw him again, her life would be an empty stretch of meaningless years.

He considered, nodded. "Soon."

"Is it horribly confining?"

"Huh?"

"Visiting our world. In your world," Tia waved at the dream other-world, "you can stretch to your full size. In our world, you're only six feet tall. Just another person."

His smile showed the thousands of years of pain he'd suffered.

"It doesn't work that way, Tia. I'm myself no matter where I manifest. Just because you see me in only three dimensions doesn't mean that the rest of me isn't still there. It's just out of view. I'm like a snake, poking its head out of a hole in the wall, but the rest of me is coiled behind."

That was not a mental picture she wanted to keep, so she changed the subject. "*Can* we stop them, Ewan? Iconic had to know you were coming because Sam and Hank attacked me within hours of when you arrived. They must have been watching, waiting. They know what to expect."

She hoped that he'd laugh, tell her that he had their measure, that no mere mortal could stand up to the power of a god enraged. That was the way it was in the Thor comic books her nephew was so fond of. In fact, why not simplify things? If he really was a god, he could watch what they were doing from his magical universe and stop them with a word of power. *Shazam.*

Now that she and Joe-Hill had patched so much of him up, Ewan should be good to go. He wouldn't need her help any more—other than what manna she sent him. Time for him to go into full god-mode and save the day.

He didn't laugh, didn't tell her anything of the kind.

"In some ways, Travers was right," Ewan said. "Gods are energy creatures. People named us gods, but *your* concept of God doesn't match what I am. Maybe there is a higher level of the divine I know nothing about, but that's not me. We exist in symbiosis with humans. You sustain us with your faith and we protect you with our powers. Iconic Security figured out how the symbiosis works. Using that knowledge, it created a way to drain us of our energy, and a way to protect themselves from us. I can't touch them. I can't even see them without first creating a physical presence in your human universe. When I was in N-dimensional space watching you in Travers' apartment, you and Lori were clear, but I could only see Travers by the empty space he manifested. He was a hole in the universe. When I reached for him, my hand went through emptiness." He paused, then continued. "It wasn't just emptiness. It was worse than emptiness because he sucked energy from me even as I tried to attack him."

Her heart beat a bit faster. Ewan *had* tried to help. She hadn't even realized she'd resented him abandoning her to Travers, but she must have. Now she knew he hadn't. "If there's a hole—"

"I can't detect them unless I know exactly where to look. Even when I find one, I can't touch it."

He paused again, for what seemed like an eternity, looking into Tia's eyes. Then he brushed a knuckle against her cheek. The apparent warmth of his hand, so different from the sub-arctic feel of that same hand in her own universe, reminded her that they were in a dream. Or in a multi-dimension where nothing felt as it really was.

"We are so screwed."

He didn't argue. Instead he dropped his hand from her cheek and held it toward her. "Pull me across, Tia."

Chapter 12

In her dreams, Tia inhaled the scent of pine forests and snuggled closer to the hard muscles and furnace-like heat of the man/god/being she felt so weirdly and fiercely attracted to. She really should try to awaken and figure out what was going on, but she didn't want to. She wanted to stay here with him, savor the touch of his body against her own.

His heart beat strongly, a slow lub-dub that gave her hope that he'd be all right despite the injuries he'd sustained. How could anything horrible happen to someone as vital as he? His arms, muscled and cut, pulled her more tightly to his chest and she wished she'd gone into the dream world naked. Instead, she was still wearing the clothes she'd collapsed into Joe-Hill's bed with.

Ewan *was* naked. The rigid length of him pressed against her bottom. Feeling it raised her temperature, sent pulses of moisture to her core as her body prepared for lovemaking.

But she wasn't dreaming. She was back in Joe-Hill's clinic. When Ewan had asked her to bring him through, she must have done something that had worked. He was there, lying next to her, in all of his nude physical glory.

Her heart raced and her breathing accelerated as if she were running a marathon, but Ewan's heartbeat remained slow and steady.

She didn't know, couldn't tell whether she twisted her body to bring her breasts into his hands or whether his hands sought them. Either way, it happened. She was grateful she had, at least, shed the blood and ichor-soaked shirt she'd worn when she and Joe-Hill had sewed Ewan up.

Her breasts seemed to swell, her nipples hardening, pushing against the thin fabric of her sport's bra as Ewan's hands absorbed the heat from her body, then reflected it back. Warm hands. He'd changed, although he still looked haunted by hunger.

Through her bra, Ewan's fingertips brushed against the very tips of nipples--that lightest of touches was enough to send surges of pleasure and pure sensation down her spine. It flooded downward, accelerating until it hit her womb with a splash that combined with the pure desire already gathering there in a knot that packed itself tighter and tighter. Ewan's arms pulled her more tightly into him, his hands caressed her breasts, his hardness pressed against her bottom. Unexpectedly, irrationally because she was definitely not that responsive, Tia felt an orgasm building within her.

Without consciously deciding to do so, Tia pressed her hips against his erection.

His breath stopped for a millisecond, then started again, faster.

She pressed again. She was on the edge, just the slightest added pressure, the brush of his lips against her neck, the warmth of his naked thighs against her own would have pushed her over the edge to completion.

His hands grew warmer and his entire body seemed to swell.

Then she realized what was happening. He was using her sexual arousal to get her to pump manna his way. He turned her on in exchange for her power.

In all her life, Tia had never felt like a whore. Now, she did.

Ignoring her body's desperate craving, she yanked herself away from him. Ewan vanished.

She pulled herself together, splashed water on her face, and went out to the clinic.

Ewan sat at a table, staring at her from across the room.

Still naked, his body showed the scars of Travers's attack. Newly healed skin was pink against his pale flesh. His hard stomach would have made the editors of men's fitness magazines drool with envy and his broad shoulders and sculpted pectorals guaranteed that he would never have to go looking for a job as long as male strippers were in demand. His hundreds of years of hunger meant that every muscle and tendon was cut and displayed in beautiful relief. Yet his skin held a hint of color. Between the manna the gods had lent him and what he'd stolen from her, he was stronger.

"Your anger makes you poison."

"You were exploiting me."

"Can't you see? This is another path. You don't have to worship me, you can share your power through passion."

"Do you know how that makes me feel? Like a kept woman. I give you sex and you give me protection."

He looked genuinely puzzled. "What's so wrong about that?"

"Can't you see that I'm an individual? I need to be appreciated for myself, not because I'm some freak of nature."

"If I don't get more power, neither of us will be alive long enough for that to matter."

He was right. If she were logical, she'd drag him back into bed, sex him up, and completely let herself go. Even the limited contact they'd had convinced her he'd be special, that he'd open doors she hadn't even imagined existed. The funny thing was, she'd always thought of herself as a very logical person.

Evidently she was wrong.

"I guess we should go out and spell the others," she said, breaking a silence that threatened to go beyond discomfort. "Then we need to plan what to do next. If we've only got two weeks, we need to take advantage of every moment."

"You heard about the two weeks and the other gods?"

"I was dreaming, but I was aware."

"Incredible. Before, I've only been able to reach those who worshipped me, who sought me out because I was their god. You are an amazing woman, Tia."

"Yeah, I'm full of surprises, all right."

* * * *

He hadn't dreamed that lust, sex, passion could empower him. Sure, when he'd been a fertility god, back in the days when chipped stone was still high-tech, he'd gotten a mild charge from the priestesses. But they'd been his priestesses, already filled with his faith.

As it was, he'd discovered the perfect solution, one that didn't even ask Tia to abandon her original faith, and she'd slammed the door on it.

Still, he could work on it. Even the best poker face can't hide thoughts or feelings from a god, and Tia didn't come close to having a poker face. She wanted him, craved his touch. All he needed to do was wait and she'd capitulate. Unfortunately, the one thing they didn't have was time.

He followed Tia into the clinic's operating room and took charge. Remembering human weakness, he agreed with Big Red that sleep was the first order of business. He sent the aging radical, Lori, and the protesting doctor to sleep on Joe-Hill's cots.

"What about my patients?" Joe-Hill protested, but not too hard. He had to be tired, concerned that he'd make a mistake.

"I'll handle them. Tia will help."

"Do you know anything about doctoring?" Tia demanded.

"Doctoring, no. Healing, yes."

"But—"

Time to twist the knife just a bit. "If you can see your way to sending me a touch of manna, I wouldn't complain."

"I'll do what I can, as long as you don't touch me."

He didn't like the deal but he nodded anyway.

People came to Joe-Hill's clinic open for intervention. He projected the form of Joe-Hill to the patients, listened to their complaints then used his N-dimensional senses to determine their true illnesses and help them if he could.

Some of the patients were past help. Weak as he was, he couldn't reverse the impact of aging. He could heal poisoning, but toxic environments would simply poison them again, undoing his work.

Still, he could help some. He could offer the tired a few more years. He could take away pain. He could repair the worst of the battering human bodies had endured. To his surprise, he took pleasure from doing those little things he could.

Tia had covered her distracting body with a set of scrubs that didn't do enough to hide her curves but at least let his mind *occasionally* consider other things.

"You ready for the next one, doctor?"

"Show him in."

"Harold here is complaining of a cough. He says he has trouble breathing," Tia read from a file. "You've seen him four times before, so you probably remember him."

That last was a reminder to him to repair his Joe-Hill disguise. He made the adjustments to the way light reflected from his face and body to improve his semblance of the doctor and smiled at Tia. "Let's have a look at him, shall we?"

Harold tottered in, wheezing from the short walk from the waiting room into the examination room. He was elderly by human standards, dressed in a wool-blend suit that hadn't been fashionable in the seventies when it had been made and was far less so now. He held his few strands of white hair in place with a glue-like hair tonic and his nose looked like the Nile delta with purple veins drawing patterns through pale skin.

He coughed when Ewan pulled on the roll of paper that protected Joe-Hill's examining bench, then struggled to climb the short step up.

"You've been poisoning yourself with cigarettes, haven't you?"

"About the only pleasure I have left, doc."

"If you stopped, you could find other joy."

"Who we kidding? I've got maybe six months to live, tops. And I'm going to be sick all through that."

"I'd hate to fix you up and have you just poison yourself again."

Harold gave a rasping laugh that transformed itself into another hacking cough. "You stop the cough and I'll quit smoking. I promise."

"I'll hold you to your bargain."

Ewan had it easy compared to human doctors. His additional dimensions meant he didn't have to cut or use clumsy x-rays to see or touch what went on inside a patient. He didn't have to damage healthy tissue to reach diseased organs.

Harold had poisoned himself with cigarettes until his throat and lungs were covered with black and cancers exploded through his body. Harold's guess that he had six months to live was tragically optimistic. Unless Ewan could help.

Ewan pressed his hands together, forcing the ichor from the fingers and letting cold more absolute than the reaches between the stars flood through his fingertips.

"You look a little different, doc."

Ewan met Harold's cataract-filled eyes. The cataracts clouded his vision of the three-dimensional human universe, but that loss sharpened his sight into the deeper reality.

"I am different."

"You're the angel of death, ain't-cha? You here to take me away?"

"You've got me confused with someone else."

Harold squinted at him. "I'm not so sure. Something about you squints up my eyes. Don't worry about spilling the beans. I'm old and nobody listens to me anyway."

Ewan shook his head. The man was old, yet his entire life had been nothing but a flicker in Ewan's existence.

"I'm not the angel of death. I'm going to help you."

"Sick as I am, I'd thank the angel of death for his help right now."

"Maybe you'll thank me more. Hold very still."

He reached past the three physical dimensions that were all this man knew and brushed his superchilled hands against the cancers, freezing them, destroying them, eliminating them from Harold's body.

Ewan couldn't restore dead flesh, but he could hunt down renegade cells that had been invaded by cancer viruses and were cannibalizing the man's body for their destructive purposes. He did so ruthlessly, freezing each of them as he found them until he'd emptied out the man.

"You'll need to drink liquids, wash the dead poisons from your body," he said.

"I can drink?" Harold's voice sounded healthier already and when he coughed, he got rid of poisons rather than stirring them around.

"Water or fruit juice. Alcohol won't help."

"Water? In this neighborhood? Trying to poison me?"

Ewan didn't bother answering.

"Well, thanks, Doc."

"Do you want to be able to see again?"

"Sure like to be able to read my *Bible*."

Another touch. "Done. I've given you more time. Try to use it wisely rather than throw it away on cigarettes and wild women."

"I'll give up the cigarettes. I already promised that. I get a chance with wild women, though, I'll take it. Say, you happen to know if that new receptionist of yours is single?"

"I think she's pretty busy."

"Well, I can't say as I blame you for wanting her all to yourself, doc. Or should I say angel?"

"Don't say angel. Pay Tia whatever you can afford on your way out."

Harold stared at him. "Funny. You look more like the doc now that I can see better. But I saw what I saw. And I've never had a doctor who just looked at me and made his hands disappear."

Ewan smiled. Harold shouldn't have seen what he was doing but he'd underestimated the man. Well, he'd underestimated humans in the past. In the past, though, it hadn't mattered. Underestimating the humans who opposed him now could be fatal—both to himself and to those who depended on him. "You just rein in your imagination, Harold. Any doctor in the country would tell you what you're describing couldn't be."

"Maybe. But a priest might not agree, huh, angel?"

* * * *

The rest of the day was more of the same. Too many poisons, too little exercise, too much of the wrong kinds of foods. Those he urged to exercise more looked at him as if he'd suggested they sacrifice their first-born children. Those for whom he suggested healthier food choices tuned him out. They'd heard that message before and either couldn't, or wouldn't, respond. Still, occasionally he got through.

A pregnant woman worried about her fetus. He was able to assure her that the baby was developing normally--that the drug habit she'd kicked hadn't damaged her fetus.

A kid had lost a finger in a knife-fight and carried the finger in. Ewan reattached the nerves and set the finger back in place.

A little girl had been beaten by her stepfather. Ewan healed her body, comforted her mind, and put such a fear into the stepfather that he'd never strike another child.

Then there was a moment of quiet. He looked up, waiting for the next patient. He could understand why people became doctors, now. Despite the problems, despite the fact that everything a doctor could do was ultimately doomed to failure because every patient would eventually die, medicine was the closest thing humans could experience to being a god. Even the manna-flow he'd picked up from a few of them, definitely not including Harold, had been close to worship. He should have been exhausted after reaching so often across the dimensions. Instead, he felt only a pleasant fatigue. He could go on like this forever.

"I'm ready for the next," he called out.

"You've seen them all." Tia crossed her arms in front of her abundant chest.

He recognized the look. "What? Did I do something wrong?"

"I don't know. Did you help them, or did you just play with their minds and make them feel better like a cheap faith-healer in a tent revival?"

It sounded like one of those questions with two wrong answers. He gave her the truth. "Many couldn't be helped: their bodies had given up the fight. For others, I could do more."

"Why bother? They aren't your followers. Or did you make them sell their souls in response to the healing?"

Would the exchange of valuable healing for useless manna have been so unfair? But he hadn't insisted on that bargain. "I made a bargain with Joe-Hill. I said I'd care for his patients. When a god makes a promise, it means something."

Her expression told him she knew he was leaving something out, but she didn't press it. Which was lucky because he didn't want to look too deeply into the matter himself. He hadn't demanded it, but he'd gotten something out of his work. Some of the patients had sent a manna stream his way that was vaguely akin to the manna he'd received from his tens of thousands of worshipers back in the days of bronze and iron. But he'd definitely expended more than he had received. He'd explain what he'd done to Tia—if he could figure it out first.

Tia finally turned away. "We might as well wake the others. If we've only got two weeks, we need to use every moment fully."

She rushed into the rooms behind Joe-Hill's clinic without giving him a chance to answer. Minutes later, she returned with a tired-looking group.

"Don't be afraid." Big Red slapped Ewan on the shoulder and poured himself a cup from a coffee maker that had been steeping all day long. "In the struggle, our enemies always outnumber us, always have better technology, always are willing to strike first."

"Which might be why the revolution keeps losing," Joe-Hill reminded his father.

"Now *that* is negative thinking. When the revolution comes, nothing will get in its way."

Joe-Hill's thinking sounded more like realism than negativity to Ewan, but he didn't think bringing that to Big Red's attention would help.

"We've only got two weeks," he explained. "That doesn't give us time to launch a liberation war or even a serious protest movement. Not that we even know what we're protesting against."

"Iconic is trying to exploit you and that's wrong," Big Red said. "Simple as that."

"People always exploit God," Joe-Hill said. "Use him to justify whatever they want to do anyway."

"Or use him to open the doors to other possibilities," Big Red answered. "Christianity inspired both Crusaders and Quakers."

"Not to mention founding lots of universities to spread knowledge," Tia added.

It was discussions like this that proved to Ewan that god/man had been made in each other's images. Iconic Security was on a quest for absolute power and those who knew enough to confront them squabbled over philosophy. The Roman gods had similar discussions before they'd lent him their manna, and now Tia and her friends were doing the same. "The two weeks is going away fast," he reminded them.

"Do *you* have a plan?" Tia demanded.

"One thing for sure, I'm not taking you into danger again. I hope we both learned our lesson from one of the two times you ran in with Travers."

* * * *

Two hours arguing meant two wasted hours. Tia felt as if a huge clock ticked away the seconds until Ewan lost his power and vanished.

When it looked like they'd all argue for another two hours, she stepped outside.

The short winter day was dying, the sun setting behind the tenements and office buildings that made up this part of the Bronx.

She'd been gone less than three minutes when she heard a pop in the air and Ewan stepped out from around a corner. "Running away?"

Rather than admit that she was doing exactly that, she went on the offensive. "Why don't you just appear in front of me? What's with the pop-around-a-corner thing?"

He shrugged his broad shoulders. "It's about energy. You, or anyone, collapse a probability front by observing it. Since the probability is collapsed to a certainty under observation, popping up in front of you would alter an existing reality rather than just a probability field. More inertia to overcome."

"Sounds like quantum physics. Sort of like, it's easier to make sure Schrödinger's cat is alive than bring it back to life once it's dead." Lori delighted with reading physics magazines and reporting to anyone who'd listen that quantum physics proved her New Age faith.

"I guess it's like that."

Tia remembered Lori saying that Einstein had famously argued that 'God does not play dice with the universe,' only to be proven wrong, figuratively speaking of course. If Ewan played, she suspected he'd load his dice.

Given that, what were the odds that a bullet could kill a god, could damage Ewan as extensively as Travers' had? Shouldn't Ewan have been able to exploit the slight probability that Travers would miss him, or the larger probability that the bullet would miss anything significant and simply pass through his body? Why not the proverbial flesh wound so often used in the romance novels Tia's mother favored?

"Tell me about the bullets Travers shot at you. Should a bullet be able to tear so much god-stuff out of you?"

"What's done in one dimension shouldn't impact other realities. Which is a reason gods are generally thought of as immortal. But Travers hit me with a singularity, a mini-black hole. Since it had no dimension of its own, it ripped matter from every dimension. Such a weapon should be impossible. It wasn't." Ewan shuddered with the memory.

Tia looked down the street and tried to imagine a black hole hitting New York. "You're talking about physics that's way beyond anything I know. No private company has the resources to create a mini-singularity. Which means that Lori's paranoid concerns are on the money. Iconic Security has to have government ties."

He didn't even have to think about that. "All the more reason why you should stay here where it's safe. It's your government, not mine."

"We've been through that."

"We haven't been through it at all." He smiled. "I talk and you don't listen."

"Don't play games with me, Ewan."

"No games, Tia. I'm trying to keep you safe. If you stay here with Big Red and Joe-Hill, you'll be out of Iconic's reach."

And she'd be there for him to use like an ant uses aphids. Tia wasn't a god, but she wouldn't stand around doing nothing, either. "No—"

"I'll check out Travers." Ewan charged ahead as if she wasn't there—which she might as well not have been from his divine perspective. "I'll track him from his apartment to wherever he works, track the connections through him. Then…" he paused abruptly. "Uh-oh. Look at that."

"What?"

He gestured at a newspaper so swiftly propelled by the cold winter wind that Tia could barely make out that it was a newspaper rather than a gray rat or something even more disgusting.

She sighed. If he was going to hang around with mere humans, Ewan was going to have to learn their limitations.

"I see a bit of paper blowing down the street. Is it supposed to mean something?"

"It might if you read it."

She turned to tell him she couldn't read anything that far away or moving that fast, only to have him hand her the newsprint.

The blowing paper had been at least fifty feet from him when she'd seen it last, moving away quickly. But then, what did ordinary three-dimensional distances mean to a god? Evidently, not much.

Hunger

"Local businessman found murdered," the headline read. Tia scanned down the page to the photo. It wasn't just any local businessman, it was Travers.

"He was nervous when the corporate security guy, Winsor, called," she remembered. "He must have become a liability. We've just lost our only link."

Ewan's smile showed his teeth. It was a hungry, predatory look.

"They can't clean up their tracks that easily. I'll follow the traces of whoever killed him back to his lair. And then—"

"And then you'll be caught another trap—a better one this time. That's exactly how they almost captured you last time."

Ewan glowered at her, his mouth working but with no words coming out. Instead of talking, he folded the newspaper, turned it over and folded it again.

Another diamond? Tia wondered.

He kept folding until it was a cube about an inch in each direction. He set that cube in his fist and squeezed.

Flame exploded through his closed fingers and the newspaper vanished leaving nothing but memories and a sudden surge of warmth to show her it had ever existed.

"I presume you read that the police are looking for two women. Descriptions match you and Lori," he finally broke the silence. "The apartment security guard must have talked."

"We were covered with blood when we left. At the time, he was sympathetic, thought Travers had abused us. He'd probably seen similar damage in the past. But when they found Travers dead, he would have blabbed."

Ewan moved toward her until he was just a bit too close for comfort. "You've got to lay low now. The police will be looking for you, not me. Even if common sense doesn't dictate that you stay out of the investigation, you'd hurt more than you could possibly help if you insist on coming along."

He made sense, but it felt wrong to her. She took a step back so her brain could deal with something other than sexual appeal. "Iconic Security is trying to keep us away. They must know we can do something to help you and they're trying to take us out of the game."

He paced away, then whirled back toward her. "They're doing a damned good job."

"No they aren't." This time, Tia closed the distance. Unlike him, her feet splashed through the muck and slush but she didn't care. She grabbed his hand and squeezed it, ignoring her fear, and the brief wave of chill. She didn't believe Ewan would hurt her, even involuntarily. And she needed his touch, his support, even if it meant his taking her manna. She'd never been a murder suspect before and didn't like the idea at all.

"There's no way they'll tear me away from you," she said. "For the next two weeks, you might as well call me *shadow*, because that's how close I'm going to be."

"But—"

She took a deep breath. "And Ewan?"

"Yes?"

"I'm sorry I can't do the sex thing. I'd like to give you power, I just can't do that kind of bargain."

Chapter 13

"Any way you could tell if it's a trap without walking into it?" Big Red demanded.

They'd left Big Red and the others alone for a couple of hours, but clearly nobody had made any progress. Which didn't surprise Ewan.

To his surprise, all of Tia's friends wanted to throw themselves into danger, pissing away their lives as if those weren't the most precious things in their existence. And for what? To protect him?

He wasn't their god. It didn't make sense that they would care whether he survived as a slave or simply vanished.

"I don't understand why you mortals value your lives so lightly." He didn't raise his voice, but he made sure it reflected the intensity of his feelings. "If I'd been given only a few years of life, I'd treasure them."

"Since we're only given a few years, we try to make them count," Big Red explained. "Now, back to the trap."

"We don't know it's a trap. Travers recognized Winsor's name when he called. Even if it wasn't really Winsor coming up the elevator, that has to mean that there is a Winsor in Iconic's Corporate Security. They made a mistake. They didn't know that the women were listening. That gives us two angles we can use to--"

"Of course it's a trap," Tia interrupted. "Exactly like last time, they left a trail to lead you into their hands. This time they'll have a professional on the other end of the trap rather than an incompetent like Travers. *They'll* have learned from their failure, which is more than you're willing to do."

"Tia is right," Joe-Hill said. "We've got to outthink these guys, not rely on force."

"I'm open to suggestions." Ewan had to grit his teeth to admit it, but he wasn't an idiot. It was just that gods overpower people. Outsmarting them wasn't important.

Now that Tia had slowed him down, he could see she was right. Of course Iconic would set a trap.

"How about we go around the trap and see what's behind it," Tia suggested. "We didn't have much luck finding Iconic Security, but there has to be more to it than just a mail drop in New Jersey."

"You Googled them?" Joe-Hill asked.

"Googled, did a D&B Credit check, and searched all of the officers listed in their incorporation papers," she said.

"We also searched the other companies registered at the same mail drop," Lori said. "I wondered if they might be connected. Sort of like how the CIA uses the same mail drops for a lot of their cover companies."

"And?"

"Nothing that set off warning bells. Travers seemed like the easy way in."

"Sounds like we need a hard way in, then," Big Red said.

"Dad? You can't be thinking—"

"Unlike you, I'm no atheist." Big Red said. "I believe in gods and believe they have rights. The movement exists to prevent any kind of exploitation. So, if the guys won't help on this one, what the hell did they sign up for in the first place?"

"Guys?" Tia sounded dangerous.

"Sorry about that. It was mostly men in my day. Lot of women are involved now, though. Wanting a better future is not about what sex you are."

"You get on the phone or Internet or however you need to contact your revolutionaries," Tia said. "Meanwhile, it's time for us to use a little feminine logic on this situation."

"Meaning?" Ewan demanded. The woman wasn't backing off at all.

"Meaning we've been charging head-first into their traps. Once we were just ignorant. That was when Sam and Hank tried to kill me. Once we would have known better if we'd just told each other the truth. That was when they set our apartment on fire. Since then, we did know better and were just plain stupid anyway. Like when you and I walked into Travers and his gang in Harten's house, and when Lori and I took the elevator into Travers' apartment. We're doing the same thing over and over and expecting different results."

"So, what's your plan?" Joe-Hill was setting Tia up, Ewan knew. Still, the god wouldn't mind a plan, either. Thousands of years of interacting with humans had taught him was that the human imagination was practically unlimited. Gods were so used to power, lightning bolts, storms, pillars of salt, devastating diseases, earth-covering floods, that they often forgot about subtlety. Humans lacked the sheer power of a god, just as they lacked the strength of many of the animals their caveman ancestors had hunted. To kill a mastodon, to chase down and tame a wild auroch, to stand up against a tiger or a bear, humans had become sneaky. Far sneakier than even the weakest god ever needed to be. Considering how weak he was after thousands of years without a dependable manna supply, Ewan needed to take advantage of that all-too-human sneakiness.

Tia's smile looked deadly. "Don't you think it's time we set a trap for them rather than the other way around?"

Chapter 14

"Do you have faith, sister? Faith that God can restore your sight?" Big Red wore a suit so white it glistened in the dimly lit makeshift sanctuary they'd constructed in the abandoned storefront in one of the buildings across the street from Joe-Hill's clinic. The religious socialist drawled out the word *God* into three syllables, *Ge-auh-de* as he prepped both the small crowd and the aging and long-blind African-American woman for the miracle. A miracle that was going to be perfectly real, perfectly divine, and perfectly not at all what the crowd or the woman thought they were getting.

Tia winced at Big Red's expression. He believed all right, but he believed in the Liberation Theology popular back in the sixties. It wasn't the kind of faith that inspired megachurches.

Whatever Big Red believed, pretending pray to God and using Ewan to perform real miracles edged painfully close to violating the First Commandment.

"Don't think about it that way," Lori's religious friend Marti whispered to Tia. "Do you really think this is all an accident? The Lord *sent* Ewan to you. Remember this? 'You shall know them by their fruits.' Ewan and Big Red are doing good, which means they're on the side of the true Lord even if they don't know it. Ewan's miracles are being used for healing, not destruction. 'I have other sheep too, in another fold,' as Jesus said. Who's to say that Ewan and those other beings aren't part of that other fold?"

Tia's minister back home would have told her what was wrong with the logic, but she didn't argue too hard. After all, a trap had been her idea.

Marti, Tia and Lori wore golden choir robes and stood well behind the pulpit where Big Red was mixed liberation theology with old-fashioned barn-raising oratory to whip up the crowd and generate a flood of manna.

"The big corporations are poisoning you. They spout words of faith, but their god is profit. They'll poison all of you for a nickel," Big Red admonished the fifteen or so cautious visitors in the storefront chapel. "You have to organize, to—"

Tia cleared her throat loudly.

Big Red shot her a surprised look but got back on track. They weren't here to create a consumer's union, they were there to enable manna by working miracles.

"I want you to close your eyes and pray, sister. Pray with all of your faith that those who poison the people will see the light, that those who labor shall have their just rewards. Pray hard because I need your help here. You know that I'm just a man, human as you or anyone. You know I'm not the one who heals. I'm here as a witness that's all, same as every person here. We'll all witness and then spread the good news."

He gave the signal and Joe-Hill fired up a hymn on the cheap organ they'd rented from a rent-to-own furniture place a couple of doors down from Joe-

Hill's clinic. The three-woman choir of Tia, Marti, and Lori joined in.

Marti and Lori, with their theater training, sounded good. Tia didn't wander too sour but she sure didn't try any of the complicated harmonies Lori put in.

"Now maybe you've been to revivals where quack ministers mock the faith and pretend to heal." Big Red's voice was soft, but it penetrated over the music. "You've heard those big-tent preachers shout about demons, about evil spirits they claim are causing diseases." He shook his head. "I've seen enough not to mock any man's beliefs, but I'll tell you the truth about Sister Betty here, brothers and sisters. There are no devils in this woman's eyes."

That got some surprised looks. But Big Red insisted on sharing the truth as he knew it.

"Sister Betty," Big Red continued, "is no angel, but her loss of sight isn't God's punishment. Oh, no. This blindness is not God's punishment at all. It comes from the poisons spewed into our environment by companies who grind their workers' bones into profit. God isn't punishing her but she's not beyond the power of divine healing. Join your prayer to mine and ask that Sister Betty here be healed."

Every candle in the makeshift church flared and Sister Betty blinked, brought her hands to her eyes, removed the black shades she'd worn even in the dimness of the chapel and rubbed her palms into her eyes. A beatific smile crossed her lips. "I can see! I thought you were a scam-job, but I can see for real."

"Keep your money in your pockets," Big Red thundered as the mood of the small congregation shifted. "You think I'm looking to extort profits from the suffering of others? Do you really think we'd charge you for a miracle, as if we were dispensing burgers and fries from a fast-food restaurant? Read the *Bible* and tell me how many times our Lord held out his hand for payment when he walked among the poor and told them of a better life?"

On cue, Tia, Lori, and Marti shouted "Never." To Tia's surprise, their denial was drowned by the louder shout of the congregation.

"That's right, he never did. Faith is not a corporation, sucking money from those least able to afford it. Your money's no good here. Keep it. Spend it on yourself if that's what you need. If you have extra, share it with those who are hungry and shivering on the streets because they have no place to stay. Three days ago, I was in a homeless shelter myself. I know how many hundreds in our great city have nothing. I don't want your money, but I call on you to witness. Go out from here now and tell everyone what you saw. Tell them that there's a better future coming. Tell them to bring their sick to us and we'll all pray together for another miracle."

He lowered his hands. Joe-Hill cut the organ music off and the few people who had seen the miracle leaned forward to hear Big Red's wrap-up.

Nearly half a century of working with the people, of proselytizing his beliefs, gave Big Red an uncanny ability to read his crowd. He knew he had their attention.

He dropped his voice to a whisper. "Most of you know Sister Betty. You've seen her, blind as a baby kitten all these years. You know in your hearts that this is no fake where they heal some actor over and over. Faith doesn't mean you're stupid, or that you'll fall for their cheap tricks. Don't stop questioning. Question those who tell you miracles can only be bought. Question the corporations who tell you they're bringing jobs when they're really bringing disease. Question me, test me, don't let one lucky break make me seem like more than just another guy.

"Come back tomorrow and bring us the worst of your sick and injured. Because what we're sharing with you here in the Bronx is real, and it will work again. And remember, keep praying. Because prayer has power."

Chapter 15

Manna spewed all around, like water from a fire hydrant left to cool the children on a muggy summer day.

Two healing services a day, over a period of three days, gave Ewan a pins and needles sensation through his body.

Like Tantalus in the legend, the manna all around him stayed just outside his reach. When he tried to consume it to assuage the hunger gnawing at his gut, it drained away, leaving him emptier than ever.

Their plan depended on Iconic Security not knowing that. Unless they sensed the trap, Iconic would believe that Ewan was generating manna for himself, growing beyond Tia until he could stand against them and destroy them. He wanted them to believe he was hoarding that power. He needed them frightened, reacting, desperate.

When Iconic attacked him, he hoped to be ready.

As plans went, it was a long shot. But Big Red had the knack for stirring up manna. If Iconic could detect that, they'd know something was going on. Surely they wouldn't believe he'd be stupid enough to let all that manna just fade away.

As he did every few moments, Ewan reached around in N-dimensional space feeling for the kind of distortion he'd felt in the manna when Travers and his scientists had trapped him.

He'd felt something earlier that morning, but it had faded before he could reach it. Now, he encountered only Tia's nearby presence.

Their congregation numbered in the hundreds after only three days of preaching and miracles. Its manna was a palpable force, distorting the world around them. None of the congregation was a standout like Tia, but the combined power would be a beacon to the sensitive instruments Iconic must have.

The outpouring of manna teased his weakness, sharpened his need for Tia.

He hungered to take her in his arms, to make love to her, as he'd made love to his temple priestesses so long ago, glorying as Tia's manna redirected itself to him alone. The mere thought of claiming *all* of that power, now showered on a deity who seemed impossibly distant, churned his hunger into a raging fire.

Trapping Iconic didn't matter much if he couldn't have Tia. Sure he'd prefer Tartarus to being a slave to Iconic, but either way, he'd vanish as a sentient entity. With Tia, though, he could repay the manna he'd borrowed and grow strong.

He'd nearly forgotten being a fertility god, thousands of years before as the Neolithic age had yielded to the Bronze. Then, Ewan had been called on to bring pleasure to thousands of priestesses. He'd learned every secret spot on a woman's body. Tia would not be disappointed with his loving.

Was it such an unfair exchange that he'd take something in return?

A tiny quiver in the manna flow told him that Tia was troubled.

Hunger

He knew he was as likely the cause as the solution to her trouble, but he couldn't resist his inexplicable need to bring her comfort.

He twisted across the dimensional barrier and came up behind her, putting his hands on her waist, savoring the firm muscles of her abdomen, her obliques.

"What?" She gasped the question.

"I thought we might go out somewhere. Take a break."

"We've got plenty to eat here." Since they wouldn't accept money for their services, members of the congregation had begun bringing food—both to share with attendees who had nothing, and to feed Big Red and the others.

This wasn't going well. But he was a god and she a human woman. He wanted her and she wanted him. How complicated could it be? "I thought we would go somewhere where we could be alone."

"Again, why?"

For a god, even a starving, diminished god like Ewan, desire was as easy to read as a Times Square headline. And Tia positively dripped with it. Did she want to be wooed? Did she want him to lie to her, pretend a merely human love? He knew enough about women to know he couldn't just ask.

He saw no downside to wooing her, though. Being with Tia, becoming the focus of her attention, of her penetrating gaze, enhanced the painful pleasure of the rush of manna that surrounded her like an electrical field. If wooing led nowhere, he would be no worse off and he would have enjoyed the process. If she became his worshiper, he would be powerful again.

"Does there have to be a reason? I like being with you. Isn't that enough?"

He hadn't dropped his light grip on her waist, so he sensed the tension fade from her body.

"Do you think our gang will be safe if we leave here?"

He cast his senses around them one more time. "They won't attack when we're not here to catch."

"I guess I do need to eat. Give me a minute to get changed." She slipped from his grasp and headed into the woman's dressing area, an area he'd been told in definite terms that was off-limits to his N-dimensional vision.

It was a prohibition he observed in spirit only. He didn't intrude into the women's privacy, but he continually checked to be certain that no one else intruded upon them, that Iconic didn't, once again, attempt to turn the woman into a lever to control him.

While he waited for Tia, he tracked down Big Red.

"Hey, Ewan. I was just looking for you."

"I felt Iconic earlier, but I didn't pick up anything odd in that last crowd."

He'd recognized the bitter taste of the manna as coming from some kind of device. And the only organization he knew of that had developed manna technology was Iconic.

Big Red stared at Ewan for long enough to make the god wonder if he'd missed some part of the conversation. "What?"

"I'm thinking about Tia."

That made two of them. Ewan decided a simple nod was the safer response.

"I told you before, I'd hate to see her crushed. Don't fall for the strong act."

Tia didn't seem strong to Ewan. He was continually amazed that humans survived given that their bodies were formed of near-random collections of self-interested cells. Almost anything, an accident, a toxic microbe, a fall of a mere dozen feet could damage or even kill a human. When Ewan had become self-aware as a god, he'd had to learn to respect human fragility. It was a lesson that some gods, like those of the Aztecs and Carthaginians, never bothered learning. As death-gods gleefully reminded the others, there were always more humans. And death-manna was far easier to capture than the manna generated by faith. It was also a one-way street. Once a god tasted death-manna, he could no longer taste that of living faith. Which was why Pluto, among the Romans, had so few living worshipers.

Big Red still stared at Ewan and he realized he'd have to say more.

"I'm working to keep Tia, and all of us, safe."

Big Red scratched his bald head. "That isn't what I meant. I'm talking emotions here."

With his N-dimensional talent, Ewan could read emotions as clearly as he could hear spoken words. That didn't mean he understood what Big Red was getting at, though.

The aging radical picked up on his confusion. "I'm not her father, but I feel protective, all right? I don't think it's right that you go—"

Ewan always knew where Tia was, just as an astronaut would know where to find his closest supply of oxygen. Clearly Big Red didn't have the same advantage.

"If you're talking about me, you can stop it right now. I'm a big girl and I can take care of myself."

Tia's anger blazed hotter than the fire that had destroyed her apartment, manifesting her manna like a halo around her. She looked magnificent.

"Hey."

"Come on, Ewan. Let's go out on our date."

* * * *

Okay, she'd dolled up for him.

After living in jeans, sweats, and cheap rayon choir robes for the previous few days, Tia enjoyed the chance to go more girlie.

As far as she could tell, Ewan didn't even notice. Uh-uh. He might be a god, but she still expected some positive feedback when she'd gone all-out.

If she thought he wanted her for her, she wouldn't find his bargain quite so disgusting.

She decided to cut him just a little slack and be explicit about her needs. Maybe Neolithic gods hadn't been trained in basic date manners. Maybe he needed a clue.

"So, do you like what I'm wearing?" She let the short black dress flirt around her thighs.

Ewan stared at her blankly. He was still such a guy.

"I'm not, shall we say, *current* on female fashion. But you always look stunning to me."

Stunning was good. *Always*, not so much. She'd seen herself in the mirror too many times to fall for his 'always stunning' line.

"So, where are we going, anyway?"

"One of the visitors left a pass with us. She wanted to pay us back for what we'd done for her father." He handed over a handwritten note inviting whoever could come from Big Red's makeshift church to an all-expenses-paid dinner.

She stared at the address, then laughed.

"What?"

"This is for a restaurant in Florida. Maybe Florida hadn't been invented when you were doing the god thing, but it's a thousand miles away. A little inconvenient for a quick lunch?"

"I read the woman's emotions. There's no fraud and no trap."

"I wasn't thinking about the danger. Don't you get it? We're in New York. The restaurant is in Florida. Do you hear the difference?"

"Ah." His grin lit the room. "So, we'll need a shortcut if we're going to walk."

As so often was the case, Ewan's answer was completely weird. Her mouth popped opened but nothing came out.

A surge of wind blew sharp points of snow and she shivered.

A man walked by, his eyes staring at the sidewalk, and she wondered why she was certain he'd been looking at her.

"Did you see him? He looks familiar."

"Whom?" Ewan stared directly at the man's retreating back. "There's no one here."

"Him." She pointed. Abruptly, she remembered the man who'd passed her after she'd sent Ewan away all those nights ago. It had to be the same guy.

"You can't see him because he's one of them. Iconic."

"We know they're watching." He paused. "I need more manna to see them clearly."

"Another gust of wind blew and the man was gone. She pulled her coat more tightly over her too-short dress, and huddled closer to Ewan.

Sensing her chill, the god put an arm around her. Abruptly, she felt protected from the elements, as if not his arm, but some feather-light cloak surrounded her, warmed her, protected her from any harm.

She was an independent woman. But given what they'd been through in recent days, she didn't chastise herself too much for savoring a moment of comfort.

Ewan kept walking, pushing his joke way past when it stopped being funny. Two blocks from their mission, he turned abruptly into an alley that smelled of garbage and that didn't, as far as she could see, lead anywhere anyone could possibly want to go.

"What's going on?"

"I said we needed a shortcut."

For just a moment, the protection he'd wrapped around her seemed to break down: a sharp wind cut at her eyes like a sandblaster.

She blinked, and the world changed.

"It's around this corner"

Tropical warmth replaced New York's gray skies and ice-cold temperatures. The sun beamed down from a cloudless blue sky and the smells of the city, garbage, sweat, snow, were replaced by those of citrus and tanning lotion. Tia's coat felt like it weighed a million pounds and she shed it, handing it to Ewan when he offered.

The restaurant sign matched the name on the note, down to the Key West address.

"You're trying to impress me, aren't you?"

His look was slightly cocky, definitely challenging, but also interested. "Did it work?"

She had to laugh, this time at herself. Oh, yeah, she was impressed. Walking down an alley and ending up a thousand miles away was not the trick an ordinary street magician could pull. "I'd never admit that to a guy."

Ewan shrugged. "Healing the sick is more difficult. This is simply a matter of understanding dimensions. It took no more energy than climbing a flight of stairs. But, you said you were hungry. Let's eat."

The wait staff fawned over them the instant Ewan handed over the pass. A parade of chefs, puffy white hats on their heads, came out from the kitchen to thank them for what their mission had done for the owner's popular father. None of them, chefs or wait-staff, would take a penny, even for the tip.

There was one small problem eating out with a god. Despite the feast, Ewan contented himself with moving food around on his plate.

It had to be the best meal Tia had ever tasted—her fish had been caught only minutes before, the herbs cut from the herb garden in back of the restaurant, and the vegetables fresh from nearby greenhouses, but it wasn't Ambrosia, whatever that was. It might taste like food for the gods to her. From Ewan's reaction, it wasn't close.

It was hard for a girl to eat in the face of that, especially since living with stick-thin Lori made Tia conscious of every ounce she carried.

Ewan was in good form, though. He chatted with the chefs, who came out to make sure their food met his approval, flirted with the waitresses, charmed the elderly couple sitting at the next table over, and amused Tia with a series of stories of confusion between gods and humans that had, invariably, resulted badly for the gods.

After a couple of bites, Tia forgot about calories and fat grams and concentrated on the pleasure of food, of having the best-looking male in the restaurant across the table from her, and in the delightful sensations she got when he took her hand, touched her shoulder, or spoke her name.

Ewan even *insisted* that she have dessert.

* * * *

"Shouldn't we get back?"

Lunch had taken longer than she'd planned. After she'd eaten, Ewan had suggested a walk along the beach. Turquoise waters and glowing white sand reflected the shimmering light of the sun. She'd slipped off her shoes, letting Ewan carry them. Now she savored the feel of warm sand beneath her feet.

"No."

"We shouldn't get back?"

He grasped her by her shoulders and turned her to face him, his jet-black eyes gazing straight into hers. "That can wait. You and I can't. I want you. Here. Now."

Okay, she was going to have to help him improve his technique. Still, there was a certain attractive caveman directness to it. And he said want, rather than talking about a bargain. Still—

"We're in the middle of a public beach."

"We're completely alone."

The restaurants, the wharfs, the sailing boats and jet-skis, the bikini-clad females and weightlifting musclemen that had been ubiquitous only moments before were as gone as if he'd taken an eraser and eliminated them from existence. Ewan had taken them elsewhere.

"We might walk into an Iconic trap."

"If they have the power to reach this place, they don't need a god. Besides, I don't want to talk about Iconic. I want to talk about you. Talk—and more."

Her body responded to the compelling desire in his voice. Her ex-boyfriend had always claimed she was unresponsive. If she ever saw the jerk again, she'd let him know it wasn't her problem. With the right guy, she could catch fire. And she had. She took back her earlier thoughts on improving Ewan's caveman technique. He was doing just fine.

She opened her mouth to tell him that, but he cut off her answer by lowering his lips to hers.

She already knew Ewan was a great kisser.

She'd forgotten how good.

His hands left a trail of fire and ice as they traced a path from her shoulders down her arms to her waist.

He pulled her closer against his body. Ewan might not be a man, exactly, but he was very obviously male.

Her body was ready to forget everything and make love with Ewan, to keep making love with him forever. But her mind couldn't stop worrying.

Since his lips had finally left hers, if only to create a trail of kisses to her shoulder, she could talk. Sort of. Thinking was hard, though. Or rather, thinking of anything but making love was purely impossible.

"We can't just do it on the sand. That's gross."

He stepped back but left one hand on her waist as he pulled off his coat, shook it, and spread it out on the beach like a blanket.

Like a blanket? It was a blanket. And how had he gotten it off at all, considering that he hadn't moved his hand from her body?

"Cheap magic trick," she said.

"Compared to you, all magic is cheap."

"You're laying it on thick now, godling." *But don't stop.*

Ewan's smile should have been illegal. Her knees got wobbly and she felt as if she'd drunk three glasses of wine with lunch rather than the single glass of iced tea she'd actually had.

"We're on a world where humans never evolved. We have time, an eternity if you wish, before we need to be back in New York. I can read the desire in your body, Tia. I wouldn't ask this if you didn't need it as desperately as I do."

Desperate. That was a good word. It was hard for her to believe that Ewan really could be desperate for her, but he'd told her that gods couldn't lie. So she believed him. And if she believed that, she had to believe everything.

"Yes."

"Yes?" Despite his self-assurance, her capitulation caught him by surprise.

"We may not make it through the next few days, Ewan. Why should we deny ourselves?"

He didn't argue.

Chapter 16

Ewan shuddered as he brought his lips to the curve between Tia's neck and shoulder, first kissing, then biting lightly.

Her skin, soft as sea foam and heated by the tropical sun of this forgotten and empty world, tasted of musk and flowers.

Her manna surrounded him, encompassed him, suspended him in a whirlpool of sensation and pleasure unlike anything he'd experienced before.

Surprisingly, though, her manna wasn't all he wanted. He wanted her, the essence of woman that Tia had become for him.

He'd imagined his long-ago encounters with temple priestesses over so many thousand years made him indifferent to the appeal of a woman. That was so wrong.

Tia wrapped her arms around him and pulled him toward the blanket he'd manifested to cover the fine dry sand.

He let her take the lead for the moment, but seized the initiative when he lay beside her.

She'd seemed disappointed earlier that he hadn't really noticed her clothing. Tia didn't yet understand that his multidimensional vision let him see the true person far more clearly than the external packaging. To him, Tia herself was more interesting than any dress. Still, up-close, he could appreciate the way her little dress seemed designed to be opened, like the packaging on a precious gift.

A light tug on a tie in the back and the wisps of fabric that covered her breasts were gone.

He reminded himself to send warming ichor into his hands before caressed each of Tia's breasts.

With each beat of her heart, it became easier to do so. Her manna bathed him in abundance.

Her breasts swelled at his touch. Her nipples, pink and pretty, hardened still further as he brushed his thumb against them, then carried brought his lips to them.

She gasped, then squirmed, grasped his erection and squeezed.

Unlike hers, Ewan's clothing was insubstantial—a part of himself rather than something bought and discarded. He simply let it dissolve back into N-dimensional space and let his skin touch hers.

It was Tia's turn to shudder. "You're not going to be a normal boyfriend, are you?"

He didn't, couldn't answer. The time for talking was over.

Tia's legs parted for him as he brought his hand to her center, slipped her panties into the same N-space cul-de-sac where he'd put her unneeded winter coat, twisting her dress into temporary nothingness. Then she was naked beside him.

"Oh, my." This time when she squeezed him, there was nothing between her hand and his need.

She was hot, wet, ready.

He forgot the tricks he'd learned all those centuries before and let his need rule him.

Fighting his body's hunger for speed, he turned to her slowly, knelt between her legs—and waited.

"What?"

His voice had been steady at battles where thousands of warriors had battled for control of their world but it shook now. "Ask me to enter."

"You are like a vampire, after all."

"Tease me later, if you must." He sounded almost in pain. "Not now."

"I'm asking, I'm begging."

* * * *

She'd never made love before.

She'd thought she had, of course. She'd lost her virginity years earlier in college and her relationship with her ex-boyfriend hadn't been sexless despite his whining about her unresponsiveness. But Ewan was Ewan.

Ewan was bigger than Bobby had dreamed of being. He filled her completely. But size was only the beginning, the least important difference.

The god halted when he hit her limits. His clenched teeth told her of his need, his hunger for his body, but he stopped, waited for her body to accommodate itself to his size, before continuing.

When he did continue, her body combusted into heat and desire. His movement was slow at first, but became faster as he recognized and matched the rhythm of her body, her desire, her need.

He kissed her as he made love to her.

His clever hands, not cold at all now, caressed her breasts, stroked her bottom, and ran through her hair. Although he used both hands to caress her, she had no sense his weight pressing down on her.

She'd felt that she would explode when he'd first entered her, but now she squeezed her inner muscles and laughed as *he* shuddered with pleasure.

Until he continued on. Then pure sensation washed all thought away.

Later, she would decide that making love with Ewan was weirdly like the N-dimensional space where he had taken her—all of her senses running together and confused. Impossibly, she could see everything Ewan did to her and what she did to him—inside her body and outside. At the time, she was mostly aware of his scorching heat, the impending explosion of her orgasm, the scent of wild dark forest on his breath, and the urgent need swelling inside of her. A need that devoured everything she was.

She wrapped her legs around his rock-hard waist, urging him ever-more deeply into her as her body conformed to his bulk. Finally, she screamed as her own orgasm took over, raised her, or reduced her, to something not completely herself but a creature of need, sex, desire, and love.

His own explosion came scant moments later and she felt the spurt of his seed as it entered her body.

A golden glow surrounded Ewan.

He looked like a medieval paintings of an angel. Travers had been wrong. Ewan wasn't *just* an energy being, whether symbiotic as he claimed or parasitic as Travers argued. He was something not of the human earth at all. Something that floated near that earth but that remained separate from it.

She loved him, she realized. But that moment of realization carried tragedy. They were too different. Even their lovemaking highlighted the impossibility of the two being together.

Still, she would savor what she had.

She ran her fingers through his thick black hair and noticed that the glow infused her body as well.

She would ask him about that. But not right away. Now was about enjoying the aftershocks of an orgasm unparalleled, unimagined in her life experience.

Until he moved inside her again, still rock-hard.

"You're supposed to roll over and fall asleep," she said.

"This is a good thing? Why?"

Since she didn't know the answer to that, she decided to keep her mouth shut and pay attention to what *he* did instead.

One of the world's shortest conversations was followed, somewhat distantly, by one of any world's most prolonged, powerful orgasms.

She had only one question? Why had she waited so long? She could have insisted that he come home with her that first night after he'd rescued her from Sam and Hank? They could have made love after he'd rescued her from the fire? They had only two weeks and she'd let day after day of it get away.

Just because of her foolish pride.

I love you, Ewan. Only a momentary flash of sanity kept her from saying the words out loud. She knew men feared to be pressed for words they weren't ready to say. While Ewan might not be a fully human man, he had the whole male-thing down in spades. But his silence was all right. She loved him and that was what mattered.

* * * *

Ewan gave her time to recover after their second lovemaking, feeding some of the abundant manna she showered over him back to her in the form of healing. Despite his care, her body was not used to him.

An hour after they'd first made love, though, Tia was ready—ready and demanding.

This time, Ewan took Tia into the sea's bath-warm water, submerged, and let the salty water support them in perfect weightless. He kissed oxygen into her system so that she could breathe underwater. There, as he entered her again, he gloried in the pure sensation of her body, her soul, her manna merging with him.

He enjoyed the small surges of manna she hadn't been able to deny him when he'd touched her, brushed a hand against her back, pressed her foot against his leg during a meal. But sex was as different as a horse from a seahorse.

Each of Tia's precious, eternal, climaxes showered tsunami waves of golden manna over him, filled him with a power beyond anything he'd experienced in thousands of years.

With this and time, he would be young again. He could reclaim his place in the hierarchy. He could carve out a place for himself, create a new people, dominate a part, at least, of the world.

Manna mattered. So, too, did the way she gave it to him, generously and without stint.

While Tia briefly swam away from him to take care of something private, he considered turning Big Red's chapel from the worship of the deities each member brought with them to the explicit worship of Ewan. That was what Iconic expected. With the manna from hundreds of devout and with the vast abundance that was Tia, Ewan could work major miracles. He could call up storms again, direct the lightning, separate the seas, rain destruction down on his enemies, and shower wealth and rewards on those who worshiped him. With Tia at his side, the possibilities were infinite.

That had been his goal in seducing her and he was now closer to that goal than he'd been in thousands of years. He should be satisfied. Oddly, some part of him felt—could it be guilt? Impossible. Guilt is a human emotion. For gods anger and love were pretty much full emotional spectrum.

He cut off that fruitless line of thought when her energy glow signaled Tia's approach.

Her manna fed him, her manna reaching parts of him that had been cut off, starving, dying for centuries. His divine body tingled with the return of circulation.

He hungered still, of course. He had starved for two thousand years. A single feeding, however abundant, couldn't fill the emptiness that had nearly consumed him.

He wasn't complete, but he was closer than he had been since the Roman legions had smashed his mounted archers and the Roman gods had restrained his lightning. It felt wonderful.

He stared at her, wondering.

"Oh, shit."

That hadn't been the reaction he'd been hoping for. "What?"

"We didn't use protection. Could I get pregnant?"

He smiled at her concern. He'd forgotten that conception, for humans, is a weird sort of gamble when once, he'd heard thousands of prayers on the subject each week. "I'm not Jupiter."

"Meaning?"

"Gods don't create children by accident. Between gods, conception takes place when *both* want it. Fair or not, between a god and a human, conception takes place when the *god* wants it. Jupiter always wanted it. He thought the world should be filled with his children. I never believed that an unasked gift was such a blessing."

She looked at him questioningly. "So, no kids?"

"Even if I were willing to father a child with you, I wouldn't plant one unless you asked. And that isn't going to happen. But the manna was wonderful. Sex freed up your manna flow, gave me the power I'm going to need to survive Iconic and go reclaim my place in n-Space."

She should have been comforted by his answer. After all, his power meant her safety, and surely she didn't want to get pregnant at a time like this. Instead she seemed disturbed, proving, as if he needed proof, that he didn't have a clue how Tia worked. It had to be that she was still recovering from the emotional high of their lovemaking.

He thought he understood. The bond they'd created was unlike anything he'd known. Impossible though it was, it had seemed, at least for a moment, that he had reflected manna back to her, and she to him, magnifying it with each sharing. That couldn't have been the case—such a manna feedback system would have destroyed anything human. Still, he lacked words or concept to understand what had happened.

"I don't see my clothes," she said.

"I put them somewhere safe." Thanks to Tia's gift, he had enough manna now that he could have manifested them new, out of thin air. But he didn't feel the need to show off and feared he'd need every bit of manna he hoarded when Iconic put in its appearance. He pulled his blanket from the sand, shook it back into the shape of a coat, and reached into the pockets.

Her clothes weren't in the pockets, of course. They would have gotten wrinkled and, besides, the blanket hadn't even had pockets. But the newly created pockets served as temporary portals into N-space.

He tugged her panties, dress and coat out and handed them over.

"What about my shoes?"

Wearing shoes with heels like that didn't make much sense in icy New York. It made even less sense on a sandy beach. "When we reach the grass."

Tia glared at him but said nothing.

Okay, he hadn't been imagining the arctic freeze that had come over her. "Want to tell me what's wrong?"

"Nothing."

It wasn't nothing. Their day had gone from perfect to horrible in moments. Her manna, which had flowed around him like the sea when they'd made love, now recoiled from his reach and her eyes similarly refused to meet his own.

What had they been talking about when she'd changed? Oh, yes, pregnancy.

"You didn't want me to make you pregnant, did you?" Tia would be a good mother, but mothers of demigods rarely came to happy ends.

"No. Of course not."

He sensed truth in her answer. Okay, that wasn't it. "Why not just tell me what's got your knickers in a knot."

She turned on him, her eyes blazing, her hair flowing around her face as it reacted to the tropical breezes. "I said I'm fine, bozo. So back off and give me some space."

He begrudged every wasted moment in the few days he had left but she'd made herself clear. For reasons as logical to a human as they were illogical to a god, she wanted him gone.

She jerked away from him when he took her arm.

"It's time we get back."

"Who's stopping you?"

"It's easier if we're in contact." Easier, but more painful. Her manna burned rather than healed.

She grasped his elbow. "All right. What are we waiting for?"

"Close your eyes."

"I don't trust you."

"We just spent three hours making love. Of course you trust me. You're just mad for some reason you won't explain. Now close your eyes."

His answer surprised her into momentary acquiescence and he dimension-twisted back to New York.

Uninhabited tropical worlds might be nice places to visit, but without people, they were without manna. And without manna, they were no place a god could stay. Especially when Tia was sending out manna vibes colder than anything he'd ever experienced.

* * * *

She was wrong to blame him. He'd told her from the beginning that he was looking to exchange sex for manna. She'd deliberately blinded herself to that, let herself pretend that she meant more to him than a dairy cow who needed to be pampered to provide good milk.

It wasn't as if she wanted a child, even. But he'd hurt her when he'd laughed off the idea. Well, maybe it was laughable. Tia wasn't set up to be mother to a divine child, and she wasn't constructed to be girlfriend or mistress to a god, either.

She should be grateful that he'd given her the time he had, sexing her up so thoroughly that afterwards any merely human male would forever be inadequate. She should continue to give him all the manna she could, and take the compensations he offered, no matter how little they meant to him.

Feeling that in her gut tore her to pieces.

The instant Ewan magically teleported them back into The Bronx, she headed for the dressing room in back of the chapel, threw her date-dress on the ground, and put on a pair of bulky sweats.

Lori gave her a confused look. "I thought you guys were going to lunch."

"We did."

"Must not have been much good then. You weren't gone more than ten minutes."

Ten minutes? No wonder the god had said they had plenty of time.

"Ewan messed with time while he was messing with my head. We were gone at least six hours." With maybe four of those hours involved in mind-boggling sex.

"Good thing you weren't. We're going to have a big crowd for our next service. We're on in another hour and a half."

"I didn't notice."

116

"Are you sure you're okay? You look—" Lori paused and really looked at her. "Your lips are puffy, you're flushed, and you look like you've been out in the sun. And you had a six-hour lunch? Ohmigod. You finally got lucky with Mr. Stud-God, didn't you? I am so jealous."

"It was a mistake."

Lori's eyes widened. "Don't you dare tell me he was a lousy lover." She inspected her friend more closely. "No, I just won't believe that."

"He was fine." Tia paused, realizing she wasn't being fair. "All right, sex was wonderful, really. I've never experienced anything like it."

"But—"

"But nothing. We did it. It felt great. Now I won't have to worry about what I was missing."

"Don't kid a kidder, Tia. After the late service tonight, we're hashing this thing out. You know I'm on your side, but I've seen Ewan look at you. He may not know it himself, but he's a goner. He thinks you hung the moon." Lori giggled. "It's funny when you think about it because he might actually know who hung the moon. I mean, he's a god, right? Anyway, I don't think he's the kind of guy who changes the way he feels when he gets laid. Unlike most of the guys I've dated in this city. I mean, at least back in Rockwall, once they get lucky, guys tend to come back for more. Here they just carve a notch in their bedposts and go on to the next female. Since there are, like, eighty single girls for every straight single guy, they don't have to worry about where their next blowjob is coming from."

"I don't want to hear this."

Lori batted her eyes innocently. "But I'm saying that Ewan *isn't* like that."

"Please don't—"

"We really do need to go out for that drink. Too bad we've got church coming up. I don't think Big Red would be too happy if we got drunk before his service and Ewan had to heal us."

"That would waste his manna."

"Yeah, poor Ewan, huh?" Lori didn't sound sympathetic. "Now put on your robes. Word must be getting out about what we're doing here because I've gotten six calls from other actors. Our friends are asking how come we didn't have a casting call when we put on this choir. So, guess what? We're holding auditions."

"It isn't like there aren't a thousand church choirs in the city dying for talent. Did you tell them we don't take collections and we can't pay them?"

"We're actors, Tia," Lori admonished her. "If we were interested in money, we would get practical jobs like being paralegals or something. They heard we're getting the crowds and they *need* to be a part of it. Now hurry. Joe-Hill is working in his clinic so I'm on keyboard. You and Marti can put the herd through their paces. Then the three of us will make the casting decisions."

Lori had mentioned six calls, but at least fifty women gathered, ranging in age from sixteen to sixty, each clutching 8x10 headshots with their career high points printed on the back.

Throwing herself into a project turned out to be exactly what Tia needed to pull out of the funk she'd fallen into.

Every woman at the audition was talented. Several had sung in gospel choirs before they'd come to New York. Others had sung in the choruses in Broadway hits. One of the older women had been a megastar years before, and was trying to make a comeback after a failed marriage to her producer.

"They're all better than me," Tia admitted to Marti when the three women headed back into an office in another of the suddenly resurgent buildings near Joe-Hill's clinic.

She wasn't sure if it was Ewan's manna or the positive philosophy Big Red spouted, but in the three days since they'd started the church, several boarded-up business, including a sandwich shop, a hair salon, a photographic studio, and a lawyer's office, had reopened. The one enterprise that had thrived before they'd come, a bustling illegal drug business, had evaporated. Big Red was busy checking out all of the abandoned buildings in the neighborhood looking for a larger venue for his services—and Ewan's healing.

Lori flipped through the stack of headshots. "I always thought those cattle calls were tough on the actors. They're tough on the casting crew, too. How are we supposed to decide?"

"Let's pick the top five," Marti said. "More than that and we'll overpower Big Red. I wish the man would wear a mike, but he won't and that's what we have to deal with."

"Why not make it six," Tia suggested. "You don't need me singing when you have a choice of talent like that. I'll just back off and let the professionals handle it."

Lori laughed. "You're forgetting something, girlfriend. *You're* the reason we have this thing. You and the godling. Even if your voice were completely horrid, you'd still have to stand up there and lip-sync. And it isn't *that* bad." She paused a beat. "If you wanted to improve, you could put a bit more gut into it, sing from your diaphragm rather than from your throat."

Lori hurried on when she caught Tia's glare. "Even without that, you've got a nice little voice and you hit the notes. So, let's pick five more and stop being silly. Just because you and Ewan had a fight on your ten-minute lunch, that's no reason to sabotage the plan. Remember the saying about hanging together or hanging separately."

"Sorry."

"I don't want sorry. I want five names."

All she really needed was a couple of tiebreaker votes.

By their next scheduled service, their choir was up to eight members.

The crowds were bigger, the singing was more professional and Joe-Hill got a new keyboard

Big Red picked twenty of the biggest and fittest regulars to be ushers, helping people find seats and reminding them to turn off their cell phones. They also, Tia noticed, scanned everyone who came in. Nobody said what they were looking for, but Tia figured whatever it was had a *made by Iconic Security* sticker somewhere. They didn't know everything, but they knew the mission was under threat and they'd fight to protect it.

What had begun as a simple idea of trapping Iconic had turned into a train plunging down a mountainside. She couldn't see the destination, but she sensed that they were approaching it quickly. When they got there, she suspected the crash would be horrible. Yet, she could think of nothing that could slow the train or protect the growing crowd of those who'd be hurt when it finally did smash off the rails and into destruction.

Chapter 17

Off and on for the two days since he and Tia had that unforgettable lunch, Ewan had felt the manna detectors, the metallic tang, the electronic whine that twisted the flow of manna into something that tore at his gut and made him want to retch.

Iconic was watching, but they'd done nothing. And time was running out.

Ewan looked around their newly claimed former movie theater and picked out the faces that didn't fit. Even with the manna he hoarded, he could see nothing unusual.

Joe-Hill cranked up the volume on his keyboard and the theater rocked.

The choir belted out a song that had most of the audience tapping their feet while they waited for their healing. They'd added five new singers the day he and Tia had made love—and since then, the music had gotten more complex with every service.

Now, the choir didn't just sing, it created harmonies that called out the melody, and hit notes he hadn't believed were in the human range. More importantly from his perspective, seven highly trained singers surrounded Tia, their voices magnifying the impact of her manna flow like a lens magnifies the rays of the sun.

When that manna hit him, it burned worse than any focused sunshine ever could.

Big Red waited until the introductory song of praise concluded, then raised his arms in welcome. And a roar of applause shook dust from the hastily cleaned theater's ceiling.

The revolutionary's message had sharpened until the growing throngs were ready to change their lives. Despite what he'd claimed when he and Ewan first met, he'd moderated his message. He spoke of rebuilding communities, of rebuilding bodies, not of violent utopian revolution. The revolution he taught now came from within.

The long-abandoned movie theater Joe-Hill had found was a treasure, and a perfect setting for the trap.

Once, it had been a glorious and gaudy retreat for the tired and entertainment-needy. Faded crimson and gold paint decorated carved plaster friezes. Huge velvet curtains had rotted on the walls in the decades the theater had been boarded up since the 1950s.

One afternoon's work by a thousand members of their swelling congregation had left it clean and usable.

To deal with the huge numbers of sick and injured, Ewan came out from behind the stage, nominally Big Red's *assistant*. The revolutionary shouted hope and cooperation, complete with condemnation of corporate greed. Ewan handled the healing.

If Ewan had been a holy-roller minister, he would have been overjoyed with the progress of their ministry. They were running four services a day, seating two thousand in the huge theater, and still turning people away at the door.

They could have minted money.

But Ewan didn't care about money.

He cared about time and manna. And he was running out of both.

He'd been sure Iconic would react. They couldn't know he had only two weeks. They had to know he was gathering huge volumes of manna. If they waited much longer, his trap would be empty and Tia and the others would be exposed to their revenge.

Tia had shut down. Her manna, which had sustained him even when he'd been able only to consume the spillover from her abundant faith in the God of her upbringing, was poison to him now. The manna coming from the crowd cut him like acid.

He'd consumed everything the Roman gods had given him just staying alive. Now he was running low on even that abundant flood Tia had sent him while they'd been making love.

Every person he healed, every tiny alteration in the quantum physics of reality, every moment he sustained a physical presence in the three-dimensional world of the humans cost him manna he couldn't replace.

Every hour that Iconic Security waited, he grew weaker.

Perhaps they were so confident of their technology that they actually wanted him filled with manna before they struck.

This was the fourth service in a row where the detectors had been present, and so far, Iconic had made no move, had done nothing that could allow Ewan to identify the leaders.

Rather than fight, he would heal once more.

He studied the line of sick, maimed, injured and unhappy. The physically wounded joined with hypochondriacs, addicts, depressed, and mentally ill in a throng that stretched all the way up the center aisle of the old theater. Hundreds of people looked to him for the healing they needed so desperately. As he watched, more stepped, shuffled, were wheeled, even crawled to join the line.

It took no effort for him to empty his hands, to bring the cold of intergalactic space to his fingers now. Warming them would have been the problem—if he'd had any reason to warm them. With Tia's rejection, he didn't.

He reached inside of himself again, found enough manna to reach into the next in line and de-activated the virus that had attacked her system.

It fought back.

He had to step far back into the dimensions to gain a touch that could penetrate throughout her system. Once there, he inspected each of the uncounted billions of cells that made up her damaged body. Destroying the poisoned ones was the easy part of the job.

He reeled back from her, drained and empty, as the woman stared at him, eyes sunk in her head, her face still covered with paper-thin skin. She waited for that marvelous glow of health he couldn't afford to give her.

He'd worked a miracle. He'd probably given this woman another forty years to live. But from a theater perspective, he'd wasted his energy. She looked just as weak as she shuffled away from him as she had when she'd stumbled up. In a couple of hours, she'd feel even worse as her body emptied itself of all those dead cells. It would take days before she felt noticeably better, weeks before she was really healthy. He'd be long gone before her manna flowed deeply enough to do more than sustain the flickering coals of her soul. But he'd resisted the temptation to give her a cheap shot of energy instead of healing—and he couldn't afford both.

He swayed slightly, feeling reverberations through the N-dimensional space that should have held his body upright. Daggers seemed to pierce his gut.

After his brief feast on Tia's manna, hunger hurt so much more.

Gasping for breath, Ewan reached out to Tia for any splash of the manna she so abundantly threw everywhere but in his direction.

At that moment, he abruptly felt himself seized.

"Federal Agents from the Food and Drug Administration," the man, who'd innocently stood in line as if he too needed healing, announced. "You are under arrest for practicing medicine without a license."

"I'm a doctor." Joe-Hill abandoned his organ and hurried over to where the fake-patient had been joined by four other men who attempted to wrestle Ewan's arms into strangely shaped cuffs. "Associate Reverend Ewan is operating under my guidance."

"Then you're under arrest, too." The agent twisted Ewan's arm in a move that would have dislocated any human's shoulder.

Ewan's body didn't work that way, though. He might be weak, but his body bent where he wanted. Human joint locks didn't affect him at all.

Then again, the handcuffs the self-proclaimed agent tried to snap over his wrists gleamed with anti-manna energy. They weren't designed for ordinary humans.

"Iconoclast," he said. His voice, carried across N-dimensional space rather than through merely terrestrial sound waves, would reach everyone in the church simultaneously. The word would mean nothing to most. To a few, it would refer to a convulsion in the history of the Christian Church. But Big Red's carefully selected ushers, this was the signal for the attack. Time to release the trap.

The Iconic Security team had planned well when they'd pretended to be government agents. Respect and training for authorized peace officers was ingrained into American minds.

Most Americans, anyway. Big Red reacted instantly, slamming a bony fist into the man who'd grabbed him, and reclaiming his lectern. His booming voice shook the old theater to the rafters. "Money-grubbing corporations have sent their thugs to stop us, but the people, united, cannot be defeated."

Ewan shrugged away from the man with the cuffs. Would Big Red would forget their agreement and incite the mob to violence? With an effort of will, the aging radical pulled himself back on plan.

"Don't try to fight them, brothers and sisters," Big Red urged. "Remember our Lord's teaching to turn the other cheek. But send us your prayers as we battle for you."

The acid taste of manna eased a bit—into something barely usable. Ewan sucked it in even though he knew he'd pay a price later. His hunger could not be denied.

The cuffs were an adaptation and improvement of the clumsy hyperbolic dishes Travers had used to immobilize him. If he hadn't already faced Travers, he might have let them trap him.

But they hadn't abandoned the older technology. Throughout the congregation of thousands, small handfuls of men stood and pointed dishes at him.

Each dish, as it came on line, added to the suffocation that threatened to overwhelm him, drained that small flow of almost indigestible manna the congregation sent him.

What little manna he still held trickled away like water through open fingers. It drained more slowly than it could have.

Iconic's machinery was not as discerning as he. The congregation's manna formed a buffer between machine and god. The dishes had to suck it in before they could incapacitate him.

He was weak, but he could act.

He let a second man reach for his arms, shifting his shoulders ever so slightly when the thug lunged.

Instead of his robe-covered arms where the attack had aimed, the fake agent's hands landed on Ewan's sub-zero fingers.

The thug's scream pierced the theater and his body jerked away from Ewan.

A mistake. The thug's hands remained frozen on Ewan's. When the rest of his body pulled back, his fingers and palms stayed where they were.

He screamed again in horror when he saw the stumps of his wrists.

Ewan shook the hands off, shattering them in another fake agent's face.

"Since you don't approve of my healing, you'd better see a real doctor." The near-absolute cold of Ewan's hand had frozen the blood in the goon's arms, temporarily cauterizing the wound so no great spouts of blood covered the floor, but the man would die of shock if he didn't find help.

Which wouldn't bother Ewan especially. Iconic's thugs were not his people and, like most gods, Ewan cared only for those he'd chosen, those who had chosen him.

Another goon pulled on a pair of insulated gloves and carried a weapon—some sort of clublike electronic device.

He feinted toward Ewan's face, then swung at his body.

Ewan watched his muscles, read the flashes in his brain, stepped away from the weapon when the man attacked.

The goon adjusted a knob on his weapon and hefted it. Perfectly straight teeth gleamed from a face that should have been handsome but was distorted by need. "Say goodbye to your freedom and your little harem, energy beast."

The weapon didn't make a sound, exactly. Rather than vibrations on air, it oscillated the entire manna field.

The manna in their church had been poison to Ewan, but the weapon made it worse. If that thing touched him, Ewan suspected it would transform his own manna into something alien, just as the virus he'd so recently cured had taken over the woman's cells, using her own body to kill her.

He needed strength.

Tia gave him nothing.

Ewan's knees buckled from weakness, from hunger. The thug with the weapon closed the distance between them.

Manna, usable manna, clung to the fake agent like honey to a hive. Ewan was no death-god, but his people needed protection and he saw no other path.

Iconic's shields protected their agents from his remote touch, but physical contact would open them like an ax cracking a watermelon and exposing its fruit.

His hand moved, reached for the fake agent's forehead.

"Don't do it, brother." Big Red had seen his movement and somehow guessed its meaning. "Don't destroy yourself for them."

It wasn't greed that drove Ewan—it was need. The need to protect both himself and those who had fought for him, risked their lives and possibly their souls for him.

Without manna, Ewan would implode into nothingness. As the Roman gods had known, Iconic didn't need him. They'd simply move on to the next god. Without him, Tia and her Niagara of manna would become their slave.

He twisted at the last moment letting the manna weapon pass by him—and claw through the back of another thug.

* * * *

It was her fault.

Tia had seen that man before, but she hadn't been able to remember when and had assumed he was just another member of the congregation. She could have called out warnings, but she'd done nothing.

Memories flooded through her, now that it was too late. She remembered seeing his face. He'd followed her that first night, after Sam and Hank had tried to kill her. And she'd seen him again before Ewan made his detour to Florida.

If she'd made the connection five minutes earlier, she could have warned Ewan, launched Iconoclast. But she hadn't.

Ewan's skin clung to his skull like shrink-wrapped plastic, hiding nothing, exposing his weakness, his hunger. The man attacking him, muscular, tall, and moving with a cat-like grace, would kill him and Ewan couldn't fight back.

And it was Tia's fault.

Tia knew that, but knowing the problem and finding the solution were two different things.

No matter how badly she wanted to fill Ewan with her manna, she didn't know how.

Big Red was a formidable brawler from his years in the movement, but he was in his sixties and he'd turned aside all of Ewan's offers to heal him. The erstwhile preacher landed some good punches, shouted something to Ewan, and went down under a thrashing sea of fists.

Big Red and the ushers were supposed to distract Iconic while Ewan worked his magic, but she'd left him so empty, the trap had no teeth.

Iconic Security guards sprang up like the proverbial soldiers sown from dragon's teeth. Everywhere she looked around the huge theater, clumps of Iconic agents set up their equipment to destroy the god-man who owned her heart.

Lori plucked her arm. "We've got to get you to safety."

"If they capture Ewan, they'll do anything they want."

"Ewan springs the trap. We stay safe so they can't use us against him."

"He *can't* spring anything. He can hardly stand. Can't you see that? There isn't enough of him left."

"We already proved *we* can't fight worth beans—those guys know lots more Kung Fu than I do. We've got to stick with the plan."

The plan hadn't contemplated that Tia would cut Ewan off from manna in a fit of what she had to admit was purely pique. So what if he still dreamed about ruling the world and didn't see her as proper girlfriend material? His penalty shouldn't be death. "I don't care about the plan. I'm going to fight them."

"You want to fight them? Then do it right. Worship Ewan. Give him what he needs." Lori turned her back on Tia and spoke to the choir. "Come on, girls. Ewan needs our help. We need *A Mighty Fortress is our God* about now. Uh, skip the second verse, about Christ Jesus though."

Worshiping Ewan came easily for Lori. After all, Ewan didn't demand exclusivity from his worshipers. And Lori held room in her pantheon for one more god—a god who happened to be her roommate's boyfriend.

Even *a cappella*, and since Joe-Hill had been belted down by one of the goons he wasn't any help with the keyboard, the choir's harmonics filled the theater, rising over the sound of struggle and violence.

Ewan was no mighty fortress. His walls were breached, his weapons rusty, his power exhausted by his efforts to help those around him.

Still, he perked up his head as their voices filled the air. Incredibly, Tia actually sensed the manna field, felt a change in the taste of the manna flowing through the theater as the choir's music spread its transformation. Without her standing in the middle, poisoning everything that came from them and diluting that tiny pure trickle with her huge volume of hatred, perhaps this tiny source of faith would help Ewan.

She'd let the choir do their job—while she took the fight to the enemy.

She couldn't help Ewan directly. Iconic had surely sent their most deadly agents to tackle him. But she could do something about the others.

She looked around for a weapon and spotted the state flag of New York, the figures of Liberty and Justice on a deep blue background.

A piece of cloth isn't much as a weapon, but the flagpole had a spiky brass tip. A spear was just what she needed.

She yanked the flagpole from its stand, lowered the point, and poked it through the nearest satellite dish.

A cloud of sparks shot toward the ceiling. A pasty-faced man of about forty stared at her. "Hey." His voice cracked as he addressed her. "What do you think you're doing?"

Not all scientists were nerds. Tia knew that. Still, most scientists use their brains rather than their fists for a living. And if this guy was typical of those holding back and pointing their dishes at Ewan, she might be able to take out a bunch before they stopped her.

"Hold that man under arrest," she shouted at one of the ushers. "He's one of them, Iconoclast."

"Yes, ma'am. Frank, lock this loser in the room we set up at the back of the theater. George, gather up some of the guys and help Miss Tia. Move."

The next scientist's attention was split between watching Ewan battle the Iconic goons on the stage and making adjustments in a palm-sized computer built into the base of the dish. He didn't even see Tia as she ran her spear through the dish, jerked it to the ground, then pointed the scientist to Steve the usher. "Him next. If you can find some more sticks, I could use help disarming these guys, too."

Tia hadn't dreamed Iconic would be able to send more than a hundred men to capture Ewan. She also hadn't dreamed that the congregation itself would figure out that their ministers were under attack and turn to defend them. By the time she'd taken down the fourth satellite dish, the others had vanished as well.

* * * *

They were supposed to hide.

Ewan didn't have a problem with female warriors. His problem was with completely untrained people pretending to be warriors and throwing themselves into danger.

This was not the bargain. It shouldn't have come as any surprise. Humans always break their bargains with gods.

"A mighty fortress is our God, a bulwark never failing." The choir belted out the words, every ounce of their feeling behind them.

He felt anything but mighty. And they'd have been a lot closer to tell the truth if they'd left out the 'N' and called him "a bulwark *ever* failing." Still, the first trickle of unpoisoned manna in days reached him.

"Surrender and we'll leave the women alone." the goon with the manna weapon backed off but Ewan could see he was still completely confident.

He was also lying. Tia remained the perfect bait and they'd have to use her.

Ewan absorbed the trickle of manna and magnified himself, creating a subsonic resonance to his voice.

"Surrender if you don't want me to snuff your life out a cheap candle."

The man's lips pulled back from his teeth in a skull-like gesture. "Our technology protects us from you."

"You're Winsor, aren't you." He recognized that voice over the phone in Travers' apartment.

The security chief gave Ewan another perfect grins. "That's one names. *You* may want to call me Nemesis."

He shook his head. "I know Nemesis. She is a lot scarier than you."

"Idiot." Winsor swung his manna stick again.

Ewan looked for a chance to disarm him, but the man knew what he was doing. Like all the Iconic Security people, Winsor kept Ewan dimensionally blind, prevented him from simply reaching within him.

Still, the human was right in front of him. Ewan didn't need his N-dimensional senses to track him. And he certainly didn't need those capabilities to capture him. A mere human with one lifetime to live could never learn all of the moves, all of the secret strikes, all of the lost arts that a god, even a famished god, remembered.

The choir was still singing, still sending him every drop of manna their limited bodies could generate. Even better, with each passing moment the drain on him lessened. Something had changed. Something else that was not in the plan.

He had to look.

Out in the theater, Tia led a mob of ushers and ordinary people who'd stopped in to check out the excitement in taking out the guys with the hyperbolic dishes. With each one they eliminated, a tiny portion of the tap on Ewan's system vanished.

Winsor saw the brief movement in Ewan's eyes as he checked on Tia and struck.

But a god's vision isn't limited to two physical eyes. Ewan had fought opponents far more dangerous than Winsor. He watched his enemies no matter what else was going on.

He swirled his robes, tangled Winsor's weapons in the silk-satin fabric, and drove a fist into the security chief's jaw.

Ewan had to give it to the man. He had a hard jaw and knew how to take a punch. He even managed to hold onto his tool. But he still reeled back from a strike that was far weaker than Ewan had wished, but that drew on thousands of years of training.

Winsor spat out blood. "So, we're going to have to play rough?"

Ewan smiled. He needed Tia's strength to survive for long, but he could take Winsor without it. And Winsor would know where the bodies were buried at Iconic Security. By the time Ewan had wrung him dry, they'd know everything they needed to shut it down, and to keep Tia and her roommates safe.

Winsor must have made the same calculation. The security chief took a step away, turned off his weapon and put it under his jacket, then took out the pistol that Travers had used—or one just like it.

"It would have been easier if you'd come with me, but I won't let you ruin our plans."

Ewan had been stronger when Travers had shot him. Even then, two mini-black hole shots had nearly destroyed him. He wouldn't survive another.

"You can't use a god you've destroyed."

Winsor shrugged. "There are more gods. There's only one me."

"Your bosses might not think that way."

"When this works, I'll be the boss. They'll take orders then. Everyone will."

A trio of Winsor's men sat on top of Big Red, making sure he didn't get into the fight. Joe-Hill was breathing, but barely. And Tia was halfway across the church smashing the hyperbolic dishes as fast as she could reach them with some sort of brass-tipped spear. She looked great but was too far away to help him. Winsor and his gun were up to Ewan.

He faked dejection. "You'll leave the women alone?"

"Cross my heart."

Winsor's lie made no difference. Ewan had no intention of surrendering.

The heart-crossing gesture distracted the security chief just enough to let Ewan let a bit of manna out of his own reach.

During the fifty years the theater had been abandoned, termites had gnawed at its wooden structures. The crew from the congregation had marked some of the worst spots, but hadn't cleaned out all the rot. A tiny probability flux put one of those rotten segments directly under Winsor.

Ewan watched the strain in Winsor's eyes, the tightening in his shoulders as he prepared to fire.

Across a million dimensions, Ewan ducked, until it took every ounce of his concentration to keep his three-dimensional earth-image upright.

Making Winsor miss him wouldn't be enough. If the mini-black hole even came close, it could destroy him. If it got close to anyone else, they would die, too. Maybe it was because he was so weak himself, but he cared more about short-lived individual humans than he had before his return.

Winsor was smooth. An ordinary human would have missed the slight catch in his breath as he decided Ewan wasn't going to surrender, that he'd have to fire. An ordinary human wouldn't have seen the practically invisible tension in his wrist as he squeezed the trigger.

It took more than one sneaky man to fool a god.

Ewan let the N-dimensions of his body snap his three terrestrial dimensions to the ground. At the same time, he let the random rot collapse under Winsor's feet.

As Winsor's body fell, his arm jerked up. The gun fired, the mini-black hole drilling a five-foot wide hole through the elegant rococo plaster of the old theater.

Winsor landed like a cat on the concrete surface four feet beneath the old wooden stage and dropped the weapon back into firing position, pointing to the right and then to the left as he sought Ewan out. And saw nothing.

Rather than stopping at the wooden stage, Ewan had kept going.

Every high school physics student learns that matter is mostly empty space. What appears to be a solid piece of wood is actually a few molecules of carbon, oxygen, hydrogen, and trace elements, locked in a sort of lattice and floating in a vacuum.

Hunger

Ewan simply dropped through the empty spaces between the atoms. Which meant that he, unlike Winsor, didn't leave a hole behind him.

Winsor's head, arms, and gun remained above the hole that had dropped him to the subfloor. He didn't even see Ewan as the god crouched down under the stage, closed the distance, and drove an ice-cold fist into Winsor's groin. Hard.

Iconic Security could protect their men from a god's ability to reach across dimensions. But they couldn't block Ewan's ability to touch them in the three directional dimensions of the Earth-plane. Not if they wanted to be able to touch Ewan. And they definitely wanted to touch him.

Winsor was a tough man. Still, an unexpected fist to the groin, especially one thrown by a being with thousands of years of experience learning exactly where humans are most sensitive, is beyond the requirements of toughness.

Winsor's knees buckled, and his stomach convulsed, smashing his already injured head into a portion of the wood stage that Ewan had thoughtfully left intact.

Ewan passed back up through the stage, disarmed the security chief, and pulled his unconscious body out of the hole he'd made. The battle was over. They'd have to repair both the roof and floor before they held another church service, but incredibly, nobody had died except that one security guy Winsor had pushed at him.

He sent out what power he could spare to help Tia and the ushers as they rounded up Iconic scientists.

Some got away, and Ewan squandered manna he couldn't afford putting traces on them. But they captured forty of the invaders. It would, he hoped, create a huge hole in whatever defense network Iconic had in place. And Winsor was surely the key. Without him, it would be stuffed suits like Travers who led the defense. Once he knew what he faced, Ewan could go through them like a white-hot spear through a desert dust cloud.

He had to believe he could, anyway. Because time was running out and he needed to close down Iconic forever before his two weeks ended.

At that time, unless he'd persuaded Tia to relent, Ewan would vanish into the nothingness of Tartarus.

Chapter 18

Tia should have been happy.

None of the scientists had talked, yet, and Winsor was still unconscious, but they'd captured more of the Iconic staff than they'd dreamed possible. The thing they'd worried about most, that innocent church attendees might get caught in the crossfire, hadn't happened. Joe-Hill had amputated the rough edges from the arms of the thug who'd tried to grab Ewan and had saved his life. The guy Winsor had stabbed in the back had simply evaporated, presumed dead but with no body left behind. That, and a couple of banged heads and scraped arms, was the extent of the casualties.

Tia didn't even feel guilty about the disappeared guy or the guy with no hands. They'd attacked, after all. That their efforts had backfired wasn't Tia's problem.

Ewan, Joe-Hill, and the choir had even complimented Tia on how smart she'd been to go after the satellite dishes.

Yeah, she should be happy.

"What was Big Red shouting to you about?" She caught Ewan nailing plywood over a man-sized hole in the stage floor that definitely hadn't been there before the fight. Despite the New York winter outside, it was warm in the theater and he'd stripped off his shirt and was working bare-chested.

Multicolored reflections from their makeshift church's lighting system glistened off muscles made even more impressive by Ewan's extreme slenderness. He held a sledge-sized hammer in his work-gloved hands and had a mouth full of large nails.

I won't be distracted, she lectured herself. Following that common-sensical advice wasn't easy. All his muscle and naked skin reminded her of making love with Ewan, of the way he'd played her body like a musical instrument reaching notes she'd never imagined even existed.

"What was Big Red shouting?" she asked again.

Ewan gave the sheet of plywood he was nailing over the hole a final tap, put down the hammer and nails, then cocked his head as if listening. "I don't hear any shouting."

"Don't be obtuse. During the fight. You were reaching for Winsor and Big Red yelled something at you."

He brushed a gloved hand across her cheek but she batted it away and tried not to think about how sexy the combined scents of fresh-cut wood and highland forests could be. She'd never be able to walk in the woods again without being reminded of Ewan. It just wasn't fair.

"Don't trivialize me," she said.

"I would never trivialize you, Tia."

Gods don't lie. Ewan was telling the truth, *as he saw it*. But she knew how wrong he was. To a god, any human was like a pet cockatiel with an unusually developed sense of conversation.

"He stopped you from doing something. What were you going to do?"

Ewan's jaw worked. "I needed manna. I considered taking it from Winsor."

"I thought you could only take manna from worshipers."

His smile was completely unconvincing. "I took manna from you, and you never worshipped me."

She kept her face stoic. She *had* worshiped him. He'd moved the earth for her when they'd made love, and she'd been ready to give him anything within her power. Until she'd learned how he really felt about her. It had been easy to walk away from Bobby when she'd realized he thought of her as a convenience rather than an equal and partner. Walking away from Ewan was harder, but the logic was the same. She demanded some basic respect. That didn't seem too much to ask. "Stop avoiding my question."

He considered, reached a hand toward her, then abruptly stopped with it still inches from her. "I was going to rip the death-manna from his body and consume it."

She shuddered. "You can do that?"

"It would turn me into a death-god."

"I don't know what that means."

"Once a god consumes death-manna he can *only* use death-manna. Even other gods shun death-gods."

She tried to summon up some anger that Ewan would even consider that step. But had she given him any choice? If she hadn't been caught up in hurt feelings, he could have drawn the energy he needed from her. Thanks to her pique, she'd abandoned him to their shared enemy.

Still, that ability and that decision served as vivid reminders of their differences. To her, Ewan was a purely sensual delight. To him, she was, well, food.

She searched for the words to describe her feelings—and came up empty. "I'm glad you didn't do it, then."

"Me too. Big Red saved me from myself. I owe Big Red. And..." his face grew deathly serious and he tilted his head to the side as if listening to a distant voice.

She leaned forward to hear what he'd say next, hoping it would be something personal, something about her.

"Winsor is awake. I've got to go." He pulled a shirt out of the air and shrugged it on.

"I'll come with you."

* * * *

The security chief was a mess. His chin bore the unmistakable imprint of a large fist. His expensive suit was ruined and his skin abraded beneath it.

He should have been handsome, Tia thought. He was built, had regular features, nice dark hair. But his eyes looked like cold chips of steel.

Ushers had tied Winsor into a solid wooden chair with fishing line--the only sort of binding they could find on a moment's notice--and the thin plastic strands cut into the thug's flesh.

He glared at Ewan as if seeing the devil incarnate, his muscles bulging against the ties even though he had to be hurting himself.

Ewan met his gaze, simply staring at him for a good minute in silence.

Winsor didn't even blink back.

"I'd like to propose a bargain, Mr. Winsor."

Winsor's damaged face jerked back as if he'd been struck. Of course, if Ewan ever used that ice-cold tone to Tia, she would have done the same. Winsor might be scary, but the god was far more dangerous.

"I've got time," the security chief said. "Feel free to make an offer."

"Your company appears to be working on a project that puts me, and my kind, at risk. I *will* eliminate this threat. If you help, I could be grateful."

Winsor narrowed his eyes. "How grateful?"

"Grateful enough to let you live."

Winsor laughed out loud. "You think I'll live if I turn on them? They're the government, idiot. The CIA."

"I'm sure you have emergency plans to get away from them," Tia said.

The look Winsor gave her was similar to what he'd probably give a cat that produced a submachinegun. Surprise, contempt, and a tiny bit of fear.

He covered up that fear so quickly, Tia had to remind herself she'd seen it.

"It's not just the company. Nobody gets away from them all."

"Whoever they are, they're humans," Ewan said. "I can protect you from them. They can't protect you from me."

"You, protect me? Don't make me laugh. You're the test case, the one we could get safely. You're nobody. When we're done with you, we'll get some of the big guys. Then we'll see what real power can do."

For the first time, Winsor's eyes sparkled with real animation. "Imagine it. Real gods in my yoke, powerful gods, I'll make myself immortal, become a god myself." He turned his attention to Tia. "Don't you see, Tia? Imagine leashing the power a billion worshipers or more. I could solve every problem America faces. I'd build a shield so powerful, no enemy attack could penetrate. With a divine shield in place, defense spending would be unnecessary and I could divert that money to help the poor. The poor *and* the homeless. Imagine the kitchen where you volunteer feeding thousands instead of hundreds. Imagine being able to offer Ewan's type of magical healing to everyone in our country— perfect health for a hundred, maybe two hundred years for every single citizen. More for you and me. And you're wasting time with maybe a dozen people a day who are lucky enough to live near an abandoned theater in New York."

"Enslaving gods is no way to—"

"Enslaving? Gods? Come on, girlie. If they were real gods, they wouldn't need us."

"That's true. But—"

"Energy beings like Ewan are vampires. You've seen where their energy comes from—they take it from us. Don't you think it's fair to ask for it back? It is *our* energy, after all. *Our* manna. And we could use it to solve *our* problems. rather than simply let some parasitic race of energy beings suck it from us with nothing but an occasional miracle, or plague, to pay us back."

Hunger

Tia waited for Ewan to correct the security chief, to explain that gods weren't parasites. The god remained silent.

"People like you are treasures," Winsor went on when it became obvious that neither Tia nor Ewan would refute his claims. "These false gods are a conduit, that's all. Once we productize the conduit, we won't need them. But your country will definitely need people like you. You will be rich."

"I don't—"

"Did you like Travers's apartment? You could have it, or one twice as nice. Want to bring your parents from Omaha to join you here in New York? That could happen. Want this god-thing as your personal love-slave? Done. You can have him when we're finished with him. Once this experiment is over and we trap the big ones, I won't mind sharing."

Despite the bonds holding him to the chair, Winsor leaned closer to her, dropping his voice as if imparting a secret. "You'll do yourself a favor, Tia. But you'll do more than that. You'll do a service to your country."

Ewan laughed, breaking the hypnotic spell that Winsor's promises had cast over Tia.

"You think everyone is like you, Winsor. That everyone is motivated only by greed and power. Tia isn't like that. If she were, she would have worshipped me from the beginning. She knows *I* can give her everything she craves, and that I, unlike you, keep my promises. But her integrity forces her to resist me. Do you really think your cheap bribes can persuade her into evil?"

"People must have been more innocent when you were a real god," Winsor said. "Or maybe you didn't understand humans, even then. After all, you didn't have to, did you?"

Abruptly, Tia couldn't stand it any more. She rushed out of the projection room where they'd been interviewing Winsor and raced down to the choir dressing room.

* * * *

Lori looked up from her computer when Tia burst into the room. "Hey, guess what I found. An entire website devoted to choir robes. We can get rid of these ugly things and get something nice. I mean, check this out. Think how sexy we'd be wearing these."

Tia couldn't not look. And yes, Lori had found a beautiful set of pale blue and silver robes that would set off Lori's dark hair and skin and make her look like an angel. The light hues would wash out the blondes in the choir out completely and leave even Tia sallow, but Lori would look good.

Was that what it was all about? Were people really put on earth to stab each other in the back and claw their way to the top?

"I guess you don't like it."

"It would make me look jaundiced and make Marti look like spilled milk. Is that what you had in mind?"

Lori opened her mouth, but nothing came out. Abruptly, she slammed the lid of her laptop, walked over to a wall unit, and yanked out a bottle of Scotch and two glasses.

"I'm not thirsty."

"I don't give a damn," Lori said. "You've been acting weird ever since you and Ewan made love and we're going to talk this thing through."

"I don't know—"

"Shut up and drink, Tia. I don't want excuses, I want the truth. And if there's *veritas* in *vino*, the strong stuff should get to it faster."

A part of Tia wanted to snap back. She hadn't asked to be put in this position. It wasn't her fault she'd fallen for a god. And she'd never even heard of manna until Ewan had walked into her life. But if Lori thought something was wrong, that she was acting weird, then she probably was.

She took the full tumbler of Scotch and stared at it. The golden color reminded her of honey, but the fumes were anything but sweet.

"Bottoms up," Lori said.

"I'll get sick."

"I'll help you clean up the mess. Come on. One glass won't kill you."

Tia closed her eyes, raised the glass to her lips, and drank.

The Scotch burned going down, its smoky taste calling up mental pictures of the fire that had raged through their apartment.

Ewan had saved them, then. Just as he'd saved her when Sam and Hank had mugged her. Remembering all of those things gave context to her emotions. She wasn't in love with Ewan, she'd been fooled by his fabulous body, by the way he guided her to heights of pleasure that no mortal man could hope to reach, and by the wish she held in common with most women to find a soulmate. She couldn't love him. All those feelings had to be simple gratitude and a normal sensual response to a male as powerful, as beautiful, as protective as he.

She slammed the glass down on the door propped up on a couple of sawhorses that they used as a makeshift table. "Okay, I get it. I'm not in love with him at all."

"Oh, really?" Lori sounded dubious. "What insight brought forth this brilliant conclusion?"

"Don't you see? He saved my life, so I feel grateful. I mistook that for love."

"Funny. He saved my life too, but I never thought *I* loved him. Think I have better insights into *my* emotions?"

Since Lori famously fell in love with just about every guy she met, for a day or so, anyway, Tia was pretty sure she was being mocked.

"No. You fell for Joe-Hill."

Lori sputtered into her drink. "I didn't. And if I did a little, it's not just because he rescued us."

The Scotch had hit Tia's gut hard. Almost instantly, the alcohol insinuated its influence into her system. She felt dizzy and decided that standing up would be a very bad idea.

"You think I'm in love with Ewan, don't you?"

"Of course," Lori said. "He's your one. He just happens to be a little different.

"Like Joe-Hill is the one for you?"

Lori looked down at the floor, refusing to meet her eyes. "Maybe he asked me out. Maybe he's a good man, doing a good thing in a rough neighborhood."

"Not to mention, he's hung like a racehorse and a monster in bed," Tia said.

"And exactly how would you know that?" Lori's claws were on display.

Tia giggled, knowing the alcohol was fueling this discussion. "I didn't until right now. But think how cool this is. I mean, we live together for more than a year and the only guys we meet are metrosexual actors and narcissistic businessmen. And all of a sudden, I've had hot sex with a god and you've found your soulmate. How lucky is that?"

"It'll be lucky when you admit to yourself that Ewan is more than some mysterious rescuer, that he's your guy."

"He can't be my guy. I saw the real Ewan. Ewan is sexy, but love with him is strictly a one-way deal."

"At least you're using the word," Lori said. "That's progress."

"Give me that bottle."

* * * *

Winsor had shut up after Ewan had given him the truth—that Tia wasn't bribable.

He knew he should kill the man. But he put off the decision hoping that he'd find the leverage to make the man talk. The Chief of Security for the whole Iconic Corporation could be a huge asset if he could just find the key to unlock him.

Meanwhile, Ewan let Winsor stew while he worked on the technicians Tia and the ushers and caught.

They weren't easy, either. Apparently Iconic had guessed that some of them might be captured and had filled them with threats to themselves, their careers, their families, and their nation's safety if they talked. But they weren't professional tough-guys like Winsor, and their N-dimension protection wasn't as perfect.

It took longer than it should have, but gradually Ewan discovered an angle, a corner, a point of leverage. One by one, he popped them.

Sure enough, Iconic's main lab was in New Jersey, but nowhere near Holmdel. The scientists had been working for years on what they initially thought were spy radio detectors but were really manna-stealing dishes.

With Big Red's help and input from dozens of the scientists, none of whom had seen the whole corporate campus, Ewan painstakingly created a 3-D map of the office park where they worked. Over a period of hours, he, Big Red, and Joe-Hill interviewed each scientist, piecing together the security precautions, the staff levels, and eventually, using a computer program called AutoCAD and digital maps from *GoogleEarth*, he rendered an architecturally detailed depiction of the entire campus, accurate to the best memories of the scientists whom Tia and the ushers had captured.

"What do you think these things are?" Big Red pointed at humps set at regular intervals on the earthen berm that surrounded the campus.

"Part of the security system," Ewan guessed. "Do they look like anything you'd see in a standard top-secret site? You know more about government programs than I do."

Big Red took out a pair of reading glasses, looked around to be sure nobody else saw him using them, and studied the fuzzy computer images. "They look a bit like those satellite dishes your friendly scientists were carrying. You know how you couldn't touch Winsor or Travers from your N-dimension stuff? Seems to me they'd want to keep you out of their labs, too."

In the old days, Ewan would have called up an earthquake or a flood to handle that kind of obstruction. Of course, in the old days, nobody even imagined tools that could keep a god out of anywhere. Lacking the power to create an earthquake larger than a fat guy could manufacture by stomping his foot, or generate a flood much bigger than the same fat guy could manage by pissing, Ewan had to find other options.

He'd been certain he would have more of Tia's manna by the time Iconic sprung their trap. He'd believed that the challenge was finding the hidden enemy.

Instead, he was empty. With every minute that passed, he grew weaker and Iconic would be reinforcing their defenses, replacing the men he'd captured. He tried to envision defeating Iconic without using manna he didn't have—and came up blank. Even a god needs something to work with.

From the way Big Red was practically pawing at the ground, though, he figured his *friend*, he still had trouble imagining a human as a friend but there was no other word for it, had a suggestion.

"Yeah, Red?"

"Not everyone in the Liberation Theology movement will think it's cool helping some pagan god, but I can get some to help. How about we set up a picket line around Iconic's campus, not let anyone in."

Ewan shook his head. "A couple of dozen aging hippies are no threat to a company with military connections and a security boss like Winsor. No wonder they hate the idea."

Big Red laughed. "You got *that* dead-wrong, Ewan. These guys love a lost cause. Being right is enough for them, and getting beat up is just part of the price."

There had been a time when Ewan would have said to go ahead. They were merely humans and would die soon anyway. So what if the gesture was pointless? Being with Big Red, Lori, Joe-Hill, and especially Tia had changed him, though. Human lives were short, but they packed such intensity into them that they seemed complete. "They wouldn't just be beat up, they'd probably be disappeared for knowing too much."

"We need more allies."

"The Roman gods gave me all I'm going to get. The other gods are either empty or not responding my call.

"I was thinking people. Honest, church-going, God-fearing folk."

"They'd rather let me starve than lift a finger. And their manna is useless to me."

Big Red shook his head. "It's not all about manna. And there are a lot of people who would agree that is perverting everything they stand for. You heard Winsor about putting the yoke on the big guys. You know who those big guys are and that's purely blasphemous no matter where you stand on the political spectrum."

"I am an atheist," Joe-Hill put in. "And it seems wrong to me, too."

Ewan raised an eyebrow. "You're still an atheist? After everything we've gone through?"

"Sorry, Ewan. It's a political thing. No disrespect to you, of course."

Chapter 19

Tia's stomach clenched. Ewan was growing weaker by the hour, Big Red was fantasizing about mobilizing the fundamentalist community, and they had forty antsy prisoners to worry about. Despite assurances from Ewan, she couldn't believe that none of the people who'd been at their service would contact the police, and they'd all be in trouble if the police raided and found they'd kidnapped an army of government-sponsored scientists.

They shut down services after the attack. Even with Ewan's emergency repairs on the stage and the ceiling, the old theater was too badly damaged, and too full of prisoners, to be put into use. Which would have been okay if they'd been able to go into attack mode as they'd planned, but now they seemed stuck waiting for a miracle.

The morning after the attack, hundreds of people lined up outside the old movie theater to get a second chance at their lives. Rather than turn them away, Ewan and Joe-Hill saw them in the clinic. With each patient, Ewan faded just a bit more.

Ewan's weakness was her fault. She wouldn't give him what he so desperately needed.

Just as she needed what he could never give her.

She willed herself to pump manna his way, but her manna didn't operate on demand. Her irrational anger at him for seeing her as a tool for his power rather than a friend, lover, partner, poisoned everything she could offer him no matter how much she wished otherwise.

She had to have it out with him.

Joe-Hill finally closed his clinic doors at nine in the evening, long hours after the sun had set and a dank misty cold had lit into the city like an invading virus.

Ewan stumbled slightly on his way out of the clinic, and Tia grabbed his arm. She wasn't sure if she was trying to support him or just gain his attention.

"We need to talk."

He nodded. "I'm always anxious to talk with you."

Which made one of them. Since they'd made love, she'd avoided him even though doing so damaged both of them.

"I'm hungry. Keep me company while I eat and we'll talk."

He didn't need food, of course, at least not the kind of food he could get at the Indian restaurant where she took him. But she really was hungry. Besides, she'd be able to talk better if she had something to distract herself with. Keeping her hands busy with food meant she wouldn't wring them together like cheap dishrags.

The restaurant was part of the enterprise zone that had sprung up around their church. Recognizing Ewan as associate pastor, and Tia from the choir, the manager hadn't wanted to let them pay, but Tia had insisted. Her Visa card still had some room left on its credit balance and she worried that once Ewan vanished, the restaurant would need everything to go its way to survive.

Hunger

"I suppose you want to talk about the plan," Ewan said, once the food had been delivered to the table and the waiter had installed a small privacy shield that let them eat in peace, as if in a private home rather than a restaurant in one of the largest cities in the world.

"The plan, to give it a grand name it doesn't deserve, is in shambles. You're so weak you can't do anything even though we've taken out most of their manpower. And every day we wait, they'll be replacing those. Things went perfectly on the trap, except that I'm not giving you what you need."

"You're giving me what you can."

She hated it when he was reasonable. "That means nothing."

Ewan nodded. "You're right about them replacing the men we captured. Considering we have only a few days before the Roman gods come to collect, there's no point in waiting. Tomorrow, I'll attack Iconic's headquarters. In the meantime, we've got to figure out a way to get you to safety."

"You said you couldn't lie, but if you think there's anyplace I can go and be safe, you're lying to yourself. I'm seeing this thing through."

He raised a single eyebrow. "If you've decided everything, what do we have to talk about?"

"Us."

He'd picked up a glass of water, but he set it down quickly as crystals formed on both sides of the glass. "Ah."

She watched his glass as it stretched to hold in the expanding water, then shattered.

Absentmindedly, he waved a hand, causing the glass molecules to bond together again, undoing the damage he'd done. Altering quantum probabilities like that wouldn't cost him much manna compared to summoning an earthquake or a hurricane. But Ewan could ill-afford any loss.

She sensed he was looking at her, so she got busy with her food for a bit. Anything to avoid meeting his jet-black eyes or seeing the way hunger had tightened his skin over high cheekbones.

"Obviously you've had a problem using my manna," she said when it became obvious he wouldn't speak until she did.

"Although I'm certain this isn't your intent, your anger poisons your manna for me. It has ever since we were—together on the alternate earth."

Ever since they'd made love, he meant. It shouldn't hurt her that he couldn't say the words, but it did. Because she knew it wasn't just *saying* the words, it was feeling them. She cared about him, he cared about her energy.

"But while we were making love?" She tried to make the question light. "What then."

A smile lit his face. "It was a feast. Glorious. You have a great gift, Tia. The power of a million worshipers wrapped into one beautiful person. For me, it felt like being buoyed on the flood of a great healing river. Your manna swept everything before it and I felt stronger than I've felt for many hundreds of years."

She'd only taken a few bites of her curry, but abruptly her hunger vanished.

Or rather, she hungered for Ewan rather than for anything as mundane as food.

"You're going to need manna for tomorrow, aren't you?"

Ewan's gaze was completely expressionless. "It may not be so bad. Perhaps Iconic will, as your poker players say, 'throw in its hand.'"

That wasn't a lie, of course. He'd said perhaps. As in, perhaps world peace would break out, cancer would be cured, and all the cattle in the feedlots back home in Nebraska would print up picket signs and go on strike. None were technically impossible. Betting on any was a shot so long she couldn't begin to calculate the odds. Which Ewan knew as well as she did. Iconic would go forward unless someone stopped them.

She swallowed, then looked at her hands. "If I made love to you again, it would give you the manna you need."

Ewan froze with surprise for the second time in that brief conversation.

"Did you say—"

She didn't stop to think, forcing herself to meet his gaze. "Let's make love again. You need to be strong before you face the enemy."

She wished the desire so clearly written across his face were desire for *her* as a female, as a woman, rather than merely a hunger for the manna she offered him. She wished she didn't feel cheap, like a whore selling her body for money. But wishes were cheap and had a limited impact on what really was. Win or lose against Iconic tomorrow, they only had a couple of days before the Roman gods collected and Ewan vanished. She would settle for what Ewan could give, rather than holding out for the impossible.

"You've tried to worship me, haven't you? I've felt you straining to send me manna. It hasn't worked despite all of your attempts, and certainly despite my desperate need. Why would sex be any different?"

Because I love you, idiot. There was no way she could humiliate herself by saying those words out loud.

"What can it hurt to try?" She asked her question as if it were merely a rhetorical device, with the implication that it surely couldn't really hurt anything.

But trying would hurt, whether it worked or not. It would hurt her like the devil when Ewan consumed what he needed—and then moved on.

The time she'd spent with Lori had persuaded her of one thing, though. She was going to hurt no matter what. She might as well get some joy out of their relationship while she could. Besides, Ewan needed her manna and this was one way she felt certain she could give it to him.

* * * *

Tia was a churning mass of frustration, anger and sexual desire. So much so that it hurt Ewan to look at her. Her emotions tangled with her manna, turning the flood into something that both tantalized and tortured him, while remaining completely outside his reach.

She was right about one thing, though. He needed the manna only Tia could give him. Needed it so horribly his knees quivered across a million-million dimensions at the thought of receiving her avalanche of power and desire.

If he'd been sane, if he'd been himself, if he'd had any power at all, he would have said no. Sex between them had turned him inside out, had twisted things until her manna ripped at him rather than strengthening her. More sex might make things worse, might turn her into the human equivalent of one of Iconic's manna sumps. But he had no power, was walking to certain annihilation if he faced Iconic without it. He couldn't afford to turn down a chance, however slight, that something might reverse what had happened.

Logic said to go forward but he realized that this was only *his* logic. What about Tia? He knew he had hurt her, although he couldn't understand how. He didn't mind taking a chance on himself—he'd survived for thousands of years. But did he dare take a chance on destroying Tia completely?

"First you need to tell me why—"

His thoughts had been marshaled, the words lined up and ready to say, but then Tia stood, leaned across the table, and kissed him.

His words and thoughts grew muddled.

Badly muddled.

Her manna hit him just as her lips did. Sweet manna, not the bitter power that had eaten at him like a corrosive acid. Intoxicating manna was the strongest drug.

The double-sensation of her physical touch and that mental-psychic force of hers pushed him from the realm of thought to that of absolute sensation.

He caught her in his arms and dimension-twisted. Not to that tropical world but to N-dimensional space—to his home.

Tia struggled for a moment when she realized where she was, but he'd given some thought to her distress when they'd been there earlier and come up with a solution.

He filled her bloodstream with oxygen, giving her the ability to filter it from the N-dimensional aether. Tia could now survive here, for at least a while.

And he wanted her there with him.

She relaxed, leaned against him, and kissed him harder.

In the three-dimensional world of Tia's ordinary human senses, he was limited in the ways he could reach and touch her. In his own space, his entire body could touch hers, bring her the sensation she craved, and that he so desperately needed.

She wouldn't be able to do the same to him, of course. Not fully. He didn't mind that. Her manna was a more precious gift than anything he could give her.

But he wanted to give her everything.

He grasped the trickle of manna that started flowing the moment she kissed him and sent it raging into his hands, bringing them to a safe temperature before dissolving the gloves he'd worn on Earth whenever he wasn't healing.

She deepened her kiss and the river of manna swelled like a mountain stream after a downpour.

Surrounded by manna, it almost seemed that Tia could use all of the dimensions available in the field of the gods, as if he were making love not to a human female alone, but to the kind of soulmate few gods even bother imagining.

Ewan needed more. He grasped her bottom, pulling her more tightly against his body as he continued the kiss.

Her clothing simply didn't get in the way once they were in N-dimensional space. He could reach around it, touching her wherever he pleased, wherever would bring her pleasure.

She shuddered as he caressed her bottom, sliding his thumb down the cleft below her hips, brushing close to her core.

Her knees shook and he transformed gravity letting the aether as well as the ground support her, taking the pressure off of her and letting her savor the sensations as he savored them, without concern for mundane details of three-dimensional physics. Falling became impossible.

"It seems different here." Tia's words and their kiss existed simultaneously under the weird rules of this reality. "Do you know that I can see both your front and your back?"

"I didn't dream a human could see things as they really are," he admitted, "but you must be doing that. In N-space, ordinary three-dimensional directions are meaningless."

"And I can talk. I haven't been able to talk here before."

"Can I give you the tour later?" He was happy that his efforts had succeeded, that she could survive comfortably in his native environment, but his purpose in doing so was not as a science experiment, but to allow both of them to experience lovemaking in its full power. Just as each dimension added a root power to hyper-volume, so, each dimension would multiply the impact of sex. Three-dimensional sex could be wonderful. N-dimensional sex was the precious plaything of the divine.

He'd never brought a human woman here before Tia. Sex with women had been more about overwhelming *their* bodies, and he could do that well enough in the limited dimensions of Earth. For Tia, he wanted more. He wanted both to give and take a level of sensation that was reserved to the gods alone.

For all the thousands of years he'd been self-aware, and notwithstanding the temple priestesses and other women he'd had sex with, he was about to experience something he'd never tried, never even considered.

His body trembled across all of the billions of dimensions in anticipation and pure desire. He wanted this, hungered for this, *needed* this—although he'd never needed anything in the thousands of years of his existence.

* * * *

Ewan had been holding back before, Tia realized.

Their earlier lovemaking had been so overwhelming that she found it hard to believe, but it was true. He'd been holding back when he'd taken her to that otherworld beach. There he'd been fulfilling her fantasies rather than his own.

Now, at what was almost certainly the end of their time together, he was finally opening up. He'd taken her to his universe. With every touch, she learned more about herself, about him, and about the way love could be. Or at least, how love could be when you loved a god.

Hunger

She'd seen those statues of Indian gods with their dozens of arms and hands and thought them odd, maybe even silly. Now, though, they made sense as three-dimensional representations of N-dimensional reality. Because in N-space, Ewan wasn't limited to touching her in just one place.

She hadn't undressed, but her clothing simply seemed to be in a different world, not getting in Ewan's way when he decided to touch her. Which he did.

A lot.

Simultaneously, his hands were on her breasts, her hips, her thighs. In a single moment, his lips met hers in a kiss, laved her nipples until they stood in points as rigid as any soldier at attention, and explored the folds at the apex of her thighs.

She ran her fingers down his chest discovering that his clothes, too, had conveniently vanished from the equation. In all of the dimensions, his clothes retreated to only three.

Ewan was far too lean, his skin flayed over chords of muscle. But he was incredibly sexy to her, strong, capable, and more male than anything her wildest fantasies could have envisioned.

Her knees turned to jelly and she would have fallen if the weird air-analog hadn't buoyed her. She barely gave that a thought—with so much happening, she could only concentrate on sensation, on pleasure. Merely human logic had no place in Ewan's universe.

She slid her hands further his body, floating over his flat nipples, past his ribs, across the rigid muscles of his stomach, down to where his erection jutted.

She'd taken him before, but she still quivered in response to his size, his hardness. Anticipation and desire battled the fear of physical pain and the certainty that she was stepping of a precipice and that nothing could prevent her fall. Then there was the issue of putting all of that inside of her.

Ewan shuddered as she stroked him. Slowly, but as inexorably as a massive hurricane, he pressed his entire body near, to, and into, her.

In N-space, his body surrounded her, caressing her everywhere. His erection strained against her hands, but also pressed against her stomach, her hips, her bottom and most especially her womb.

Being surrounded by a *man* would have been frightening, claustrophobic. Being surrounded by a *god* was warm, even freeing. Oddly, although all of her was held and surrounded by him, all of her also remained unconfined, free.

Abruptly, she needed to surround him as he surrounded her. Not encompassing him in some N-dimensional game, though. Rather, she craved the ancient, eternal way a woman engulfs a man and brings him inside of her.

Her feet seemed grounded, but no weight descended to them. She could relax entirely without fear of physically falling, without the need to lie down.

With every touch, every one of those millions of contact of his hands, his lips, his erection against her body, heat rushed through her. Her muscles transformed to mush so she couldn't have stood without the weird things Ewan had done to their gravity. Her center became a liquid ball of pure need.

Warmth radiated from her into Ewan, and his beautiful body glowed as he received it. He reflected it back, multiplying her desire as it did so.

"Make love to me," she demanded.

"Yes." She *heard* his answer with her tastebuds as much as with her ears.

One of his long slender finger touched her core, readied her lips for his entry. And then he was inside of her. Or rather, he was becoming inside of her. Entering wasn't the word at all because he was simultaneously without, within, and through. She lacked words.

Rather than name her feelings, Tia leaned back, found support in what passed for air in his weird universe, and savored pure sensation.

Ten-thousand hands caressed every part of her body. His thumb caressed her clitoris, two more thumbs tweaked her nipples, forcing them to ever-harder points, one hand slid along her bottom, teasing it with sensation.

When he moved, awareness exploded. For an eternity of bliss, her senses merged, each sensation feeding on the last. His lips caressed her toes and she quivered with pleasure. He licked her clitoris and chills raced up her spine. His erection filled her core and she teetered instantly and completely at the brink of orgasm.

Then he kissed her lips as simultaneously his teeth bit ever so tenderly into the soft curve where her neck met her shoulders.

Her hips spasmed as he withdrew, and she wrapped her arms around him to pull him back. But he wasn't leaving, only finding that tidal rhythm of thrust and withdrawal that turned pleasure and tingles into tsunami of erotic need. She shut her eyes, but nothing diminished the blinding flavor of color that flowed from her body and poured back, reflected from Ewan, then flooded from her once again, transformed and heightened. With every turn it became more powerful until she felt that her whole body had engaged in a conflagration larger than the largest grassfire that had ever raged across the Nebraska plains of home.

Time lost meaning.

She'd read that cliché, but had never really grasped that time was merely another dimension, another way of seeing the world. In Ewan's universe imminent/now/forever/eternity collapsed into a singularity of fire and pleasure. A thousand years passed in a single breath. Her body's shiver lasted a fraction of a second—and forever.

She pulled Ewan even more deeply into her as she fell off the edge of the universe into an orgasm that wasn't mind-blowing so much as it was universe-creating.

It seemed, she realized as thought became possible once more even in the midst of her body's convulsions, that they shared more than pleasure. Their hearts found a shared beat, a hard pounding that echoed through the universe. Ewan's ichor mixed with own blood as it ran through Tia's veins, and her blood in his. His thoughts, his memories of ancient times and of days of glory, mingled with her own.

She tottered over the edge of another orgasm, one that went so far beyond her experience that she wondered if she could ever recover, questioned whether

her mundane life would be worth living after having experienced the ultimate.

She sighed, then, prepared for him to withdraw and to return to the ordinary world. Impossibly, though, Ewan upped his tempo.

As he continued thrusting into her, building to his own orgasm, her body achieved a new level of sensation. It caught fire; orange and blue sparks flared from her into the eternal now of Ewan's universe.

With each thrust, each moment of time and space, Ewan filled. His face grew less haggard. His muscles remained hard and cut, but they seemed less flayed and more solid. And he glowed, sending light through the piece of the multidimensional universe they alone inhabited.

This is for Ewan, she assured herself. She knew better than to expect to achieve higher levels of sensation than when she'd climaxed herself. She knew better, but it happened anyway.

Finally, just as she realized that Ewan could continue until her own body was a small pile of charred ashes hanging between the stars in N-dimensional space, he climaxed.

His spasm of pleasure pushed her over the edge once again, into an unreality of pleasure, where pure feeling flowed around her like a racing glacier, overwhelming her and threatening to engulf her into something other than herself. She clawed at his back as he shouted out his own pleasure, trying to surround all of him as she surrounded his erection, as his god-body surrounded her.

What she achieved was nothing so simple as one more orgasm. Instead, the first mind-blowing orgasm simply continued to throb, grow more intense, throughout their lovemaking. This transcended any meaning of completion she'd ever even guessed at, wrapping her in bliss so intense she knew why humans had both yearned for and feared, in those ancient legends of making love to the gods.

It lasted a million years.

Then Ewan kissed her on the lips again, before, finally, pulling back to look at her.

For the first time since she'd seen him in the homeless kitchen, the barest hint of warmth glowed within his midnight-sky-black eyes.

She sighed for her loss of innocence as well as for the experience.

She could never again be the person she had been. She had experienced something not meant for mere humans. She had eaten from the tree of the knowledge of good and evil. Like Buddha in her Comparative Religion class, she'd transcended the order of the universe, its dharma.

Weirdly, and without Ewan saying a word, she knew she faced a choice. He'd prepared her for this. He'd changed her so she could breathe what passed as air. She could draw sustenance from it. She could stay in this god-universe, surrounded in this eternal moment, protected from anything Iconic or the other gods might do by the transformative power she and Ewan had summoned. By transcending the mortal world she could remain here, seemingly with Ewan because for her, the moment would be eternal, making it eternal for some aspect of him as well. A billion subjective years could pass and she would still be here, still savoring a type of pleasure that could never grow old.

Time hadn't lost meaning so much as it had lost relevance. Just as her earlier six-hour episode of lovemaking had translated into only ten minutes for Marti and Lori, so she knew that she could simply delve ever-deeper into this fraction of a second, turning the single vibration of a watch crystal into an eternity of fire and ice, pleasure and sensation.

The temptation to stay and continue to savor the bliss of divine lovemaking tore at her like a tiger's claws.

Ewan would be grateful that she was safe when went to confront Iconic—and he would go, even though he would seem to stay. As a god, he could live in the moment and also respect the river of time.

This was his gift to her—what anyone would admit was a more than complete repayment for the manna she'd given him—manna she had no particular use for anyway and spun out like chaff from a combine back home.

Her friends would call her crazy if she turned away from Ewan's gift.

Lord how she wished she could hold onto that one perfect moment.

So she did. For one more moment, one more brief eternity, she savored it.

But even while it remained perfect, sorrow touched that moment.

Even while clinging to the pleasure, she knew she had to return.

Possibly their lovemaking had changed nothing. Possibly she would still be poison to Ewan once they returned. But she had been able to give him just a little strength before. Surely she could do that again. That small increment was unlikely to make a difference against the destructive nihilism of Iconic, but unlikely was not the same as impossible. If there were anything she could do, no matter what it cost her, she would do it.

Big Red, his friends, and the religious leaders they'd assembled had risked everything. She could do no less. Ewan might need her help.

She savored Ewan's touch for another eternal moment, kissed the god on his mouth and inhaled his scent for what she was certain would be the last time, ever. "We have to go back."

Chapter 20

Winsor was gone.

Ewan used his N-dimensional sight to view the past and shook his head when he saw how the security chief had managed his escape.

He'd known that Winsor was a snake, but the man still surprised him. He'd shaken off handcuffs, picked a lock that should have been completely inaccessible to him, subverted one of the choir actresses who shouldn't have been within miles of the abandoned theater, and then stolen Joe-Hill's Volvo to make his escape.

"With Winsor free, they'll be prepared for us," Joe-Hill said. "Nobody told him, but he probably knows we've figured out their location. For sure he knows we're holding his scientists. He can figure out what that means. I was responsible for keeping him captive and I failed."

"Oh, babe." Lori stroked Joe-Hill's face, the contrast between her dark skin and his pale flesh sharp.

Big Red's laugh wasn't completely convincing. "They already knew we're coming. People will talk. Think of all those priests and ministers we talked to. Not all of them believed me. Some of them probably contacted Iconic for confirmation. They know we're coming and they'll know when we're coming, too."

"But Winsor is a murderer. He's the one who came closest to stopping Ewan." Joe-Hill looked from person to person without much hope. "We can cancel. That way, fewer people get hurt."

"*You* should cancel." Ewan let his power seep into his voice. "I've depended on you for too long already. I am a god. I will go in alone."

For the first time since he'd returned, Ewan had power. Not just cheap trick power like turning newspaper into diamond or summoning a chain saw, but the kind of power that can shake the earth. Manna radiated through him as it hadn't for two thousand of year. He could, once again, pull lightning from the skies or turn a trickling stream into a flood that would make Noah salute.

Beside him, Tia glowed with sexual satisfaction. Since they weren't making love any longer, most of her manna had redirected toward the God who centered her faith, but she spared him her spillover once again. Beyond his hope, she was no longer poison to him.

He could handle Iconic. Then he could begin to make plans to handle the Roman Gods. Maybe survival wasn't impossible after all. Perhaps his oldest, fondest dreams of carving out a place for himself, of being worshiped not just by thousands but by tens of millions, might finally be attained.

"I guess you were too busy in god-school to get the message," Big Red said, "but no man can stand alone. We need to work with each other."

"I am no man."

"We're doing this together," Tia echoed.

Ewan didn't like it.

"Why put yourself in danger?"

"Stop arguing, Ewan. You shook my hand, you made the deal, and god's don't lie, remember. We're partners."

Once again, clever humans wanted to manipulate him. Yes, he'd agreed to partners. But he hadn't meant this.

They would slow him down. Protecting them would spread his power. Besides, he wanted them safe.

He would need to focus on Winsor like a child focusing the sun on a trapped cockroach. As Joe-Hill had said, Winsor was the danger. With him in charge of the Iconic defenses, danger multiplied.

"If I go alone—"

"Together," Tia repeated.

Ewan raged inside. Finally, though, he nodded. They deserved a chance to see this through to the end. While he would happily have let them walk away, he couldn't deny them what they'd earned by working with him. There was no safety in that path, but what safety is there in any human path—where even the most healthy can barely live a hundred years?

Their chances of success were small, but their best chance came if they consolidated their forces. Perhaps they could help. It was even vaguely possible that the faith of dozens of devout would create a manna blanket that could confuse the electronic detectors Iconic deployed as it had done in their theater. Winsor hadn't been back for long. Ewan just had to hope he couldn't implement new defenses based on what he'd learned. Not too many, anyway.

He still hated putting his friends at risk.

"Right. Let's roll," Big Red ordered, not letting Ewan rethink his decision.

With Joe-Hill's Volvo missing in action, they went with his backup car, an ancient Volkswagen van that still sported the peace signs, painted daisies, and 'Ban the Bomb' stickers of an earlier era.

A winter storm had hit during the night while he and Tia had explored their passion, and New York's snowplows had not yet made it into the Bronx neighborhood that they'd made home.

Joe-Hill's lightweight van fishtailed as its tiny engine putt-putted it through empty streets covered by a blanket of soft snow.

A group of the homeless looked up from a garbage can fire as the van passed. A pair of them waved the peace sign 'V.'

Big Red waved back, completely in his element.

Ewan spent a little of his manna holding the van's tires on the slick roads as they navigated through narrow streets, heading steadily south.

Tia smiled and fed him more.

The winter cold grew more intense as they left the artificial warmth of the city and headed into the relatively open spaces of New Jersey.

Even with the van's inadequate heater blowing as hard as it could, the humans in their small group shivered with cold, their breath steaming in the vehicle's interior.

Joe-Hill, who was driving, pulled a rag from under his seat and handed it to

Lori sitting beside him. Repeatedly, she wiped down the windows, but it steamed up almost as quickly as she could clean it as the moisture from five breathing humans collided with the icy cold of outdoors.

It didn't feel especially cold to Ewan. He'd clothed himself in the black pants, white shirt, and long black coat he'd shaped when he'd first met Tia, but he'd done so for convenience rather than because he needed any protection from the weather. Compared to the cold of the vast emptiness between the stars, a chilly mid-Atlantic day was positively balmy.

As they approached Iconic's lab, a different kind of cold penetrated even him.

The faith and prayers of all the billions of humans create a manna field that circles the globe, penetrates the darkest spaces, and fills every vacuum with a kind of background radiation that warmed, even if it didn't sustain.

Like the atmosphere itself, manna was simply everywhere. That universal manna field provided a part of the framework in which a god operates. Just as humans depended on the air to breathe, so a god depended on the background level of manna to sustain his existence.

Here, a huge gap ripped through that universal manna field.

Whether intentionally or as a side effect of their experiments, Iconic's machines created a hole of emptiness where manna should exist.

Which should have been impossible. Even a god can't consume <u>all</u> of the manna in an area. More manna would rush in from the surrounding areas, refilling any void created by the Iconic experiments. But it hadn't happened.

That emptiness was too much danger for the others. But Tia just stared at him when he suggested he would explore on his own.

A small herd of church vans sat, engines running, in front of the convenience store they'd set as their rendezvous.

Big Red ignored the cold and dragged Ewan out of the van to make the rounds. He gripped hands and pounding shoulders of the older men and politely introducing himself to the younger men and women.

One skinny minister welcomed Tia and introduced himself to Ewan as Rev. Thruston from the church that sponsored the homeless shelter. While he and Big Red didn't agree on every scriptural interpretation, it turned out that Big Red had encouraged Thruston to open the shelter in the first place.

The ministers and their flocks sipped on jumbo-sized cups of coffee from the convenience store, talked softly, and glowed with the power of their faith.

Big Red demonstrated one of the hyperbolic dishes the technicians had used on Ewan, showing that its purpose was to drain the power of faith out of its victim.

A few seemed horrified, but most merely nodded their heads and blew on their coffee. They had heard Big Red's stories, didn't need physical evidence to back up the words of a man they trusted.

Big Red's radical buddies straggled in over the next half-hour. Unlike the clean Ford and GMC vans used by the church groups, their vehicles reflected a broad range of income—Mercedes Benz SUVs mixed with Harley Davidson motorcycles, an ancient International Harvester pickup truck, and a pair of home-converted electrical cars.

The antipathy between those in the church vans and those in the hodgepodge of vehicles surprised Ewan until he remembered that humans create fear and hate out of small differences. Big Red was a member of both groups, of course. But although both felt separated from the mainstream, each was fiercely protective of their rights and freedoms.

Ewan's insight saw mostly similarities despite their different cars and different clothing. As he'd told Tia so long before, clothing wasn't something a god noticed first.

All burned with the fervor of their faith, the certainty of their rightness in the face of a world that doubted everything, rejected so many of their goals. All believed in creating a better world, in pursuing the goals of peace, in helping those who were less fortunate, who needed a hand. Yet they lacked a language that would let them communicate their shared wishes.

He could, Ewan thought, bridge that gap. These two groups could be the basis of his new way.

Even as the thought presented itself, though, he couldn't take it seriously. Iconic was strong—stronger than he'd imagined. They'd prepared themselves to harness gods far more powerful than he—even now that he was reinforced with Tia's power. And the Roman gods still waited, impatiently, for manna he'd bled out over the fields of N-space.

He wouldn't give up on his dream—no god could. But he had to face the odds against it—odds even control over the quantum state could do little to change.

Big Red dealt with the differences by pretending they didn't exist. By simply assuming that the two groups could work together for what was so clearly a shared goal, he shamed them into going along with his plan as they'd already agreed.

* * * *

When she'd been in her early teens, Tia had gone to a Moody Blues concert. It had seemed then that many of the fans must have pulled themselves out of museums. You just didn't see people who dressed like that, who talked like that, who consumed drugs like that on the streets of the Omaha.

The aging radicals that Big Red had assembled must have dug themselves from the same secret closet of America.

Although several people from the church vans rolled their eyes, most paid attention as a couple of silver-haired women, tie-died shirts worn over thick layers of thermal underwear, proceeded to give a quick lesson to the church members on how to stay together, what to do if the enemy used dogs, guns, or tear gas against them.

The church members stared, their mouths gaping, but they lapped up the knowledge.

Tia almost lost track of Ewan during the briefings, but she checked on him when she could, and did her best to pulse him manna with every heartbeat.

He looked pale, which was strange because he'd been pumped full of energy and strength when they'd left New York.

It seemed as if the lecture could go on for a while, so she angled toward the god, anxious to check on him firsthand.

Before she got to Ewan, though, Big Red glanced at his watch and announced it was time to move.

Everyone climbed back into their vehicles and the motley caravan headed the few blocks to the Iconic campus.

"I'm okay," Ewan said.

Maybe he couldn't lie to her, but he managed to lie to himself. She wasn't reassured.

Even if she had been, the first look at the Iconic campus would have ended any positive feelings.

Seeing the laboratory facilities on GoogleEarth and in the computer aided design program hadn't prepared her for its reality. It was a gash of brown mud and black glass, cut into clean snow, an ugly brooding evil in the midst of bucolic central New Jersey.

Around the campus, a berm of brown dirt was piled twenty feet tall, then topped with rounded spirals of razor wire. Somehow the snow, which lay thick on the ground outside the berm, had melted off the berm itself, exposing the naked earth.

Not even a weed poked out of the dead soil. A low-pitched hum and the distinct scent of ozone told her that the fence was electrified.

For perhaps a quarter of a mile outside the campus itself, every tree had been cut, leaving a ring of stumps amongst the snow and mud.

Inside the berm, several small office buildings were dwarfed by a large skyscraper, covered with black glass, climbed perhaps ten stories above the trees.

A pair of vultures, wings almost perfectly still, circled the building, intent on something going on below them—something that Tia couldn't see.

Security personnel, armed with submachine guns and mini-black hole weapons, crowded into a large guardhouse near the campus's single entrance. More guards walked the top of the berms, their growling dogs straining at leashes.

"Is it too late to say I've got a bad feeling about this?" Lori clutched Tia's hand as the two women climbed out of their van and faced what could only be called a fortress.

"Way too late."

The entire team would have shut down in panic if Big Red hadn't given them assignments. As it was, everyone but Ewan, Big Red, and a couple of drivers grasped protest signs and edged nearer the gate holding their signs in front of them as if the thin cardboard could ward off dogs and bullets.

Their arrival caused a brief stir of movement within the guardhouse and, moments later, a black Hummer pulled into view from somewhere within the complex.

A muscle-bound guard climbed from the drivers seat, stepped around the militaristic vehicle, and opened the door.

Winsor emerged. His wounds had healed faster than Tia would have guessed possible and he looked strong and confident. The security chief wore camouflage, packed one of the black hole weapons in a holster at his belt and held a portable electric megaphone in his hand. He grinned when he saw them, pointed to his watch and nodded as if to let them know they were right on schedule. On his schedule.

The stomp of his booted feet on snowless concrete broke the silence.

He strode to the gate, signaled for the guards inside the guardhouse to open it, then motioned to his minions who assembled behind him in a tight phalanx.

He glared at Big Red's team silently for a good minute as the electric door slid open. With every passing second, Tia felt the intimidation he projected grow, spreading through the group.

Big Red must have felt it as well. He launched into a hymn that everyone would know. *Amazing Grace.*

Winsor sustained his glare for a few more seconds, but one by one their mixed group picked up the hymn, using its powerful message to reassure themselves. Even the aging radicals knew the old hymn, and their voices added harmony to the simple melody.

Finally the security chief gave up on his glare and thumbed on his megaphone. "You are trespassing on private property and have breached a government-regulated security zone. I have notified the New Jersey State Police and the Department of Homeland Security. They are dispatching officers and agents to apprehend you. If you fail to disperse immediately, you will be arrested and held without trial or bond."

Tia expected Big Red to respond but Rev. Thruston beat him to the punch. "Our faith belongs to God, not to any particular company or even to the government. When you attempt to steal it from us, you give up any right to protection by the law."

"I doubt that the DHS will agree with your legal reasoning, Father." Winsor turned and grinned at the group of security guards behind him. "Since the government types are a little slow in arriving, let's show our visitors the treat we put together for them."

He switched off his megaphone and there was a moment of silence, broken only by the whisper of cloth against cloth as their mixed group of perhaps ten radicals and fifty of the faith looked around.

Tia opened her mouth to start the next chorus of <u>Amazing Grace</u>, but snapped it shut when Winsor and his phalanx of guards stepped back rather than forward, opening a path to the protestors.

The sound of the dogs split the silence like a sword through silk.

Big dogs, German shepherds, Rottweilers, Doberman pincers, more than a dozen in all, snarled and barked as they strained at their leashes, yanking their attendants through the mud and slush.

In contrast to Winsor in his camouflage, the guards wore black and looked like nothing so much as Nazi storm troopers.

Tia and the church group swayed back from the onrushing canines. The aging radicals had confronted dogs before. In a synchronized motion, they flipped their protest signs over to present the approaching animals a row of sharpened wood stakes.

Tia suspected they were making a horrible mistake. Those animals didn't look intimidated and looked as if they'd been trained to hunt humans. A human with a stick might be able to defend himself against a single dog. Doing so against a pack—and against their armed masters? Not happening.

Ewan had been quiet, waiting, surrounded by a group of the faithful. His thinking must have tracked Tia's though, because he *twisted* and abruptly stood between the dogs and the waiting protestors.

From how he'd explained the way he controlled quantum probabilities, working magic like that in front of everyone had to be draining.

She tried to send a bit more manna his way and he half-turned and gave her a wave.

On some signal Tia missed, the guards simultaneously dropped their leashes and the dogs, who had been straining against them trying to get at the small group outside the gates, leapt toward Ewan.

Tia covered her eyes with her hands but couldn't help peeking through the gaps between her fingers.

Ewan stood perfectly still as the dogs approached. Then, when it seemed that they would bowl over him like a hurricane washing away a child's sandcastle, he raised one hand in the gesture policemen use to halt traffic.

The growls and barking from the dogs instantly became a series of high-pitched yaps. They fawned around Ewan like puppies who'd come across a long-lost parent.

For an instant, through some time-lapsed memory of Ewan's N-dimensional space, Tia saw Ewan through the dog's eyes. The god was larger than life, glowing brightly in a world that seemed to consist more of grays than of colors. His scent, that familiar wonderful mountain-forest scent, raised ancestral memories. Memories of hunting with their humans across lands teaming with aurochs, mammoths, and bears.

From the fairy tales she'd loved as a child, Tia recognized him in that guise. He had taken on the aspect of a nature god. To the dogs, Ewan must have seemed to be something like ancient Arawn, the Celtic deity who controlled the wild hunt.

For the first time, Tia wondered about his name—Ewan and Arawn sound somewhat alike. Could he be related, another path, taken by *that* frightening god of Celtic myth—a god who had taken the step Ewan had refused—becoming god of death?

A string of curses from the former dog handlers did nothing to return the dogs to their original duties. They formed around Ewan like a boxer's entourage, growling at every attempt to recall them.

Winsor raised his megaphone. "Most amusing, godling. I had thought to send the men in with nightsticks next, but since you've subverted the dogs, perhaps we'll move directly to more extreme measures."

"Pray," Rev. Thruston shouted. "Evil can never defeat the power of the Lord."

"Evil?" Winsor shook his head sadly. "We're no more evil than those who first built windmills to harness the energy of the winds. Back then, fools believed that those winds were gods and called millers evil. Now we know better. Only vampires like this being who's fooled you into worshipping him will lose if we harness our own power to benefit mankind."

He sounded so reasonable, Tia feared he would succeed in splitting their group. Indeed, several of the faithful turned to Big Red, questions on their faces.

Big Red just laughed. "So, now we are to render onto Caesar that which belongs to God? I think not, brothers and sisters."

Winsor shook his head in mock sympathy. "I had hoped to spare you. Oh, well." He paused for just a moment. Then, "Kill them all."

* * * *

It was too easy, Ewan thought. There had to be more.

Winsor seemed baffled by what had happened to his dogs, and had jumped several levels in what he'd apparently planned as a systematic attempt to demoralize Ewan's followers. Of course, he didn't know they weren't followers. He probably thought Ewan was the recipient of all the faith they generated.

Ewan squandered a bit of the manna Tia had showered on him while they'd made love. He countered the laws of entropy in the tiny area of the explosive shells within the guards' submachine guns, creating tiny regions of cold by shifting all heat out of the cartridge primer.

Triggers slammed into shells Ewan had chilled to the temperature of liquid helium, and the cartridges shattered rather than firing.

Tia was the first to grasp what had happened, and she rose to the occasion, as Ewan had known she would. Her laughter pierced the silence that followed the tinkle of collapsing metal. The dogs listened, their ears perking at the rich sound of joy where everyone had expected death. Moments after Tia reacted, the dogs broke into baying that sounded as if they were adding their laughter to hers.

Winsor sputtered, then turned and climbed back into his Hummer, driving back toward the ugly black building that jutted like a single rotting tooth in a sea of mud.

Without him, the guards retreated. The gate, which Winsor had opened to let the dogs loose, growled and inched closed. The guards didn't dare attack again, but they weren't going to let anyone pass them either.

Ewan partially released the dogs from his control. They leapt toward their former masters, fully intent on paying back the cruelties that had been used to twist their nature until they had become weapons to be used against humans rather than the companions that thousands of years of breeding had shaped them into.

The guards, especially those who had led the dogs and who still carried leashes in their belts, hesitated but didn't break.

The hungriest part of Ewan wanted to let the dogs have their way. For the guards, this could be the wild hunt of a million nightmares.

He shook his head, compelling the dogs to retreat. Doing that would mean he'd taken the path *they* had taken when they'd perverted the animals. And *a hunt* could become *The Wild Hunt*. That was the path to becoming death-god.

The guards kept their black hole weapons trained at the gate. He wouldn't be entering that way.

They'd planned for this. "Take down a tower."

Big Red nodded and shouted out the commands.

A pair of the younger radicals, men in their thirties, carried a long chain up the berm.

Holding their chain with insulated gloves, they wrapped it around one of the manna-consuming devices that surrounded the campus, then hooked it to the largest of the church vans.

A bearded minister engaged the transmission in that four-wheel-drive vehicle and pressed down on the accelerator.

The engine strained, and the blue smoke of burning oil permeated the bitterly cold air. The tower trembled a little, but it seemed solidly planted.

This was bad.

The minister revved the engine, trying to get a harmonic going, but the van wasn't built for detail work and the engine howled its protests.

As long as that tower stood, Ewan might as well have stayed in New York.

He reached out a tendril of manna to change the probabilities, to enhance the tiny stress flaws that form a part of every metal

The instant his manna touched it, though, he was caught. Winsor had set another trap and Ewan had jumped into it.

The machine grasped the thread of manna he'd allowed to reach too near and pulled, ripping at the very heart of the manna gift Tia had given him.

He staggered, fought the urge to hold on and attempt to recover what he'd already lost. Instead, he managed to sever the connection just as that horrible grasp threatened to turn him inside out leaving him a dusty memory on this brutal winterscape.

He was alive, but he'd lost a lot—possibly too much.

In the vast vacuum Iconic had created around their campus, Ewan could find only a few sparks of usable energy. The manna from the faithful provided a hint of a field that he could operate within, but he couldn't access its power. Lori, with her hodgepodge of New Age beliefs, sent him a trickle. Then there was Tia. Across countless centuries, he'd never relied on any one human. Humans are fickle, as likely to turn on you as worship you. Only in the combined faith of vast numbers of believers is there safety. But Ewan had been forced to rely on Tia more and more during the weeks they'd spent together. Even when she'd been angry with him, denied him access to her manna, he'd depended on her to be there, to share her ideas, her plans and her vision of a world completely changed from the one where he'd once been a power. Now, he depended on her for his survival.

He sagged back against her now, physically as well as emotionally, trusting her to support his weight, to give him everything she could as he recovered from his horrible blunder.

A loud crack indicated that something had broken and he opened his eyes again, looking into N-dimensional space to see whether the church van or the steel pole had failed.

He wasn't certain whether his touch had weakened the pole before the machine had grabbed him or whether the minister had finally created the harmonic vibrations he'd sought.

Whether it was purely natural, or natural assisted by a bit of quantum manipulation, the tall pole and its deadly manna trap collapsed.

Ewan dared not use manna to guide it down safely. He was too weak even to shout out a warning. Instead, he took a chance to use the intimacy he and Tia had created while they made love. He spoke directly into her mind, giving her the words that were needed to have these people, his people whether they worshiped him or not, move to safety.

The direct touch of mind on mind had to startle her. The words, in a language of command that had already been ancient in those long-forgotten days when Ewan has first come into awareness, were completely alien to her. He wouldn't have blamed her if she'd frozen, if she'd backed away in horror.

But she didn't. She repeated Ewan's words of command in her husky, sexy voice.

Obeying programming that built into human DNA before the fall of Babel, during the long millennia when humans had lived closely with their gods, his adopted people responded instantly, scattering to safety even as the steel pole accelerated. Controlling physical bodies had always been easier than altering their mental state.

The pole crashed to the ground and the manna-eating machine at the top of it shattered. But no one was harmed.

Seeing what he'd done, Tia opened up. A bit more of her manna flowed into him—enough, perhaps, to let him move, to work tiny miracles. He leaned on her for an eternity that lasted only a fraction of a second but proved how weak he truly was and inhaled everything Tia had to give him, picked up the trickle from Lori, gathered what little manna he could from the faithful. It wasn't enough.

Unfortunately, it would have to do. Waiting would give Winsor more time to prepare. Ewan had already given Winsor and his Iconic security forces too long. He had to move now.

He launched himself through the hole in the campus manna-eating shield. Big Red, Joe-Hill, Marti, Lori, the radicals, the faithful, had done their part. It was up to Ewan to deliver.

Chapter 21

For a moment, Tia carried the weight of a mountain.

Something had happened to Ewan when Brother Jones had pulled down that manna machine on the wall. Something brutal.

The god had sagged against her then. Only locking her legs in place had kept her from collapsing beneath him.

His emaciated form could barely weigh anything but she'd seen the real Ewan, the Ewan who existed on so many dimensions her brain whirled even trying to imagine the number. And it felt as if she kept every one of those dimensions, those aspects of Ewan, from imploding.

Moments like this, far more than his magical tricks, reminded her Ewan was something different from human.

For the first time, the ancient story of Atlas holding the world on his back almost made sense. An N-dimensional god was so fully present in the universe that he could bear the entire three-dimensional earth's weight as easily as a child can carry a large balloon. But Tia was merely human. Supporting him should shatter every bone in her body.

Yet, she wouldn't deny him, no matter what it might cost. He knew her weakness. If he overtaxed her, it could only mean he had no choice. Which meant, she *had* to summon the strength to be his support.

Her had muscles trembled, her bones creaked, and her boot heels sank into the solid-frozen earth. It took every ounce of her strength to stay upright for the few seconds he leaned on her. But she held. Barely.

She felt Ewan's desperate reach as he grabbed all of the manna around him and she opened her soul to him. He wasn't her god. He could never be her man, but he was her lover, her love and she would withhold him nothing within her power to give. She would have done that even if he hadn't been fighting a battle that was as much hers as it was his own.

When he filled her mind with words, she'd trusted him, shouted them out, and watched without surprise as people who'd been frozen, like frogs hunted by a cobra, strolled calmly, purposefully to safety.

Then, abruptly, he was gone.

Ewan's weight had pushed her feet deep into the soil. So deep she had to reach down, unfasten her boots, and pull her feet out of them, leaving the boots behind.

Lori's feet were longer and more slender than Tia's, but they were close enough. Her roommate stripped off her own boots and handed them to Tia.

"You're going after him, aren't you?"

"I have to."

"I know. Please be careful."

Tia nodded. If this were happening in a movie, Lori would be cringing, telling the heroine to stay where it was safe. If Ewan couldn't handle whatever Winsor and his thugs threw at him, what could Tia do?

But this wasn't a movie. Tia was only a manna pump to him, but Ewan was Tia's one-special-guy. She intended to stay close, to feed him all the manna he could take.

"We'll keep the outer guards occupied," Big Red promised. "And if Winsor really did call the cops, we'll delay them as long as we can. Don't know what's inside, though."

She kissed her friends, slipped on Lori's boots, and headed up the steep berm.

The dog pack joined her, adopting her as mascot in the absence of their god.

Why not? In half of the world's cultures, the lord of the hunt had been female, rather than male. Tia was no goddess, but these were no hellhounds. She and the dogs would do the best they could.

The falling tower had dragged the razor-wire into the mud. Tia gave each dog a boost, then carefully climbed through the mess herself.

A couple of the guards, left behind when Winsor had headed back to the central building, headed her way as she clambered down the back side of the berm. The dogs chased them back into the guardhouse.

But they'd call Winsor, let him know she and the dogs were on their way. She shrugged. If he believed Ewan was with her, he might think he had more time than he did. Either way, she had to press on.

A stench got to her before she reached the lab.

She'd grown up in Nebraska, knew the smells of livestock and fattening yards. This, though, was the stink of a slaughterhouse. Still, she was shocked when she saw it.

She'd imagined Iconic as a movie-style lab, with gowned scientists and flashing computers.

Instead, blood, frozen like a convenience store Slurpee, covered the lab's courtyard entrance.

Black feathers and flapping wings gave a false impression of life as ravens ripped at sacrificed flesh.

The pair of formerly white calves didn't look big enough to have generated all the blood she saw, but they had certainly created some of it. Their entrails were strewn across the entryway to the lab. Anyone entering would have to walk on them.

Tia did her best to ignore both the sacrificial animals and the hungry birds. To her surprise, although the dogs were kept almost as close to starvation as Ewan had been, they didn't seem interested either.

She hesitated when she reached the massive bronze door.

When she'd walked into Travers's unguarded apartment, he hadn't been expecting her and she'd still barely escaped alive. The Iconic lab would be far better protected than his apartment had been, and Winsor far more deadly than Travers.

Still, she had made her choice. Whether he knew it or not, wanted her or not, Ewan needed her. Like an iPod and a battery, they were a team and needed to stay close together to function properly.

She pushed open the door.

* * * *

Ewan detested the vainglorious nature of wargods and deathgods who found joy in slaughter. Still, Ewan had been god of a warrior people. He'd led their armies, taught them the tactics they'd needed to survive against vastly more powerful enemies.

Although weapons had changed over the centuries, the basics of combat remain constant. A warrior must yield where the enemy is strong, pursue where he is weak.

Winsor hadn't expected that his outer defenses would be defeated so easily. He'd been flustered, frightened, and he'd run.

Ewan had to strike hard and fast, before Winsor regrouped and remembered his defenses.

As so many armies had discovered, though, esprit and tactics only went so far. Against a vastly more powerful enemy, they could only delay the inevitable. But Ewan had strengths of his own. Winsor dreamed of becoming god-like, but Ewan was a god. The odds were bad, but a long-shot was more than he'd have if he let Winsor organize and come against him.

He'd ignored the white bullocks lay in front of the building, but he couldn't ignore the blood of thousands of sacrifices over years.

Using blood as ink, and their fingers as pens, Iconic's priest-scientists warded the building's door and glass walls.

Egyptian hieroglyphics, Sumerian cuneiform, Futhark runes, and Hebrew script, all proclaimed the site protected.

Ewan laughed. Iconic had been too smart for their own good. Powered by the death-manna of so many hundred animals, those wards could have been formidable obstacles. But the very manna vacuum that left him weak had sucked the energy out of those sacrifices and spells until they carried no more power than would fingerpaint left by ignorant children.

He *twisted* through the door, studied Winsor's trail, then froze.

Tia was following.

Through their manna bond, he sensed her, felt her presence, tasted her emotions. Now, despite their agreement, despite the danger, despite the powers they faced, she was coming to share his danger because of some remote possibility she could help.

He'd command her to return to the safety provided by Big Red and the others, but knew how futile that would be. Unless he *compelled* her, she wouldn't obey. Forcing her to return to the cars would delay the inevitable but it would and make her angry, poisoning her manna.

He sighed. Neither logic nor persuasion would work on Tia. She never obeyed him--now would be no different.

A god *shouldn't* have to learn to accept what he cannot change. A god should be able to change *anything, everything*, create a world to his own liking. But the prerogatives of a god, at least of a god of a people long vanished into history, were dramatically limited in modern times.

Accepting the inevitable meant he could plan for Tia before she plunged herself into danger.

It took him painful seconds to trigger the traps Winsor had hidden around the entrance—traps against humans because humans can't help imagining that gods would be just like them.

Steel jaws of death slammed shut. Electrical charges carved dark scorch marks across the ceiling. Lasers shot blinding rays of light and superheated the air until it exploded into plasma. Poisoned gas sprayed from concealed tubes guarding the entrance.

All dissipated before Tia arrived.

Against a human, Iconic's dark lab would have been an impregnable fortress. But both physical and chemical traps are low-entropy states—innately loaded with potential energy waiting and anxious for release. It took only the slightest alteration in quantum probabilities to trigger those traps, to leave the pathway open and safe for Tia.

Still, every second, every erg of manna he used on the traps gave Winsor that much more time to prepare and stole from Ewan's resources.

Like a bolt of lightning from a cloud-free sky, it occurred to Ewan that he wouldn't especially care what happened to himself if Tia didn't make it. That realization rocked him back on his heels—across all N dimensions.

Humans were transitory. That was *the* fundamental reality of godhead.

Religious myths might be filled with stories of the capricious nature of gods, but these myths were told from the standpoint of humans who viewed their own lives as magically precious. Gods didn't have that luxury. They had to look after the *tribes* that worshiped them, not the wellbeing of particular *individuals*. They had to plan for *centuries* rather than for the immediate *present*. For a god, no mere human, no matter how special or faithful that individual might be, could be allowed to stand in the way of the greater plan. The god, and the tribe, could survive for millennia with each individual human could be only a flash in the pan—burning brightly for a moment, perhaps, but quickly vanishing into oblivion.

Tia had altered that perspective for him. Being with her had changed him in a fundamental way that he couldn't understand.

He did understand something important, though. He had to keep Tia alive. How he'd manage, he had no clue.

Ewan translated himself up through the ten floors of the lab, past dozens of researchers at their computers and their lab stations, past the empty desks of dozens more researchers—researchers who were probably waking up in New York to find that their temporary cells had been left open so they could make their way back to the questionable safety of Iconic, if there was anything to return to.

Ewan felt Winsor waited on the rooftop. It was there that he headed.

The rooftop was another trap, of course.

Black-coated security guards formed a ring around the rooftop, aiming dozens of black hole generators.

Ewan manifested himself anyway.

Winsor jerked when Ewan appeared. He stood at an altar wearing the costume of the high priest of the ancient Israelite faith. Ewan hadn't heard Ancient Hebrew in millennia, but Winsor's accent was better than passable.

He paused from chanting for just a moment. "You're finally here."

Ewan smiled.

The security chief plunged a stone knife into an albino goat kid, then pulled the young animal's entrails out and lifted them to the sky with gory hands, offering them to whatever hungry gods might wish to partake in the feast.

Manna machines mounted on light poles rising above the rooftop tore at Ewan, attempting to seize the thin tail of flow connecting him to Tia and the others he left behind.

The high-frequency radio signals from the manna machines slammed into his weakened manna shields—and splashed. He and Joe-Hill hadn't spent *all* of the previous day healing patients. They'd analyzed captured Iconic electronics and built a radio-powered device they hoped would harmlessly siphon those energies into N-dimensional space.

It worked.

He grinned at Winsor. "Wrong prayers to the wrong gods, loser."

A couple of drops of sweat on his forehead betrayed Winsor's perfect calm. "Your immunity won't help if I order the guards to shoot."

"True," Ewan admitted. "I admire the loyalty of your men. Imagine being ready to throw their own lives away in order to shoot me." He turned his voice toward the guards. "You aren't foolish enough to think my body will stop those projectiles, are you? They'll keep going, destroying everyone within a hundred yards. Get a decent crossfire going and we'll all die together."

The guards looked across the building and saw other guards pointing weapons at *them*. First one, then several, then all lowered their weapons.

Winsor looked startled to see that some of the guards had been pointing their weapons in *his* direction. The security chief might be big on sacrificing animals, but he wasn't interested in sacrificing himself.

Unfortunately, Winsor had his own black hole generator in a holster at his belt. The good news was, his hands were full of a flint knife and goat entrails.

With a quick bit of probability bending, Ewan might be able to change everything.

Ewan reached for Winsor's belt, planning on cutting it and sending the weapon plunging off the rooftop to the concrete walkway surrounding the building ten stories below. Instead, his thread of manna ran into that blank nothingness that Iconic's people cast in N-dimensional space. He and Joe-Hill had thought their device would nullify Iconic's shields. It didn't.

All around him, the manna machines heterodyned through multiple frequencies trying to overcome his bypass device.

Eventually, Ewan realized, they would succeed. Which put a very definite, and tragically short, time limit on this encounter. He had minutes, at most, to defeat Winsor and to destroy the technology that Iconic had developed in an attempt to use gods as energy resources.

From below, the rumble of an elevator motor warned him that the elements of the standoff were about to change. Tia was on her way.

If Winsor took Tia hostage, Ewan would be helpless. His only hope was that Winsor wouldn't believe a god could be so vulnerable. Winsor wouldn't risk himself for another. Surely he wouldn't believe Ewan would, either.

He forced himself to wait, probing through the probability fields for the key that would transform this situation.

* * * *

The elevator chimed to a stop at the fifth floor and the doors opened.

A couple of scientists, coffee-cups in hand, each took one step toward the open door, then froze as a dozen dogs snarled simultaneously.

"Uh, we'll catch the next elevator," one of them said

"A smarter plan would be to evacuate the building—now."

"Right, lady. Whatever you say."

The elevator doors whispered shut and the electric motor whined as it lifted the cargo of woman and canine toward Ewan.

Making love in N-space had created a psychic bond between herself and Ewan, a bond that let her flow manna to him, but also made her aware of his proximity even when he was out of sight. She sensed Ewan above her, felt his frustration that she was putting herself in danger, yet also caught his hunger, his need for manna, power she *should* be able to give him but somehow had never been able to deliver completely. Not even when they'd made love, although that had been when she'd come closest.

The elevator doors chimed a second time when they reached the rooftop. Ducking low in a protective gesture, she stepped out—and froze.

Two-dozen angry-looking men glared at her.

Blood and animal entrails dripped from Winsor's hands and his lips curved up into a smile.

"I believe that the equation has just changed, godling." He gestured to one of the guards who held a leash that had once been used to lead the dead baby goat to sacrifice. "Jack, please bring the woman to the altar. Without her manna, this energy vampire will lack the power to oppose us."

"But…"

"Just do it."

Jack looked at the snarling dogs, then at Winsor, clearly trying to decide which he feared more.

He made the wrong choice.

The pack swarmed from the elevator like wild wolves their ancestors had been.

Jack had managed only two steps toward her before he realized his mistake. Backing up was his last mistake.

His arms made big circles as the back of his knees hit the low ledge around the rooftop, but his effort was too little and too late.

He screamed all the way down.

Tia strolled to her lover as if there for a casual meeting. Her pack took their stations around them, snarling at any guard who made a move toward a weapon or toward the hunt.

Ewan reached out to draw her close to him, then ruffled the fur of one, or maybe all, of the dogs.

She couldn't worship Ewan, but she loved him. She called up every memory of their lovemaking, of Ewan saving her, of what he'd done for the city's poor. She let her love direct every scrap of manna she could mobilize to his assistance.

His eyes widened as she hit him with that flow. Around them, the dogs' fur stood on end. Blue sparks flew from their teeth when they barked and growled at the guards.

"Impressive," Winsor sneered. "You could have been a Queen among humans if you'd joined with me, helped me become a god among men. Instead, the scientists will scalpel your brain to uncover what makes you such a source of energy."

"Calm." She sent the word silently over her link to Ewan. "He's trying to rattle you."

"He's doing a hell of a job," Ewan's words were modulated over an emotion that Tia didn't recognize and couldn't comprehend.

"You've lost, Winsor," she said. "The dogs will tear the arms off any guard who moves for a weapon. With every second, I'm pumping more power into the god. Soon his lightning will scour you from this rooftop. But don't hide in the building—it is an abomination. It's seen too much death, too much blood to be washed clean by anything less than complete destruction."

"You've been listening to too many of that Communist's sermons," Winsor sneered. "This is a manna-free zone. The false god's powers cannot reach us."

He was talking to the guards, Tia realized. Lying to the guards.

She laughed. "Manna free? That's why you sacrificed that goat, is it? You were planning a barbeque up here? I don't think so. There's a hole in the shield straight overhead and lightning will come down it like water through a downspout."

"Jeez, boss," one of the guards said. "I'm getting an uncomfortable feeling about this."

One cue, Ewan raised a hand toward the sky.

A line of white fire descended from the heavens and terminated in his fist, glowing and pulsating in a display that would have horrified Tia if she hadn't trusted Ewan completely and absolutely.

He swelled visibly, exposing more of his N-dimensional self into the three-dimensional world of Earth.

Then he launched that lightning bolt—not at the humans surrounding him, but at the circle of satellite dishes on the rooftop.

The bolt flashed from dish to dish, overloading electronics and melting plastics, blasting metal into tiny shards of shrapnel. The bitter scent of ozone mixed with the growing stench of the guards' cold sweat.

One reached for his weapon—and was swarmed by four huge dogs. They pushed him toward the edge until he threw down his black hole generator.

With their teeth firmly clenched to his jacket and black uniform pants, the dogs kept the guard from following his weapon, but they'd made their point.

The other guards froze in place.

"Impressive," Winsor hissed, his eyes filled with greed. "Imagine that power being used for the benefit of mankind rather than selfishly hoarded for use by an energy vampire."

"For the benefit of mankind? Or for the benefit of one particular man?" Tia asked. "You are planning to become Emperor of Earth or something like that, aren't you?"

Winsor laughed. "Why shouldn't those who give so much to humankind enjoy some rewards? *I'm* not the monster here. The energy vampire is. And you may think you've won, but you're wrong. Bert, come here."

He shoved the dead goat off the alter, grasped the guard he'd called, ripped his stone knife through the man's throat, and lay his still-thrashing body where the goat had been.

"Help me now," he screamed at the winds. "Remember our bargain."

The sky opened.

That expression had always meant rain to Tia. But here, a black tunnel split the cloudless blue sky like a door to emptiness. A solid ray of solid darkness slanted downward, heading directly to the altar, toward the dying guard whose blood still gushed from the arteries in his neck.

A shape, humanoid but definitely not human, coalesced from the darkness, was the darkness.

The dogs cowered more closely around Ewan and Tia, whining, in protest as the shape reached into the dying body and ripped something invisible but horribly real from the sacrifice.

The dying guard flopped once, then sank within himself. Dying no longer, he was more completely dead than Tia had imagined a human could be.

This must be what Ewan had described as death manna. No wonder he'd resisted the temptation.

"Deliver," The shape spoke the single word in such a low note that it was barely within the range of human hearing, yet it reverberated through time and space. The building they stood on quaked with its power.

Ewan pulled himself erect, met the dark gaze. "We have a bargain. I have two days before I owe you the manna I borrowed."

The shape shook the helmet that should have been a head. "That agreement has been superseded. Deliver, or I will take it."

"I had a fallback position." Winsor's lips turned up into a grin.

"Idiot. You just saw what a bargain means to a death-god."

"Quite right. It means, <u>you're</u> finished."

Tia pressed herself more closely to Ewan's side, let her warmth heat him despite the bitterly cold wind this high off the ground. The dogs whimpered.

Even the hunt was cowed by the power of the death-god because the death-god owns the true Wild Hunt.

"Of all the gods in the pantheon, I would have guessed you to be the last to surrender your power to the humans," Ewan said to the dark shape. "I would think even a *Roman* death-god would have more pride than that."

The dark god, who could only be Pluto, laughed. The sound was a funeral dirge.

"I will not be their victim. My brothers and sisters will not be their victims. That role is reserved—for you."

Chapter 22

"Deliver," the death-god repeated.

Pluto reached a claw across N-dimensional space, grasping for Ewan's essence.

Not even a death-god can easily feast on the death-manna of another god. Not, that is, unless the god has opened himself to that attack. Which was part of the reason why divine sex could be scary. But Ewan *had* opened himself when he'd agreed to accept manna from the Roman gods. Pluto's demanding early repayment might not be fair, but gods had no judges they could appeal to. They took what their power allowed them to take. Filled with the strength from the death-manna of a human sacrifice, Pluto had the power to do whatever he wanted.

Pain seared at Ewan's chest as the death-god sought his heart.

Pluto's hand burned with the heat of the center of a star, obliterating everything it touched as completely as if they had never existed. Across all N dimensions, Ewan's body crawled away from the death-god's touch—and was nevertheless consumed.

"Run," Ewan urged Tia. "I can hold out for a few more seconds. Run and keep running. Make sure they never catch you."

"Bullshit. And don't even think about giving up."

"But…"

"Which of you guys are in line to be the next human sacrifice?" Tia shouted at the guards. "Hasn't it dawned on you that you're disposable? These things escalate. Next it'll be two deaths required. Any volunteers?"

Killing a goat had grossed out all but the most hardened of the security guards. Killing one of their own number had shocked them into immobility. They had been raised with the idea of team play and Winsor had broken a fundamental taboo when he'd casually attacked within the team. That act crossed so many lines, they didn't know how to handle it. Shocked or not, Ewan knew they wouldn't, couldn't turn on their boss and on the death-god.

"It's pointless. Run," he repeated.

The death-god brought both hands together inside Ewan's chest, reaching for his heart. When he ripped that out, he'd have all of Ewan's manna, and Ewan would simply disappear.

Like a candle in a room without oxygen, Ewan's manna guards flickered, weakened under the assault.

Pluto pressed deeper.

Pain threatened to consume him, but he wouldn't give up until Tia was safe. He needed to hold on to protect his people, people who had become something he had never had in all of the millennia of his existence—his friends.

He reached deep and fired bolt after bolt of lightning at the death-god. Better that than let the manna be taken without a fight.

Pluto opened his mouth and swallowed them.

Ewan tried to twist, to head into the vastness of N-dimensional space and

166

lead Pluto away from Tia and his friends. The death-god's grip held him firmly.

She'd waited too long, but Tia finally stepped away from him.

Instead of heading for the elevator, she strode up to the nearest guard. "Oh, give me that." She grabbed the black-hole weapon from his numbed hand, turned and fired it into the death-god.

Against almost any other god, that zero-dimensional singularity point would rip a huge hole. But a death-god is already a vast hole of emptiness. Destructive tidal forces had little impact on Pluto.

The death-god simply raised his hands and batted that projectile away from his one vulnerable area—his heart.

Then he reached for Tia.

"No!" Ewan would not let that happen.

Tia's gesture hadn't hurt Pluto, but it had forced the death-god to remove his hands from Ewan's chest. That gave him a chance.

He grasped the manna link that tied him to Tia and twisted both of them into N-dimensional space.

It was a desperate, ultimately doomed move. Pluto would be even stronger in his home universe than he had been on Earth. But it bought Ewan time: time he could use to save Tia.

"We can't go on meeting like this." Tia pressed herself to him. All around, her wolfpack circled, protected by the same mechanism he'd designed to safeguard Tia from the deadly influence of N-dimensional space.

"He'll find us here," Ewan said. "He'll hunt me down and claim my essence. But we've got time to move you to safety. You and all of the others."

"I have no safety apart from you."

Ewan was used to the cryptic things humans said, but nothing had prepared him for a statement like that. "You've got it backwards. You're in no *danger* except with me."

"I said what I mean. I'm with you and I'm not going anywhere if it means leaving you in danger. Now shut up about your noble sacrifice. We need to plan."

"Every one of our plans had led us into deeper trouble."

"Or maybe every one of our plans has prevented even bigger disasters."

He shook his head. If he'd surrendered to Iconic, Tia and the others would be safe. It was too late now, though. Pluto would demand everything.

"Stop thinking like that," Tia said. "It wasn't you who made Hank and Sam try to kill me. It wasn't you who convinced me to tackle Travers and nearly kill myself."

His mind whirled. "How did you know what I was thinking?"

"I can see you think, even if your lips aren't moving."

"Fine. Well, my plan is to send you to safety."

Actually, he could think of little but making love to her again. Which was both inappropriate considering the danger they were in, and almost certainly unwelcome to her.

"Not unwelcome. But we need to talk."

Damn. He was a god. Humans weren't supposed to be able to eavesdrop on his thoughts. Still, 'not unwelcome' was good. With his existence so near its end, Ewan couldn't imagine a better way to go out.

Except he needed to get Tia to safety.

"You're repeating yourself. You just need pay back the Roman gods. That way, that Pluto guy won't have access to your death-manna, right? I mean, those are the rules, aren't they?"

"I *can't* pay them back. Even with everything you can give me, it doesn't come close to what they can claim."

"Then I'll give you more. You know I give you the most when we make love. Why not see what we can do?"

* * * *

She had no pride.

A woman isn't supposed to beg for sex, but Tia was past pride. She'd told Ewan the truth—she had no safety apart from him. She was bonded to him, imprinted on him, and would never find another love to replace him. Their bond had become an essential element in her life.

If she let Ewan shuffle her to hypothetical safety, she would spend the rest of her life in a sort of shadow existence, incomplete because half of her soul would remain with him.

Besides, regardless of his words, whether he knew it or not, he wanted and needed her. Her as in Tia, not her as in the manna pump. That realization filled her with strength, and a grim determination to see this thing through to the end.

He'd never been able to lie, but now she could hear the words his lips refused to form. He *knew* no words of love, of course. Man-woman-type love was a human rather than a divine concept. Their differences precluded him from thinking of her as she thought of him. But he cared for her, desired her, wanted her with an intensity that felt like a raging forest fire.

That was more than she had ever imagined she would have.

She willed his clothing away, and was surprised when the god-substance obeyed her mental order, melting back into the essence of the male she loved.

Her heart caught in her chest when she saw the two horrible gouges on his chest. Five-clawed hands had ripped into either side of his heart. Ichor, the precious blood of a god, poured like gold flowing in a foundry.

She ignored the biting cold of his flowing ichor, and pressed her hands to his damaged chest.

His wounds had to hurt horribly, yet pain was nowhere in his thoughts. Instead, she felt him savor her touch, soaking up the warmth and manna she offered him.

"Yes, everything I have is for you," she promised in answer to thoughts he couldn't speak.

She slid her hands down his chest, to the rock-hard muscles of his abdomen. As her hands traveled his body, wounds closed behind her touch, leaving pale scars that looked as if they had healed years before.

"I didn't know you could do that," she breathed.

"You did it, not me." He was every bit as surprised as she.

"Think about this," she said. "Each time we've made love, we've forged a stronger connection. With every caress we share, the river of manna that flows between us grows deeper. When we make love *this time*, it'll do more. Perhaps this time it will be enough for you to pay back what you borrowed. If it isn't, then we'll try a—"

Ewan shook his head. "There'll be no second chances. If it isn't, we've lost. The Roman gods have gathered like jackals snapping at a wounded animal. Only Venus restrains Pluto and the others from bursting in with us now."

"What can she do?"

"Pluto is death and horribly strong, but sex is Venus's domain and she guards it fiercely. As long as we're in the midst of passion, all of Pluto's powers cannot stand against the determination of the love-goddess."

Because love was life, the opposite of death. It made complete sense to Tia. Unfortunately, its extreme logic didn't mean she saw a way out. She did know how to make the most of a bad situation, though.

"So it's too late for me to get away and we're safe only as long as we can make love. You know what that means, don't you?"

He reached for her. "Yes. That, I think, I can figure out."

She couldn't tell if his hands were hot or cold, but they seared her as they stroked her face, her breasts, her hips.

He did something to her clothes and abruptly she was as naked as he was.

She shivered, pulled herself closer to him and he laughed. "Don't worry about the Roman gods watching--they can't see us. And the dogs see this small portion of N-space as a sort of wolf-heaven. They're chasing rabbits, defending the pack, fulfilling their wolf-dreams."

"But I don't want wolf-heaven, I want Ewan-heaven."

She'd let him be the aggressor before, defining what aspects of their sexuality to explore. If this was their last time, she wanted to overwhelm all limits, explore every inch of passion.

She ran her fingers through his thick hair and brought his lips to her own, claiming them, sucking and biting, making sure he knew that he was loved.

The silent sound of his pleasure, wordless in his thoughts, surrounded her. She extended the kiss, plundering his mouth with her tongue, then let him briefly take the lead as he kissed her back.

She was getting the hang of this N-dimensional space. She floated down his body, simultaneously letting her lips caress his strong neck, the hard muscles of his chest, the flat male nipples that peaked as she bit on them, his hard stomach.

His erection jutted at her like—well, like nothing else in the universe. She grasped it with both her hands, squeezed it until Ewan's wordless thoughts of pleasure transformed into an audible groan.

Then she took it into her mouth still squeezing, but sliding one hand down its shaft to caress his balls.

He groaned again and she tasted the sweet tang of his pre-come.

Using the connection and the magic of N-dimensional space, she savored his sensation as well as her own. When she tightened her lips around him and sucked, <u>she</u> could barely hold back a groan of pleasure from *his* pleasure. When she took him deeper, tilting her head to swallow more of him, she had to squeeze her legs together to keep from exploding into orgasm.

"I want to be inside of you."

His voice was hoarse, demanding. Yet she didn't fear him because she tasted the thoughts and emotion behind them. He needed her like a tree needs the sun and rain.

She needed him like a fire needs oxygen.

* * * *

If Ewan had been smart, he'd prolong their lovemaking as long as possible. Only as long as they blazed with passion were they safe.

Need, not intelligence, drove his relationship with Tia. Every touch, every word, every look she gave him cranked up his internal thermostat until he felt that he would combust, burning unquenchably like phosphorous. Only making love to her could stem the fires that consumed him.

He withdrew from her mouth and brought her to him, kissing her lips, caressing her beautiful breasts.

A simple thought, a tiny twist of the potentials in N-dimensional space created a bed.

Tia looked at it, then waved a hand.

To his surprise, the bed vanished. How could *she* do that? Only weeks before, she'd nearly died here.

"All we need is each other."

It was true.

He'd been drawn to Tia because of her manna. Like the great saints of history, she lit the entire world with her power. Now, he saw that manna was simply an aspect of her heart. Tia loved. She cared for the homeless, her friends. She preserved ties with her family even though they rejected her dreams. She reached out to others and had been first in line to help with Joe-Hill's healing mission. And she loved him. Her love for him was the most precious gift he had received in the thousands of years he'd interacted with humans.

Her manna sustained him, but he realized he would rather have her love than all of the manna in the world.

It was a humbling, impossible realization.

He shifted into a lotus position, floating several feet above what passed for a floor in N-dimensional space and gazed at her. Could she figure out how to deal with that challenge, with that potential?

"Yeah. That's more like it," Tia said. "God-sex."

She floated to join him in mid-aether—what passed for mid-air in N-space.

He grasped her thighs, bringing her sexual lips to his mouth, tasting, savoring her moisture.

She was fully wet—so ready for him. But he intended to give her an experience she would never forget. He flicked his tongue on the hardened nub of her clitoris, lapping at it until her body stiffened against his own. Only then did he slide his fingers into her, stretching her tight muscles.

She screamed as he brought her to climax with his hands and tongue, her body shuddering as he continued his ministrations even after her explosion, keeping her at the verge of completion until she was ready again, then bringing her over that edge a second time.

"I want you," she growled when her heart finally settled into a beat slower than a racing jet engine. "Now."

She didn't wait for his answer. Tia wasn't a demure temple priestess, compliant and anxious that the god take *his pleasure* with her. Tia gave as good as she got, offering pleasure, yes, but seizing her own joy from their lovemaking without shame, without false modesty.

She joined him in his mid-air float, then lowered herself to him, taking his rock-hard erection fully into herself.

He ground his teeth together to maintain control as her tight muscles clamped down on him, squeezed him even more tightly than her hands had done moments, and eternity, before.

Still, this wasn't going to work. Tia needed the rhythm of his erection moving inside of her. With their bodies plastered against one another, he couldn't move.

"That's where you're wrong." Her words were sexy breaths against his ear.

"Damn it, Tia. You can't keep reading my mind. It isn't right and it's humiliating."

"It's incredibly right. And if it's humiliating, get used to it. I don't intend to give it up."

She tightened herself against his erection and he bit back a curse, fighting for control.

Finally he saw her plan. She was going to pay him back for what he'd done with his mouth and fingers, making him come at her command rather than under his own control.

"Turnabout is fair play," she agreed, continuing to read his thoughts.

But Ewan was a god. He didn't intend to let Tia pleasure him without making sure that she could take equal pleasure.

"That's up to you," she continued to read his thoughts. "But you have to do it without moving from your lotus."

"Agreed." Ewan could get used to this kind of a challenge—a challenge that left him a winner no matter what happened.

He used his hands. He caressed her breasts, brought her nipples into ever-sharper points of pleasure.

He used his mouth. He kissed her lips, nibbled at that soft curve where her neck joined with her shoulders, laving her nipples, catching their tips between his teeth and biting just hard enough to make her squirm.

He used his erection, sending ichor to swell it while Tia's muscles squeezed.

He used his fingers to tease her clitoris, to bring her ever closer to another completion.

He used his toe, pressing between the sexy curves of her bottom to find more sensitive bundles of nerves.

"You're…" she fought for breath. "You're cheating."

Well, yes. He was a god. That did create unfair advantages in this business of lovemaking.

But then, human women have advantages in lovemaking over human men. Perhaps they were meant for gods all along.

She squeezed down more tightly on him and he lost the capability for rational thought.

He swam in a sea of sensation. The universe collapsed around them until there was nothing but them. Ewan and Tia, Tia and Ewan eternally at the brink, at that moment of potential, ready to explode like the primitive big bang that gave rise to the entirety of creation.

* * * *

She flooded manna into him.

She'd used the wrong analogies, before. She wasn't like a battery in a flashlight or a river. A battery is depleted as it powers the flashlight. A river empties itself as it reaches the ocean. Tia gained as she gave.

Ewan's N-dimensional body swelled around her as he filled those vast empty spaces that two thousand years of hunger had left. Some of that swelling was in the blissfully right spot.

It should have been impossible for her to have another climax. He'd brought her to two massive explosions with his tongue and clever fingers, but he'd also pushed her over the limit with dozens of smaller orgasms in between.

She was fully sated, should have been able to concentrate only on bringing pleasure to him.

Instead, he'd used his god-talents to bring her to the edge one more time.

She read the savage joy inside of him, knew that he would be ready for the upcoming battle.

As she teetered on the edge of oblivion, though, she saw it. All she had given him wasn't enough.

No matter what she said, he would squander his manna sending her to safety, heedless of the cost to himself. He would battle the Roman Gods, the Iconic guards, Winsor and his human sacrifices, but he would do so in a doomed Gotterdammerung, fighting because it was right but without a hope of victory or even survival.

He'd protect her, even when she didn't want to be protected, because he could do nothing else. And she'd spend the rest of her life as half a person.

Then she lost the ability to think.

Time froze.

Finally, his iron-hard control collapsed, and she felt, shared, savored every instant of *his* race to completion. With every squeeze of her body, with every caress from her fingers, he stepped that much closer to the edge. Like an ancient cannon with a lit fuse, Ewan had long since passed the point of no return. Now, only the explosion remained.

"Give me your child," she begged. "If I can't have you, at least give me that part of yourself."

He groaned, a sound that seemed to rip the universe.

She felt his body surge as his rigid control finally failed. And the surge of his seed pounding into her body pushed her into her own abyss of pleasure.

With her mind melded with his, she felt his pleasure as directly as her own. His climax would have driven her to orgasm even without the sensation of his erection stretching at her tight core, even without his clever fingers manipulating her, pushing every pleasure button she'd imagined and so many she would never have guessed her body could hold.

Like an electrical short circuit, pleasure overloaded the impossible link she'd created between their two minds, burning through the connection, separating them at last.

But before the connection completely severed, she caught Ewan's thought.

He'd given her the child she'd demanded.

Like a star going supernova, Tia shattered.

Chapter 23

"They're coming. Get dressed." Ewan pulled Tia's clothing from the pocket universe where he'd stored them and handed them to her.

The Roman gods had given them time to complete their lovemaking, to whisper sweet nothings as their bodies descended from the peaks of pleasure. Time for Ewan to savor Tia's body against his own, her breasts yielding to his touch one more time. Time for him to wonder what he'd done when he'd yielded to Tia's insistence he give her a child.

He watched Tia slip into the jeans and sweater she'd worn for their assault on the Iconic tower, holding the screens that would keep the Roman gods from seeing her. She looked at the weapon she'd stolen from one of the guards, the black hole generator she'd fired at Pluto himself, then tucked it under her jacket.

Her plan was transparent.

"Do *not* use that on the gods," he warned. "No matter what happens. A singularity here would be disastrous. Earth itself might not survive."

She looked shaken. "Got it."

"And Tia—"

She looked at him, her face filled with light, flushed from sex, and looking more desirable than was safe for her.

For an instant, he lost his concentration, forgot what he'd intended to say. Then the moment was stripped from them.

"Enough." The death-god's voice shook the fabric of N-space. "Deliver."

Abruptly, Ewan was surrounded by the ghosts of Roman gods.

His perceptions had been so altered by his own hunger that he hadn't really seen how faded they were. Now that Tia's life-giving manna filled him, it was obvious that they were not much better off than he had been. Tight skin clung to skeletal figures, sunken cheeks and bulging eyes told the story of starving gods. Lending him so much of their essence had been a horrible risk. No wonder Pluto had agreed to Winsor's bargain.

A part of him wanted to rebel, to dissipate them all in a shower of strength. But a bargain binds a god in a grip even he cannot escape.

He needed every bit of his manna for the upcoming confrontation with Winsor, but he couldn't withhold it from them if they demanded it.

They had come to demand it.

* * * *

Tia gasped in pleasure. The gods were beautiful.

In their white robes, with feathered wings billowing behind their backs, the Roman gods looked like, well, gods. Only Pluto, who remained as black a gash of emptiness across N-space as he did on three-dimensional earth, marred the beauty of the assembly.

Tia glanced at Ewan, looking for some sign. Were they going to fight? Was he just going to give them all of his precious manna?

He nodded politely. "Brother gods and sisters. You had promised me two more days."

"We reached a crisis point," one god replied. From his massive size, his trident, and the green seawater pouring off of him, Tia guessed this was Neptune. "We can wait no longer. Would you refuse to return what is ours?"

"I still confront our shared enemies. I still need strength to do so. That is why you agreed to help me in the first place. I'm asking you to trust me a little longer."

"And let you dominate us afterwards?" Venus demanded. "You've found your own source of strength. You've won the worship of the female. You've called on us, tapped us fully, but you need us no longer. We need to be replenished before we fade from all realities."

"I don't worship him." Tia knew she should keep quiet but couldn't help denying the goddess's accusation. "Ewan and I are only lovers."

"*Only* lovers?" The love goddess spoke the words in disbelief, as if she'd never heard the two used in conjunction before. "There is no higher form of worship than love."

Tia had grown up listening to preachers going on about that. She thought she knew the answer. Didn't the Greek philosophers categorize love into different groupings, with Eros, sexual love, at the very bottom?

"You're talking about holy love, Agape," she explained. "Erotic love is different. Isn't it?" It had made sense to her, but abruptly she wondered if all of her distinctions had been rationalizations, if those long-dead Greeks had been in denial. Had she been unfaithful to the true God, the God she'd worshiped since she'd been a young girl, just because her hormones had gone crazy when Ewan had walked into her life?

"If you demand repayment, I will, of course, comply," Ewan said quickly. Clearly he didn't want Tia to continue putting her foot into her mouth.

Since giving up his manna was deadly serious, she could only assume she'd walked into a minefield more dangerous than it had appeared. Which was saying a lot.

"You will repay, including interest to compensate for all of the suffering we've endured on your behalf," Pluto announced.

Ewan stiffened, then nodded. "If that is your demand, I shall comply. And you, in turn, will stop aiding our shared enemies."

Pluto's gaze seemed to spread darkness rather than simply absorb light. "Like you, I must uphold my covenants. The Winsor priest has offered sacrifice to me, has worshiped me."

"Everyone worships death eventually," Ewan said. "But Winsor is no true priest—he dreams of being a god himself. And he's at the very heart of the plan to tear a chasm between the gods and their worshipers, taking all of that manna for his own use. Helping him would be a slow suicide."

"No human dares harm us. Now deliver."

He stretched his clawed hands toward Ewan's chest, exactly as he had when they'd been on the Iconic rooftop.

This time, Ewan blocked the death-god's grasping arms. "You're over-reaching, Pluto. I intend to pay back all who helped me in my moment of need. No one needs your greedy hands managing the distribution."

He raised his hand like one of those Buddha pictures and abruptly the N-dimensional universe was filled with an unbearable brightness.

Manna flowed from him like an unending river. Tia gasped as the gods absorbed it and swelled like wilted plants in the rain, recovered what they'd lent him to save his life and what extra he chose to give them or what they chose to accept.

They'd been beautiful before, but watching them expand, take on added dimensions, become more solid and substantial frightened and awed her.

One by one, the gods nodded their satisfaction in the bargain to Ewan, then twisted into some other plane of the N-dimensional space that housed them.

As one of the winged ones, one that just might have been Cupid, turned to go, he stopped and winked at her.

Only then did she realize that none of them had promised to stay away from the human three-dimensional space. With the extra strength Ewan was giving them, might they break out, attempt to restart centers of worship for themselves, try to claim some of the human manna that should have been reserved for the true God of Tia's belief? She wondered what she'd done.

Finally, only Venus and Pluto remained.

"More," Pluto demanded.

"I've returned all you gave me and then some." Ewan had lost the healthy glow he'd gained when they'd made love. Although his clothing automatically retailored itself to fit his diminished mass, he was gaunt once more. He'd given too much, their vast explosion of manna had been consumed, leaving too little for him.

"I'm still hungry," Pluto demanded. "More."

"You were hungry when we ruled the earth," Venus said. "You'll be hungry at the end of time. Come, uncle. Let's leave the lovers in peace."

Pluto looked at Venus, then back at Ewan. He opened his mouth as if to say something, but a tug on the nothingness that made up his fabric caught his attention and he gave Tia a horrible smile. She hadn't noticed until then that each of his teeth was a human skull. She would have been perfectly happy to remain forever ignorant of that disgusting feature.

"Time's run out," Ewan said.

"What happened?"

"Winsor sacrificed another guard. Pluto can't help himself. He'll do Winsor's bidding as long at the security chief keeps feeding him."

"Which means—"

"That our friends are in danger. I'm going back. Venus will keep you safe her. Guard our child. If anything happens to me, she'll take you anywhere you want to go."

The beautiful goddess smiled and reached a hand to her.

It wasn't even tempting.

Instead of arguing, she waited until Ewan twisted the manna around him, then she just snagged a bit to herself.

If she hadn't ignored his orders and followed him before, if she hadn't been there to grab one of the black hole weapons and shoot Pluto, Ewan would have died on the Iconic rooftop. She didn't know she'd be able to help him again, but she didn't know she wouldn't, either. A slim chance seemed better than no chance at all.

A bark signaled that the hounds had joined her.

He dragged her along like a leaf being carried by a hurricane, probably completely unaware of her.

* * * *

"More. I'm still hungry."

Four dead security guards lay at Winsor's feet and the remaining guards had backed away from the two of them. Several even pointed their weapons in Winsor's direction.

The dogs, suddenly torn from their canine heavens, set up a howling that threatened to shake the building.

Icy winds tore at the rooftop, releasing an eerie moan as they slipped through the ruined masses that Ewan's manna blasts had created out of once deadly machines.

From what she could see of the sun, Tia didn't think they'd been gone long, but the weather had taken a turn for the worse. A few drops of rain hit the rooftop and froze, promising a slick and dangerous future.

"Winsor," she shouted. "You're guilty of murder. Guards, hold him until the police arrive."

"What the devil are *you* doing here?" Ewan demanded. "You're supposed to be safe with Venus."

"I will share your danger."

"But you have to think of the child."

She *had* thought of the child. But she thought of the father as well.

"I won't tell our child I abandoned her father when he needed me most."

"Friends," Winsor said. "The woman is all we need now. Bring her to the altar. Pluto will make sure Ewan doesn't get in the way."

One of the guards, clearly one who lacked any sort of survival instinct, took a couple of steps toward Tia. He backed up in a hurry when the dogs let him know how bad an idea that was.

Winsor raised his black hole weapon and pointed it at Ewan. "Ms. Burns, please come to the altar. My trigger finger is itchy and I'm afraid I'll shoot if you don't obey promptly."

If sacrificing herself could save Ewan, Tia would have been tempted. But throwing away her life would weaken rather than help Ewan. "Why don't you come and get me?"

Winsor's smile was a gash across his too-handsome face. "My late friend Travers had his entire apartment covered by video cameras. We watched your invasion of his home together before I killed him. I saw you fight, if you want to call it that. So, yes, I will come and get you."

He launched himself before he'd finished talking, slipping his black hole generator into a holster and drawing the flint knife in one move.

He was right about one thing, Tia wasn't a fighter.

If he'd been able to keep all of the manna she shared with him, Ewan would have been able to help. As it was, he had his hands full with the death-god. The dogs howled, but moved out of the way when Winsor approached. They recognized Winsor as too powerful to tackle.

Tia was on her own against a man who'd already killed four trained security guards and who'd easily murdered the man who'd nearly killed her. It didn't sound like a fair fight.

She looked for a way to cheat.

She sidestepped his grasp as he came at her, but Winsor had anticipated that move. He slashed at her with his knife, tearing a gash in her jacket that ripped through to her upper arm.

Pain wracked her body.

Blood trickled down her arm and Winsor licked his lips. "It won't take much more of those before you're finished. How ironic when your death-manna gives Pluto the strength he needs to kill your lover."

One of the dogs finally got up the nerve to dart at Winsor, but the security chief kicked it carelessly, and the animal whimpered and slunk away, his tail between his legs.

"Oh the amusement. You thought the dogs would save you." Winsor's voice mocked her, drained her confidence. He moved his sacrificial flint knife in a slow circle that centered on her belly. "*I* raised those dogs. I trained them to kill. If there's anyone they fear, it is I. Haven't you learned that fear always trumps love?"

She watched the security chief carefully, backing away, keeping the dogs between her and the guards. If one of the guards grabbed her now, it really would be over.

"I don't mind prolonging your agony," Winsor said when it became clear she didn't intend to answer his taunts. "Assuming you won't face reality and join me. There is a distinct satisfaction in watching you bleed, knowing that, with every moment that passes, your pathetic soul will offer less manna to Ewan, making him more our creature even as he fights one who should be his ally."

"You don't intend to keep your promises to Pluto, do you?"

Hunger

Winsor laughed. "You are so wonderfully transparent. Do you seriously think I'd tell you I planned to betray him? Of course I will keep my promises to him. There are six and a half billion people on Earth. I can give him a thousand sacrifices a day and never cut into the population—it costs me nothing. There are plenty of other gods I can put to the harness. Their power, not his, will let me rule. And having a god on the payroll will make things so much easier. And it's so hard to get good help these days."

Winsor continued moving, backing Tia up, cutting off the angles that would let her circle around him, forcing her toward one of the building's corners. He kept his knife close to his body, enough out of her reach that she didn't have a chance to grab it but ready for his next strike.

She ducked under a lazy swipe, rolled a summersault to get under his slash, and realized she'd done what he wanted—separated herself from Ewan and ended almost back at the bloody altar.

One good thing. In her attempt to escape him, she'd completed a half-circle. Now her back was to the north. Winsor faced the wind and rain.

"I'm afraid," he said, "our time for fun is just about over. Will you walk the rest of the way to the altar, or must I carry you?"

A gust of wind brought a quick shower of sleet and freezing raindrops into his eyes and he blinked.

That was what she'd been waiting for. She reached into her coat and pulled out the black hole weapon she'd taken from the guard before she and Ewan had fled, pointed it, and squeezed the trigger.

Winsor's face froze with horror when he saw the weapon.

At least she thought it was horror. Until she realized he was still standing.

He wiped raindrops and tears from his eyes.

"Oh, my. The look on your face is to-die-for. I don't think I've had this much fun since I was a kid pulling the wings off of flies. I took the liberty of deprogramming that device when I realized you'd taken it with you." His voice was conversational, almost pleasant. "And now, it's time for us to stop playing these games. Goodbye, Ms. Burns."

She kicked at his groin, but he simply shifted a hip, blocking her effort easily. Before she could retract her foot, he grasped it and yanked.

For a moment, she flew.

She landed on her butt, fighting for her breath and momentarily stunned.

He took advantage of her panic to slam his knife-carrying fist into the side of her head.

If he'd used the knife-edge, she would be dead, but he didn't want her dead—yet. As it was, she teetered near unconsciousness as he lifted her, carried her across the rooftop, and draped her over the altar.

* * * *

The death-god gripped at Ewan with a hideous strength.

179

He couldn't really use the manna he'd stolen from Ewan—it wasn't death manna—but taking it denied it to Ewan. Meanwhile, four human sacrifices and countless animal sacrifices added their death-manna to Pluto's strength.

Human death manna is limited, and animal death manna even more so. The death manna of a god, though, would give Pluto more power than he'd had at the height of Roman rule.

Pluto clawed at Ewan's heart. But by returning the manna, Ewan had honored his agreement. Pluto had no easy access there.

"A god for hire." Ewan loaded his voice with mockery. "I never though I'd see the day when a Roman god would sell himself to mere humans."

"It doesn't have to be," Pluto said. "Surrender to me. You and I can be partners. We're not really competitors, you know. You can have their worship and I their deaths. Together, we can rule this planet."

Pluto was that rarity among gods—a god who could lie. But Ewan suspected he wasn't lying this time. Pluto had never sought worship. He needed a front if he was to be supplied the sacrifices he craved. Winsor—who wanted to be a god, would do. But Ewan was a real god. He'd meet Pluto's needs even better. After all, Pluto knew Ewan couldn't lie. And he knew Winsor would.

"You'll spare Tia?"

Pluto gestured and time slowed. Winsor's flint knife hung only inches from Tia's head, and a dog floated in the air, halfway between the ground and the weapon hand of one of Winsor's security guards.

"Is that your price, little god? She's been promised to me and you hardly need her any more. You can have the worship of billions. Why should you care about one more, even if she is unusually strong?"

Pluto had a point. If Ewan joined with Pluto, he would no longer need Tia's manna. The death-god could complete the destruction of Iconic and together they could hunt down the last of Iconic's executives—and their secretive government backers.

"I need her alive."

Pluto didn't really have an expression, but he still managed to look confused. "She won't worship you. When she learns about our bargain, she'll never worship you. So, why do you care? Let her go. I can use her manna and you can't."

"I made a bargain with her."

Pluto drew himself taller. "Fine. Keep her. There'll be plenty of others for me."

It was the best deal Ewan could imagine. He'd finally have what he wanted—an end to his hunger, the worship of hundreds of millions, power. Sharing with Pluto wouldn't be pleasant, but as the death-god has said, there was little overlap between them. He wouldn't have to spend time with the god.

He looked at Tia there near the altar, felt the distant tremble of manna as Big Red led a small party through the hole he'd made in the fence around the campus. He could save all of them and have what he wanted.

And it wouldn't betray his literal promise to Tia. She would hate it, but why should that be his problem.

He couldn't make himself do it. "No."

"You're a fool. You gain nothing by this. Winsor will suit my needs." Pluto grappled with Ewan, his claws clamping down on Ewan's arms, his bulk forcing Ewan backward. "He'll make Earth a charnel house for me."

"You've always had such charming dreams, death-god." Ewan gripped Pluto's arms, let the death-god force him back, then rolled on his back, planting his foot in Pluto's gut as the god attempted to follow him down.

It was a throw he'd learned in the days when he took human form to participate in the games his people held in honor of him. A throw that a god would normally despise, relying as it did on weakness rather than strength, on yielding rather than standing firm. But Ewan had given too much of himself to stand toe-to-toe with a death-god and hope to survive.

Pluto flew over his head and smashed through the low concrete retraining wall that surrounded the rooftop.

Ewan continued his own roll, coming to his feet as Pluto spread huge bat-shaped wings and hovered in the air.

"You thought you could throw me to my death?" The death-god roared his challenge. "I am no human to be snuffed out like a candle."

Ewan let the death-god brag and checked on Tia.

The dogs whimpered away from Winsor and the security chief had backed Tia toward a corner of the rooftop.

Ewan suspected Tia had a plan—she always had some scheme working, mostly smarter and sneakier than anything he could imagine. But she sucked as a fighter and was bleeding from a wound in her upper arm.

Ewan still couldn't touch Winsor—whatever technological tricks Iconic had developed to protect their guards from his manna still held firm. But he could reach Tia. He reconnected her major blood vessels and closed the gaping hole in her arm.

Winsor came in with a low fast slash, and Ewan gave Tia a bit of N-dimensional time sense, slowing time for her, letting her react more quickly.

She ducked, but not low enough. So he lowered the rooftop where she stood, and she managed to roll under Winsor's strike.

Temporarily safe, she pulled out her weapon.

Then Pluto flapped back to the rooftop and landed hard, his feet crashing through the rooftop. He struggled, but his feet seemed immobilized.

It was an opportunity, the first mistake Pluto had made—if it was real. Ewan had faced the Romans before, knew how conniving they could be.

Rather than throw himself into Pluto's clutches, he flung a bolt of lightning. Jupiter had ruled the gods partly through their fear of his lightning.

Perhaps Pluto could be blasted. Ewan couldn't afford the manna but didn't have anything to save it for.

Pluto opened his mouth and swallowed the strike.

"You can't kill a black hole by feeding it energy. You can't harm me by feeding me manna," he bragged. "Now, little god of a forgotten people, face the wrath of Saturn's eldest son."

Pluto reared back, reached deep within himself, then threw. The wave of darkness seemed almost a part of the death-god as it roared toward Ewan.

Ewan knew Pluto hoped he'd try to swallow the death-god's strike. But Pluto's hideous power was poison to Ewan.

He stood firm, as if waiting to catch the wave of darkness, then dropped through the rooftop at the last possible moment, simultaneously shouting a message of command to Tia, the guards and the dogs.

Pluto's two-dimensional sheet of darkness sliced a line of death through the spot where Ewan had stood, then continued on toward the horizon.

High radio towers crumpled, a hillside shifted slightly, the atmosphere burned in a fine plane, and a molecularly thin line cut across Earth's moon.

Tia, the dogs, and most of the guards had obeyed Ewan's message, had dropped to the ground and to safety. Two guards had been slow.

One had simply stood still, unbelieving. He'd caught Pluto's strike at the top of his thighs. He looked at the death-god, and at Ewan as Ewan apported himself ten feet above the rooftop.

Then his torso slid off his legs. Blood, which had continued to flow through the severed arteries, spouted everywhere.

The second guard's death was less dramatic but equally final. He'd ducked on command, but not far enough. The flat plane of death had caught him halfway up his neck. His skull split as he reached the ground, opening like a shucked oyster.

Pluto didn't bother retaining his humanoid shape as he reached across the distance grasping and consuming their death-manna.

The death-god grew larger, darker and impossibly, more empty, towering above the building until he seemed like a colossus standing on a pedestal.

"Death always wins in the end." Pluto reached into himself again, this time letting go with not one but seven separate sheets of horrible, black death.

Ewan jinked higher, lower, then flattened himself between two strikes. He almost made it, but the last two came too close together and severed millions of dimensions of his substance into nothingness. The wounds were invisible in the human universe, but somewhere, elsewhere, his divine body shed oceans of ichor he couldn't afford to lose.

Because Pluto aimed where Ewan floated above the rooftop, the black planes did not destroy any more guards directly. But they caught one of the machines Ewan had ruined with his lightning. That fell silently, crushing another guard.

Again, Pluto reached out his claw and yanked the dead man's soul and death-manna into his ever-hungry maw.

"Shoot Pluto, you idiots," Tia shouted from where Winsor dragged her to the altar. "The death-god will consume all of you."

Most of the guards were in shock, incapable of thought, beyond the point where they could take rational suggestions and act on them. That was why Ewan had been able to reach them with his voice of command despite their shielding against his manna force.

A few, though, gathered hope from Tia's words.

Three, maybe four of the guards leveled their weapons at Pluto and fired.

He swatted away the first black hole and swallowed the second. The third and fourth, though, ripped into his substance, tearing holes through the emptiness that was death.

Pluto's groan seemed to shake the very world. Ichor, black as the empty space between the galaxies, spurted through two great holes in his chest.

Pluto reached for that ichor, but it dissipated as his claws touched it and tried to gather it in.

"Die," he screamed. He fired death-planes—not at Ewan but at the guards who had challenged him, dared pit their merely human courage against the god of death himself.

Hunger bit at Ewan like a raging fire. Pain tore at him where those black planes had sliced his N-space body away and destroyed it. Still, he reached deep, pulling every bit of manna together to cast a halo of light around the guards, around the dogs, around Tia and their barely conceived child.

Light met darkness—and the universe blinked.

Pluto shrank. His Earth-dimensional appearance had towered a hundred feet over the rooftop. Drained of so much of his substance, he contracted to a still imposing ten feet in height.

Ewan was worse off. His manna had been annihilated when it had collided with Pluto's. He was tapped.

His three-dimensional form crashed to the rooftop as his manna deserted him.

Simply getting to his feet seemed impossible.

One of the dogs nudged him with his nose. One of the guards offered him a hand and he leaned on that former enemy, absorbed the tiny trickle of faith the guard offered in thanks for still being alive. He staggered but stood upright.

"Kill the woman." Pluto's voice was a blast of subsonic vibration that would quiver on the edge of a human's consciousness. "I need her death. Hurry."

The death-god had lost interest in Ewan, in the guards, in anything beyond the brutal tableau before them.

Winsor stretched Tia across the altar, one hand gripping her throat and the other holding the flint knife high over his head.

He shouted out bits of ancient prayer—in Hebrew, Greek, Latin, Sanskrit, even a few words in the one true language, a language the gods though lost to humankind since the days of Babel.

Light-sucking clouds gathered over the security chief. Black lightning, horribly akin to those planes of death that Pluto had showered on Ewan, flickered down the knife's flint blade. The knife itself winked between shadow and solidity. Empowered by Pluto's manna and Winsor's magic, it became a more than human weapon. It was a weapon that could sacrifice a god.

Time froze.

For a horrible eternity, Ewan looked at a future without Tia, without hope, without love.

Unacceptable.

When time returned, it accelerated, as far beyond his control as the great Niagara Falls is beyond the control of a cockroach floating on a twig near its precipice.

Winsor's knife cut a dark gash through the substance of Earth-reality as he slashed it toward Tia's fast-beating heart.

Chapter 24

If she survived this, Tia was definitely joining the gym. Being tossed around by gods was one thing. Letting human guys do it sucked.

Of course, surviving didn't seem likely.

Winsor had picked her up, then dropped her down on the altar hard enough to knock the wind out of her.

She'd struggled for her breath as Pluto went mad, blasting Ewan and the guards with everything he had.

Somehow, Ewan had managed to protect the guards and himself, but both gods were reeling.

"Kill the woman. I need her death. Hurry." Pluto's words shook the earth.

"My pleasure," Winsor had murmured. He shouted some foreign nonsense and waved his stone knife in the air, then plunged it straight toward her heart.

A second before, Ewan had been leaning against a guard, unable to stand on his own.

Now, he interposed himself between the knife and its target.

"Not going to happen." Ewan's growl was primal, dangerous, frightening —the sound a god might make at the creation of the universe, or in an elemental moment of passion.

Winsor was past fear. He appeared drunk on the power of his words, the death and destruction around him, and the demand of the death-god for ever-more death.

He ignored Ewan's interposing body and slashed downward with his weirdly glowing stone knife.

That knife cut through Ewan's chest as if the god had no more substance than a marshmallow.

The god ignored his wound and grasped Winsor's hand, squeezing it until the knife barely hung within his jellied grip.

"Jesus."

"Wrong god, loser."

Despite his pain, Winsor grinned. "Good point. A little help here, Pluto."

The death-god nodded.

Once again, Pluto drew into himself, pulling more of that black nothingness he seemed made out of to form it into a forked sword of death and emptiness.

The death-god stalked toward the altar. He swung his black sword, knocking aside, destroying, the black hole weapons held by the two guards who dared to raise them.

This was the end.

If Ewan turned and faced the death-god, Winsor would complete his sacrifice with his left hand and Tia's death-manna would fuel Pluto's murder of her lover.

If Ewan stayed and protected her, the death-god would simply take him from behind. Winsor could complete his sacrifice at his leisure.

It was lose-lose for Ewan.

Which meant it was up to Tia to do something.

Ewan, the noble idiot, ignored Pluto's approach, continuing to squeeze the knife out of Winsor's hand while he bled golden ichor from more wounds than Tia could count.

Two rows of skulls glistened like diamonds as Pluto grinned.

His black snake-fanged sword roared as he swung it back over his head, then reversed and aimed a stroke that would sever Ewan's head from his heavenly body.

Tia knew she was getting strength from Ewan, strength he needed for himself, but she didn't complain. She didn't have much of a plan, but even a horrible and incomplete plan was better than nothing.

As Pluto's forked blade drew close, she twisted upright, grabbed Winsor's injured knife hand, then wrapped her free arm around the security director, and swung his body into the path of that horrible weapon of emptiness.

"Down," she shouted at Ewan.

The death-god's weapon was designed to kill a god. It cut through Winsor's neck like steel through smoke. Continuing downward, it sliced through Tia's body, finally smashing through the rooftop. But it missed Ewan.

Winsor's eyes rolled back and his muscles went slack.

Slowly, like a great tree dying in the forest, he sagged against her. Only her hold on him kept him from collapsing completely.

Winsor, the man who'd wanted to become a god, was dead.

She was dead, too, although the impossible sharpness of Pluto's weapon meant that her body hadn't realized that yet.

Pluto's black fork had sliced through her chest, her hips, and out her back.

Pain reared up, but she fought for consciousness.

She was dead, but she had more to do before she succumbed.

In her darkening vision, only Winsor's knife and the death-god stood out now. Everything else, even Ewan, faded into ghostly transparency.

Which made sense, of course. A dead woman should see the god of death and a weapon of death more clearly than the world of the living.

Greed and need shined from Pluto's face. His skull-grin was a grimace of pain rather of joy. Black ichor poured from two vast holes in his chest. But he had a feast before him. Death-manna from Winsor and Tia would fill him, give him the strength he needed to finish off the critically wounded Ewan.

186

He reached for her.

When she felt the black claws of his fingertips on her breast, she shoved Winsor's hand and knife into the death-god's face.

The move was too violent for her severed body and she felt herself collapse. But not before she heard the death-god's scream.

* * * *

Ewan was dying.

Repaying the gods had emptied his reserves. Pluto's black slices of death had cut him deeply. The bubble of life he'd poured over the rooftop to protect the guards, dogs and Tia had drained him of all of what little manna he'd retained. Winsor's flint knife had been the final blow. It had hacked through his chest arm like a dull hatchet through a green pine branch, exploding shards of his substance everywhere.

He'd reacted too slowly when Pluto had approached, trusting Tia because her soul had promised she had a plan.

He hadn't believed her plan would be to kill herself.

She shoved the flint knife into the death-god's face, not his vulnerable heart. There it met the diamond-hard resistance of Pluto's fabled black helmet.

She'd failed.

That would not do.

He summoned up his own death-manna, accepting the fate of becoming a death-god as he himself died, and added all that power behind Tia's strike.

The knife's rigid flint bent as it was caught between the implacable force of Ewan's death and the impenetrable hardness of a helmet of death.

The weapon skittered across the blackness, then found an opening—an eyehole.

Pluto's scream started below the human hearing range, then gradually pitched higher and higher until only the dogs, and Ewan, could hear it.

With every dog howling, the death-god twisted, then disappeared, returning to N-dimensional space to lick his wounds, to survive if he could persuade other gods to help him, perhaps even to perish. There were, after all, other death-gods.

Ewan stumbled to Tia.

She was dying.

Pluto's fabled fork was thinner than a single molecule, nearly a two-dimensional figure.

It had cut completely through her body. But its very sharpness had partially undone its effectiveness. Tia's blood continued to flow through arteries severed so neatly they didn't know they were cut, nerve synapses continued to send electrical charges across the gap.

He caught her as she collapsed, then twisted, aiming for N-space where he could see into her, attempt to heal her.

His body didn't respond. N-space was closed to him.

The easy way wouldn't work. So, he'd take the hard way. He'd be damned if he'd not find some way. Tia had given too much for him. He wasn't going to let her die.

Pluto's fork hadn't struck her brain. She could still think, could still feel. She might think she was dead, but she wasn't.

Ewan set Tia down on the cold rooftop and pulled himself around to cover her. He summoned more of his own death-manna to warm her.

"Let me help."

Joe-Hill was lucky Ewan was so weak. His natural reaction would have been to strike anyone who interfered with his healing.

"Tia is past human medical help. Only I can do this."

"We believe in you." That was Lori.

He knew she was pouring what little manna she could generate at him, but he couldn't feel it. He was a death-god now, impervious to ordinary manna. Impervious even to the flood of manna that Tia could generate.

For his purposes, though, he had plenty.

He couldn't travel into N-space, but his vision remained deep.

He transformed the dark manna of his death as it flowed from him, turning it to warmth, then flooded it into Tia.

Warmth, to protect her from shock.

He sent tiny tingles of manna to each nerve, stimulating them, refusing to let them die.

His ichor hadn't changed yet to the black ichor of a death-god and he let its golden substance flow into Tia.

Like tiny nanohealers of science fiction, his ichor scoured through her arteries, veins, and capillaries, sealing the walls of those vessels, pulling together severed muscle tissue.

Bone was easy. Pluto's blade had been too sharp to shatter. A quick shot of manna reminded the molecular bonds to regain their adhesion.

Tia would be the smallest bit shorter when she recovered, but no one would notice.

Finished. Bones, nerves, muscle, blood vessels pulled themselves back together.

Ewan teetered on the edge of oblivion, but he wasn't done yet.

Tia had looked the death-god in his eye. She, a human, had dared strike Pluto himself with a weapon designed for his service. No merely human mind could sustain that damage.

He would do what he'd dared not do from the beginning, alter her very mind.

For the first time in his existence, Ewan fully understood what humans meant by love.

He gathered the last of his death-manna into a ball, holding nothing back for himself, then fed it directly to her brainstem in a single monumental jolt.

Hunger

It was risky. A bolt like that was as likely to kill as it was to heal. But it was his only chance to tear Pluto's claws from where they still tugged at her soul.

He faded, willing his eyes to remain open long enough to see if his risk had paid off. But he failed.

Blackness swept over him.

The god Ewan was no more.

* * * *

Pain riddled her body with a thousand whips.

"Looks like she's coming back." A male voice.

"It's a miracle." A female.

"It is a miracle." That was Joe-Hill. "Ewan did it."

Ewan. His name sent warmth through her freezing body, met the pain and conquered it.

"Where is he?" Her voice sounded a million miles away.

"Don't try to talk, Tia. You're still too weak."

"Need Ewan."

Silence met her words.

"He's..." she had to stop and catch her breath. "...wounded. Need to get to N-space. Help him."

"He's past help, Tia."

She recognized Joe-Hill's voice but refused to accept his words. Gods don't die. "How?"

"He turned into a golden bubble over you. When he faded, only you were left. He's gone, Tia."

Her scream barely amounted to a croak, but it came from her heart. She'd waited her entire life to truly fall in love, waded through unsatisfactory relationship after relationship. It wasn't fair that when she finally found someone, he be snatched from her. She should sacrifice herself for him, not the other way around. She'd tried to do it and failed, even at that.

"Throw me off the roof. Don't want to live."

"Come on, Tia. He wouldn't want that." It was Lori. Her friends had gathered around her, were showering her with their love and caring.

And they were right. Ewan had given her their child. If she wasn't carrying that precious gift, she could happily end her life. As it was, she had someone growing inside of her. Just a few little cells so far, but still precious.

* * * *

He blinked into nothingness and, for the first time in thousands of years, Ewan wasn't hungry.

He'd done what he could. Tia would never be sick again. If she were careful, she'd live a long life. His bolt of lightning clarified her manna, eliminated the spill that would have made her a target for other hungry gods. She'd be safe.

He was content.

* * * *

Something stirred under her.

Earthquake?

"Ohmigod, he's alive. Who's got a gun?" That was Lori.

Hope pricked in Tia. "Ewan?"

"Ewan's dead, honey. It's Winsor. I thought he was dead, too."

He had been dead. But she'd fallen on top of his body after she'd struck Pluto. Ewan's healing must have been strong enough to bring both her and the murderer back to life.

The thought that her lover had given up his own existence to bring this evil killer back sickened her.

"We'll bring him to trial," Joe-Hill said. "If you shoot him, you're no better than he was."

Wrong. Because Winsor had killed her love. Winsor wouldn't give up. He'd use his government contacts and be out of jail in no time, recreating what he had here, trying to become a god. Winsor had to be killed.

She opened her mouth to say exactly that.

The words didn't come.

* * * *

Like Phaethon, falling from the sun-god's chariot, Ewan fell, burned, was crushed by the increasing pressure.

He'd thought death would be oblivion, a simple end to his hunger, that Tartarus could be eternal sleep. He hadn't expected to feel pain, to be squashed.

"He's alive. Who's got a gun?"

He opened his eyes and saw almost nothing.

* * * *

"Is Tia alive?"

Ice ran in Tia's veins. Winsor was not only alive, he was asking for her.

Pluto's swordlike weapon of blackness had cut right through her and Tia knew she'd be paralyzed at best, but she tried to pull herself together—and was amazed when she came to her feet.

Lori held a semi-automatic, pointing at the security chief's head.

Tia grabbed it. If anyone was going to kill Winsor, it was she.

"Alive." He seemed satisfied. Perhaps he was pleased he'd have a chance to kill her himself.

"I'll be alive long after you rot in the ground, murderer." She tightened her finger on the trigger. Could she kill him in cold blood?

"Kill it. It's too tight. Too small. It hurts."

That didn't make sense.

"Kill what?"

"This body."

"I'll kill him," one of the security guards said. "He treated us like cattle, sacrificing us even though we worked for him. No reason to get yourself in trouble with the law, lady. I'll happily spend the rest of my life in jail if it means he's gone."

Winsor looked at her, his eyes black as midnight.

Wait a second. Hadn't the security chief's eyes been pale blue?

His cheekbones shifted, growing higher, more prominent. His deeply tanned skin seemed to pale as she watched, just a hint of a flush showed he wasn't completely bloodless. What the--

Realization exploded. "It's Ewan. He must have occupied Winsor's empty body."

"Too small."

"Tough luck, Ewan. The rest of us have to deal with it, so you can too. I'm not going to let you off the hook."

"Not a god any longer. Nothing. Just occupying this body for a trivial moment. When it dies, I die."

"That's all any of us get, Ewan. A flash of life. We have to make the most of it. That's one reason humans are so impatient. And I'm losing patience with you. We've got a child coming and by God, we're going to raise it together."

When he smiled, all doubt vanished. Winsor had managed a smirk, but never a genuine grin. "Religious differences—"

"That's the stupidest excuse I've ever heard."

Winsor/Ewan stared at her. When Tia looked into his eyes, she saw the stars. Yes, Ewan was there.

"I—"

He held up a hand. "How can I saddle you with this?"

"Getting you a new identity shouldn't be a problem," Big Red said. "It's something the gang has been doing since the seventies when the Feds decided to crack down on anyone who didn't go along with their conventional ways."

"If you need a job, I always need help in the clinic," Joe-Hill added. "Now that Lori and I are getting married, I won't be able to spend twenty-four hours a day there like I was doing."

"But—"

"I love you, Ewan," Tia said. "And we're going to make this work."

* * * *

Ewan no longer had worshipers.

Even if he had, their manna would be beyond his reach.

His body was a failure-prone wreck.

He could barely touch the fifth and sixth dimensions, let alone all of the thousands he'd once been able to reach.

Yet Tia had been right. Human life was a brief flash of light, but so much could be done in that flash. Having Tia, sharing a life together, meant more than godhead. He hadn't sacrificed anything: he'd gained everything.

Her lips met his and his body warmed.

191

Maybe there was still a little manna flow because surely nothing merely human could be so magic. And fifth and sixth dimension did promise some intriguing possibilities in bed.

The End

Be sure to check with BooksForABuck.com or our distributors for more great fantasy and paranormal romance by Rob Preece.